By Accident

Mar Preston

PART I

Chapter One

Detective Dave Mason had been pleasantly empty-minded, attending to the regular cop business of nailing down people robbing people, beating each other up, and stealing whatever they could get their hands on. Nothing out of the usual. He surveyed the azure sky darkening with purple clouds above Santa Monica, eager for his next flying lesson.

Setting his Starbucks cup on the top of the black Crown Vic, the contents shivered with the force of an explosion that seemed to come from everywhere at once. The shock wave caught the edge of the car door and almost tore it off. Palm fronds crashed to the ground. Trees bent. The Secret Service agents who had been chatting to Mason and his partner a moment ago took off at a hard run toward the head of the line of vehicles where the President rode in ceremonial fashion down Wilshire Boulevard.

Mason saw his partner's mouth open in astonishment.

"What the fuck was that?" Art Delgado said, his jowly brown face draining of color.

A hit on the President was Mason's first thought. Oh God, don't let Santa Monica be another Dallas.

The radio chattered with a confusion of voices, stepping over each other.

Mason tilted his head, listening for a fusillade of

gunfire signaling the President was under fire.

A huge fireball soared into the sky south of Santa Monica's busiest intersection, billowing up and up.

Every eye turned upward toward the ballooning fireball. Chaos ripped at the crowd gathered in clumps here and there along the street to see the President drive by, creating a massive traffic jam. Dave Mason tried to think straight in those first moments where everything mattered. People ran and pushed, screaming, shoving away from the curb and into the streets. Flags and homemade signs thrown to the ground. Children clutched tight.

The Santa Monica Police Department and the Secret Service were on the same frequency. A report came that the Secret Service had stuffed the President into a building farther west along Wilshire Boulevard. Mason unsnapped the holster on his gun, drew it, and swiveled in a 360-degree arc, identifying potential threats.

Nothing. Mason pressed his ear to the shoulder mic of the radio listening for an update, for orders. Drops of rain pelted the windshield as he yanked the car door open and flung himself in.

Crowds pushed into the streets, people running amok as though pursued by a forest fire. The intersection filled with panicked presidential supporters and a lesser jam-up of protesters looking east down Wilshire. The Presidential visit had backed up traffic for miles in every direction.

Was the explosion a diversion for terrorists to swarm in and take out the President? Or worse, abduct him and spirit him off somewhere? But how? The tiny Santa Monica airport could accommodate small jets, but it was miles through neighborhood streets to get there.

By sea? The ocean at the edge of the Los Angeles sprawl at the base of Wilshire Boulevard? Getting him those few blocks down to the shore would be a crazy way to take him.

Dark scenarios from training sessions swept through Mason's mind. Squinting, he pressed the radio mic closer to his ear to hear better, sorting through the confusion, listening for orders. His partner, Art Delgado, shoved himself into the passenger seat, talking fast into the radio.

Delgado caught the news first, shouting at Mason. "Gas explosion. SoCal Edison plant near the freeway."

Power surge? A leak? A curl of gas? A spark? Was that it?

*

"Stay here," Bruce Draco, the security operative, shouted over his shoulder into the fitting room at Bloomingdale's, ignoring the screaming women emerging half-dressed, streaming past him. "Get down on the floor."

Celia Talaveras, the nanny, was from Guatemala and no stranger to public violence. She yanked the twins in her care down with her to the floor. "*Dios mio,*" she prayed.

Her other charge, Megan, the daughter of a celebrity household, sat rooted to the bench inside a fitting room, pulling on a pair of tight jeans. She was used to thinking the twenty-four-hour security force was just for show.

"Get down, Megan. Stay down," Bruce screamed again, swiveling in a defensive crouch, weapon drawn.

The twins, subdued by the sound of the explosion, crawled into the nanny's arms for comfort. Above them, the explosion triggered the fire extinguisher system. Jets of water shot from the ceilings.

Megan and the nanny looked at each other, eyes round, mouths agape.

"Celia?" Megan cuddled closer to the older girl, a question in her eyes, the air full of ozone and screams.

"What was that?"

"I doan know" said Celia. "Not guns. Big explosion. Is going to be alright. Just explosion." She looked for Bruce, who was always with them. He burst into the small fitting room.

"You okay?" he said to Celia.

"We're okay."

"Celia?" Megan whimpered. "I'm scared." She slowly eased down off the bench like an old woman onto the floor with the others.

"Is okay. Do what Bruce says."

Glass shattered. Fire alarms sounded.

Bruce screamed into his cellphone. Back Up. Intel. He listened for a moment.

Pandemonium.

"What?" Celia said to Bruce. "What we do?" Calmly she pulled Megan and the twins close to her on the floor, sheltering them with her body.

A second blast shook the floor under them.

The lights went out.

Moments may have passed or minutes.

Bruce shone the flashlight on his cellphone over the little heap of his people, pausing on Megan long enough to see the fifteen-year-old girl was in shock, the children howling.

"Come on," he said to Celia. "We have to get out of here."

Celia passed Megan her other shoe. "Put it on. Glass."

Megan squeezed her eyes shut, her hands over her ears. The twins clung to Celia, like small monkeys.

"Your shoes," she said again to Megan. She bent and shoved the shoe onto Megan's foot, then yanked the girl to her feet.

Bruce muttered, "Hurry. Hurry. C'mon."

Their personal protection officer led them out of the fitting rooms into the main store. A rack of dresses at the entrance swayed and then toppled over.

Shoppers and store employees, soaking wet, were pushing and shoving, falling, screaming onto the escalator from the second floor. A wheelchair toppled over knocking an old woman to the floor. People streamed around her.

Bruce slipped on the wet floor and kept himself from falling by grabbing onto a rack of display lights over a jewelry counter, which popped and sizzled as they burnt out.

"Where we go?" Celia said to Bruce who had a cut on his forehead from flying glass. Blood ran down his face.

"This way."

Ambient light filtered through greasy smoke from the skylight.

Holding the twins close by one arm, Celia jerked Megan by the hand to follow her and Bruce.

He led them past busted out windows and a collapsed wall into a tunnel that led to the sixth-floor parking lot.

Just ahead an interior wall weakened by a burst water pipe bulged. Megan paused, transfixed by the sight of the slowly collapsing wall.

Bruce and Celia made it past the wall. Bruce seized the twins and tried to keep his footing while holding the cellphone flashlight aloft, sliding in the rushing water.

Celia turned, just as the wall disintegrated. The nanny bounded through the rushing torrent of water and grabbed the teenage girl, hauling her with inhuman strength to safety.

"Run. Run, Megan," she screamed into her vacant face, pushing her.

The screams dimmed as they burst into the cacophony

of car alarms.

Sirens howled all over the city.

Wordless communication between the security operative and the nanny—Megan had to be dragged down and down and around each level to the street.

Bruce let the twins climb all over him to distract them while Celia comforted Megan.

"Is okay now. Is okay. Is okay," she crooned into the ears of the frightened girl.

Mason was three blocks from the Pacific Coast Highway where the streets were thick with locals and international tourists who came to enjoy their leisure in luxury hotels lining the bluff overlooking the ocean. Maybe even take in a Presidential visit. Santa Monica was an eight-square-mile money-making machine. Third Street Promenade was one of the city's many shopping meccas, and now on a holiday weekend, a car was lodged next to every single parking meter. Traffic Enforcement was out there churning tickets and fines.

A gas explosion was confirmed. Big mess downtown. Until it was determined the explosion was accidental, the department was on red alert. Mason and Delgado's orders were to liaise with the detail covering the explosion, then report back in when *The Big Guy* was safely on his way out of Santa Monica. The day's events were canceled. Just to make things worse, hard rain began to fall.

Not much chance the Presidential detail would be seeking his advice. He looked around at the crowds, wondering if he'd be needed to do crowd control. Long time since he'd directed traffic.

"We're to report to the scene. Hold on." Mason swung the vehicle through a tight turn heading west toward the ocean. "This is probably the fastest way."

Delgado snorted. "Yeah. Fastest. Nothing's going to be fast today." Lights and screaming siren didn't help. Traffic came to a dead stop at the top of the California Incline leading down to the Pacific Coast Highway which followed the curve of Santa Monica Bay. Mason forced his way around drivers frozen with indecision by driving on the grass of Palisades Park, avoiding walkers and old people whose tai chi session had been interrupted by the rain and the explosion.

The forecast predicted in its cagey way there would be highs and lows and percentages. The air glittered with the ozone of a coming storm. Mason didn't figure the weather guys knew any more about what was coming than he did. By the time he'd managed a left turn onto Colorado Boulevard, the rain had settled into a steady patter. Puddles widened in the middle of the street. He splashed through sending up rooster tails of backwash. A breeze flung the treetops about, sending down a quick shower of leaves. Wind skittered through the palms, the dried fronds rattling.

Both detectives jumped out of the car blocks away and began running, seeing the wreckage left by the explosion. The intersection looked like Aleppo after a Russian shelling. They couldn't get any closer than the corner of Second and Colorado.

Mason's radio crackled as they stood at the site of the explosion, waiting for further orders and watching the Fire Department and SoCal Edison people working the scene. This would be a day in Santa Monica that would be talked about for a long time: a presidential visit and a horrific gas explosion.

TV news crew were already there making a nuisance of themselves.

Mason fumbled for his house keys, stumbling up the stairs and opening the door of his condo at Seventh Street and San Vicente Boulevard. He heard the whine of the hair dryer from the bathroom and followed it to find Ginger, the love of his life, wearing a black wool suit with a white silk blouse. She turned to look at him. He circled his arms around her and leaned in close. She always smelled good.

"You look awful. I stayed up until about two watching the news. Can you believe this?" she said.

Mason let her go, twisted to put the lid of the toilet seat down in the Mexican-tiled bathroom and sat, elbows on his knees, rubbing his scratchy face. Mica glints of silver and white appeared on his jaw nowadays before he shaved.

"Just another day at the office," he said with a lop-sided grin. "This one's going down in the record books."

"Call your daughter," Ginger said. "They saw it on the news too and it scared her. And your Dad called. He didn't leave a message." She set the hair dryer down and knelt on the floor, putting her arms around him.

"Poor you. You're getting too old for all this adrenaline stuff."

The phone on his belt vibrated. Mason stared at it. The Watch Commander. Reluctantly he punched a button and listened for a long moment. Ginger pulled away from him, watching his face.

"You have to go? You've been up all night," Ginger said.

"Me and Delgado are next on the wheel."

"But the victim can't get any deader."

"You know that's not how it works, pussycat."

Mason stood up and splashed water on his face and

slapped his cheeks hard. He leaned forward to examine his face in the mirror, razor in hand. Women said he was good-looking, but he couldn't see it. There was an overlapping front tooth he was conscious of when he smiled. California was the land of the Dental Beautiful. After a quick shower, he changed clothes. No bespoke suits from London, but no two-for-one sales specials from Men's Warehouse either. On his way out the door, he paused to read the banner on KTLA flowing across the screen under a skinny blond breathlessly covering the latest news:

Southern California Edison today restored power to more than 900 Santa Monica customers after a power surge set off an explosion in an underground vault, triggering an outage. Gas explosion under the city. Major downtown fire.

The blond panted with excitement.

The explosion caused a fire that burned for hours, knocking out traffic lights, stranding people in elevators and leaving huge swaths of Santa Monica without power, officials said.

♆

Chapter Two

Four Months Earlier:

The house was silent. Derek Logan crept around in the dark armed with an assault rifle as Bruce Willis. He could play all of them. Play it better. Everyone said he was the best action adventure star of them all. Everybody said that. What he wanted now was a play on Broadway. Real recognition. This was Derek Logan's time.

The door was unlocked. She must have wanted him to come in. He entered the girl's room in the household staff wing, his blood carbonated, a fizzing, high, wild hilarity zinging through his brain.

Celia woke, frightened. Derek pointed the rifle at her and whispered as Hannibal Lecter, "I'm going to rape you."

She flung herself out of the bed running, her feet caught in the sheets, tripping her, throwing her off balance. Derek poked the gun at her, to halt her fall. Her arms spin wheeled, grabbing for him. He giggled watching, waiting for her to get the joke.

Celia fell heavily, crashing into a bicycle hook left embedded in the wall by the last nanny. The hook was used to hang bright cotton scarves and strings of beads. The sharp edge caught her in the eye socket, penetrating her brain with a force that brought her to her knees, dragging the hook out of the wall. Her blurting scream went silent. She fell to the floor in a low, slow slide with the hook protruding from her eye, a turquoise and pink billow of scarf swathing her face, instantly darkening. With a slow hand, she pawed at the fabric, blood spurting, gurgling, and dying.

The incandescent glow of cocaine shimmered in whatever crazy world Derek was in. Nothing was real. The blood was all computer graphics. He giggled. In a thrill of inattention, his finger found the trigger of the AR-15, and a three-round burst of automatic fire went off. Whoops.

The dogs penned up in the kitchen began barking.

The blood looked so real.

His wife was racing down the stairs. He heard her blasting through the kitchen, down the hallway into the staff quarters.

Poppy Sinclair stood at the door of the nanny's room looking aghast. "Derek, what did you do to her?"

His famous wife stepped around the pool of blood from the nanny's head, pulling up the hem of her virginal white nightgown. "Everybody in the neighborhood must have heard that. Ooooh, that's disgusting. That thing sticking out of her eye. You shot her in the eye."

"Nooooo. Honestly. I never touched her." Derek Logan's voice went higher and higher. "Look, the bullets went in the bed. I thought she could take a joke."

Poppy Sinclair looked at him, her dark eyes familiar to moviegoers went blank with incredulity. "A joke?"

She looked around the maid's bedroom, then darted back into the hallway to make sure no one was coming. Lupe Garcia, the housekeeper, had the room next door in the household staff wing and was visiting her daughter in Pacoima. None of the other staff lived in. She grabbed the gun from him and placed it carefully on the bed.

"I was doing Willis in *Die Hard*." Derek was still high enough to think he was the smartest person in any room. He was well on his way to achieving his life's goal: a starring role in a Broadway play. A role that skinny bastard Jeremy Irons would be considered for. The only time Logan became real to himself was watching himself on film.

"Look, this is Arnold's gun from *The Terminator*. I bought it from Props. Look, the bullets went into the blankets. She did it to herself." He was serenely confident that the fact that it was Arnold's gun made a difference. He hadn't yet made the link to the dying body because he hadn't meant to shoot her. It was an accident.

♁

Bruce Draco, one of Logan and Sinclair's security operatives, thought he heard a short burst of automatic gunfire, but wasn't sure. He was in the guard kiosk out at the street watching the monitors, on the phone with one of his sons. He strained to hear his kid who lived in Johannesburg, amid the frenetic backbeat of the club music. They were arguing about his kid joining the military as Draco had done when he was young and stupid. Bruce ended the call and made a sweep of the perimeter of the house. Through the glass doors at the end of the hallway leading to the staff quarters, he saw Logan with a weapon, naked and jittering. He wasn't completely sure he'd heard weapon fire, but his suspicions were confirmed when he saw Logan. He stole in through the patio doors. The wife must have heard it too. They stood arguing in the hallway. The twins and the daughter must have slept through it, their wing of the house upstairs out of earshot. Jake, Derek's son by another marriage, was at his mother's, or somewhere else. Who cared?

The security operative slowly approached his employer, hands held out in a *Stop* position. "Hey, C'mon, Mr. Logan, it's pretty late. Let's hang it up for the night," he said softly.

Derek Logan whirled, staggering, waving the rifle. "I make the rules here. You don't tell me what to do. Get out. Get out. You're fired."

Behind him, Logan's wife, Poppy Sinclair, gestured to Bruce Draco to leave. Draco watched the actor head back upstairs, toting the rifle, knocking into the walls. He edged to the bottom of the stairs behind him, watching until Logan had gone. His wife chased after him and closed the doors leading to the two huge master bedrooms. Draco made two calls: one to his boss, the head of the agency; and one to Poppy Sinclair's cell phone.

This was nothing new for Draco. He'd been fired before trying to protect the family from the worst of Logan's volatile craziness. Logan usually liked him. He'd been on this job nine months, which was a record with Logan. The agency would replace him with another guard, and a week later Draco would come back and encounter Logan who would greet him cheerfully, having forgotten about firing him.

He listened as Poppy's phone rang and rang. If she didn't pick up, Draco would have to go upstairs and see if there were other weapons lying around. Logan had guns. Lots of them. When he wasn't wasted, Logan was careful because of the kids.

The head of the security firm, Nigel Bateson, called Draco back. In the clipped tones of a veteran of the

Rhodesian Bush War, Draco reported Logan was playing soldier again sneaking through the house and was now upstairs flying high and wild. He'd convinced himself by now he had indeed heard weapon fire.

"Fired you again?" Bateson asked with a short, dry laugh.

"There was a three-round burst of automatic fire. People must have heard."

"Everybody okay?"

"Yeah."

"If the cops come by, you didn't hear anything."

"Right. Poppy's not answering her phone. But everything's quiet now."

"Make sure. Get Poppy to come down and talk to you. Call me back."

Draco went half way up the wide, curving staircase. "Ms. Sinclair. I'd like to talk to you." He hollered it loud. He waited, and stood back out of the line of fire beside the staircase. He called out again. And again. Waited.

Poppy flew out of the double doors of the French Country styled master bedroom on the second floor of the mansion. She marched to the top of the stairs.

"What?"

"Is everything okay?" Draco asked. "Nobody got shot?"

She pinched her eyes closed and passed a hand over her forehead. "You know Derek. He's fine now."

"Any more weapons around? I want to make sure everybody stays okay … You, the kids …"

"No, no. It's okay now. I gave him something, and he's just about asleep. He'll sleep till tomorrow."

"You sure?"

"Yes, I'm sure." Sinclair's smile lit her face, but the eyes remained flat and hard. Draco hesitated. Something that acted that fast? One of the other guys told him they had a pharmacy up there in Logan's dressing room. Sinclair went in for the supplements, all the vitamins, anti-aging products marketed on the Internet.

"I'll let you know if I need anything," Poppy Sinclair said, pulling a short black kimono around her celebrated legs.

"Okay. You're sure now."

"I'm sure."

Draco backed down the stairs and called Bateson. "Things are quiet. You know I'm alone here now."

"I'm about three minutes away."

Draco walked through the luxurious courtyard landscaping to open the electric gate in the stone wall surrounding the three-acre property, watching for the lights of Bateson's Range Rover. As Bateson arrived, the gate swung open. Draco leaned down into the open window of the vehicle to report to his employer about his fellow bodyguard.

"Eddie went to the ER about a tooth. He's no pussy. His face was all swelled up and ugly inside, and he has a fever."

"Yeah, yeah. I'll take over till he gets back," Bateson said. "If Logan wakes up and sees you here, he'll go nuts again."

"I don't know how long Eddie will be. He's sitting in the ER right now."

"Go on. I can handle it. You'll be paid for the rest of the shift."

Draco collected his gear, got into his white Tacoma truck, looked back at the house and waved as Nigel Bateson shut the gate behind him.

A neighborhood security company drove by on routine patrol and exchanged glares with Bateson, who stood at the gate. Draco drove onto the quiet, curving street of eight huge properties on Woodland Drive overlooking the Riviera Country Club.

Chapter Three

As soon as the security guy left, and Poppy was in her bathroom, Derek Logan tip-toed down the stairs. He picked up the dead body of the maid and ran up the stairs with her, dumping the body on the floor of Poppy's bedroom. Emerging from the bathroom, his wife looked at the body on the floor with horror. The bicycle hook was still embedded in the girl's eye, a turquoise-and-pink scarf trailing across her face. Blood was drying, crusting on her cheek.

"Why didn't you leave her where she was? Eeeeuw. Get it out of here."

Derek Logan ran to the window, seeing headlights shine in the floor-to-ceiling front windows.

"It's Bateson," Derek said, recognizing the Range Rover his head security guy drove. They treated Nigel Bateson with respect and a little fear, unlike most of the underlings who kept their lives afloat. He was ex-military with all the trimmings. Both went silent, looking at each other.

Moments later, Nigel Bateson pounded on the front door. With the master key, he opened the ten-foot tall front doors flanked by white columns. He called in clipped South African-accented speech. "Ms. Sinclair? I'd like to talk to you."

"Get rid of him. He likes you," Logan said.

"How am I going to do that? If you hadn't been hot for that girl…"

"Tell me you even care…"

"I don't." Poppy threw on a yellow silk kimono, making sure lots of cleavage and leg was showing and went downstairs. Bateson was standing at the bottom of the stairs. "Everything all right?"

Poppy nodded, looking pained. "Everything's fine. You know Derek. He got a little happy."

"Draco told me he thought he heard a weapon fired."

"Nooooooo. I didn't hear anything." She twisted one foot behind a knee and swung her body slowly left and right. The kimono gaped open. Bateson noticed.

"Nobody's hurt then?"

"No, no. The bullets went into the bed. You know I tell you whenever Derek's bought something new. You can go now. I gave him something. He'll sleep all day."

This wasn't the first occasion something like this had happened. "Okay. You catch a few hours' sleep."

"I will. I took something before this happened, and it's catching up with me now." She yawned and covered her mouth with the back of her hand.

Bateson made a perimeter check of the house and settled down in the security kiosk at the front gate, his eyes on the split screens monitoring the eight-bedroom property, the windows of the security post open to the balmy night.

※

Someone would take care of things. It would all work out somehow, Derek Logan hoped. It always did. He tried to hold his wife's hard stare and broke first. Dragging a blanket off the bed, he rolled Celia Talaveras in it while

Poppy watched. He slung the body over his shoulder and rose, bearing the weight lightly. He hesitated at the door, hoping his wife would say something to make it all go away.

"Come with me. I can't do this alone." Tears ran down his cheeks. He was panting.

"Absolutely not. This is your idea."

Derek glanced at the clock. 2:15 a.m. "I'm not doing it without you." He slumped down on the edge of the bed, Celia still over his shoulder. He pretended to let the body slide onto the bed.

"Don't get blood on my bed. You did this to her. Not me."

"Whether you like it or not, we're in this together."

"I hate you," she said, her beautiful face ugly with malice. "Let me count the ways."

♣

They crept downstairs, Derek at the head, Poppy carrying the feet, with Celia Talaveras wrapped in a blanket. On the patio stones outside, they dropped the body, which slid into a fetal position, the bicycle hook still in her eye. Derek had twisted the scarf to cover her face. He raked his hands through his hair, and skittered back and forth, pacing. He was still so high he was stuck on stupid. He watched Poppy march to the back right corner of the property past the swimming pool and the cabana where there was a small shed. A motion sensor light blazed as she crossed the lawn. Derek, realizing he was alone with the dead body, raced after her. Poppy came out of the shed carrying a shovel. Derek darted back to the patio to make sure the body was still there.

Outside there was moisture in the air, wind tossing through the trees. Shadows blew across the pools of light left by the streetlights. The streetlights provided only dim illumination. Heat lightning streaked through the inky clouds, like a lamp with a loose connection.

"It was an accident," Derek said over and over, thinking it might work, always hoping for the best. "I can't do this." He fell to his knees, arms circling his head, covering his ears, refusing to take the shovel from her.

"You've got to."

"I can't."

"Get up, you weakling. Do something. Drag her. Go get the shovel."

"Wait. Uh uh uh uh the gate in the hedge is locked."

"Get the key then, dammit."

"Where's the key?"

⚹

The motion sensor light went on as they crept out the back door, which alerted their security chief, who held his cell phone tight to his ear checking on the operative who was still in the ER. Bateson watched on the screen in the security kiosk as his employers dragged an elongated bundle through the gate in the hedge into the construction site next door. From the way the bundle sagged in the middle, he knew they could only be toting a body. He eased out of the security kiosk and around the side of the house.

They hauled the body toward the darkest corner at the back of the empty lot and farthest away from their own house. The dark house on the far side of the stalled construction site belonged to people who traveled most of the year. Poppy pointed at the ground and launched the shovel at her husband. Derek started digging while Poppy watched. Digging was harder than either had realized. The shovel clanged as the actor hit a stone and wrestled with tree roots that seemed to spring out of the ground to thwart them.

Bateson stole nearer and kept back in the shadows, shaking his head. Big money diluted common sense.

"It's gotta be deeper," Poppy instructed. Standing well away from the body, she breathed loudly from an asthmatic chest, breaking into coughs, and cursing her husband. He sobbed, moaning, regretting.

"It was an accident," Logan keened, hugging himself and rocking. He dropped the shovel, crouched and began opening and closing his fists, obsessively, over and over as if he were freezing cold.

"Shut up. Shut up. Somebody will hear you." Poppy swiped a hand across her face to wipe her running nose. "It's gotta be deeper."

Logan stepped back, tilting the shovel toward Sinclair.

"Then you do it. I'm exhausted."

"Maybe if you'd kept some of those appointments with Edgar you'd be in better shape."

"What an ugly bitch you are."

Poppy caught hold of one tail of the blanket, dragged the body over and tumbled it into the grave. The grave was still too small, crunching the body up, one arm flopped over the face. The mouth and nose filled with dirt. One knee stuck up above the surface of the ground. Poppy grabbed the feet and strenuously dragged her out of the shallow depression in the dirt while Logan watched.

"Deeper. Coyotes will dig her up."

"This is good enough," he said.

"No, it isn't. You have to dig out that big rock to make enough room."

Then you help me. It's not my fault," he screamed. "Your lip-smacking is driving me crazy."

An oncoming car's headlights curved around the street, nearing. Bateson took a step farther back into the shadows, but still close enough to listen.

Headlights picked out the shapes of darkened homes on big lots surrounded by fences, hedges, and stone walls. Derek's shovel bit into the hard ground and halted, his head crunched down into his shoulders. Poppy's breath drew in with a long hiss. Their eyes locked on each other waiting for the car to pass. Instead, it slowed and slowed, lights blazing, stopping in front of the padlocked gate at the front of the property.

"Get down. Get down," Poppy hissed, falling to her knees and pulling Derek down. Crouching, they froze.

Traffic on this street was infrequent. Maybe it was a lawyer or doctor or fund manager driving home on autopilot after a long day.

Was it a looky-loo with a Map of the Stars Homes hoping to catch sight of Logan or Sinclair in a window? The wind hissed in the dry palms overhead. Bateson held himself still.

Derek whimpered, hunching still lower.

"It's that security service patrol," Poppy said. "It's nothing."

"Shit, shit, shit," Derek said.

The car door opened. In the spillover of street lights, a dark figure in a bulky uniform got out of the car and slammed the door shut. He ambled over to rattle the lock on the gate. Then he stood there looking out into the darkness. A dim flashlight flicked on, the beam roving over the edges of the property, fenced in chain link.

"We should give ourselves up," Derek said. He reached out to hold Poppy. She pushed him away. "I can't stand this. It was an accident. Nate can fix it."

"We can't. It's gone too far now. And we can't have

anything happen here again. You know why."

The security officer walked back to the car. The interior lights came on when he opened the door. He slung his heavy body into the seat, looking out into the darkness, unmoving.

Minutes passed.

"What's he uh uh uh uh doing?"

"I don't know. Listening to the radio. Get away from me."

The car door opened again and the occupant of the car got out. He leaned against the car. The wind picked up in force, with a howl. Logan moaned. Poppy stabbed him with a hard elbow in the guts, making him cry out.

The guy never turned. He was pissing in the dirt by the car. He got in the car again and drove away.

Bateson made a decision after the security guard left. "What are you doing?" he said to them appearing out of the shadows, his Maglite held high, illuminating the scene.

Both celebrities whirled around, eyes wide. Bateson switched off the flashlight. They looked at each other in the dim light of the floods illuminating their house next door. The quarter moon lit up the scene like a 25-watt bulb.

"Don't tell me you're not doing anything. I'm not stupid," Bateson said.

"It was an accident," Derek said.

Poppy whimpered, flew over to Bateson and tried to cuddle in his arms as though she were afraid of Derek. "It's all his fault. He killed her."

"Who?"

"The maid. Celia. Her."

Bateson thrust her away from him. He hunkered

down by the body and unwrapped the blanket. "What happened?"

"I didn't kill her. She fell into that bicycle rack that was hung up on a wall in her room. She fell into that hook thing sticking out."

"And it did that?" Bateson said, uncurling the blanket away from the girl's face. He was no stranger to dead bodies. With effort, he twisted the bicycle hook out and unwound the scarf away from her face, setting both on the pile of dirt. "What were you doing in her room?"

"I was puh puh playing with her. You know…"

"Shit-for-Brains tried to rape her," Poppy said, flinging the accusation at her husband.

Bateson rose to his feet, looking at Derek. He could hear a sound like rats chewing in the walls, Derek grinding his teeth.

"What are we going to do now, Nigel? You have to help us." Poppy said. She knew Nigel felt sorry for her. He also knew she was a manipulator.

He said nothing, just gave them hard eyes. He turned his back on them, thinking. "I have to help you?"

"Please. That came out wrong," Poppy said, trying to get around in front of him.

"What I should do is report this to the police. You can't get away with this, you know. Too many eyes on you."

"Can't we work something out?" Poppy said, trying to take his hand.

Bateson shrugged her off, frowning. "I don't think so. This is serious."

"Money? Can we pay you?" Derek said.

"Money to cover up that you killed her?"

Bateson walked to the security kiosk at the front gates and shut the door firmly behind him. They ran after him,

Poppy rattling the doorknob on the security kiosk. Bateson had locked it behind him, shutting them out, alone with their paranoia.

"Or what, Nigel?" Poppy asked.

Bateson sat down at a chair facing the monitoring screens, his back to the door, thinking. He'd pulled clients out of messes before, but never murder. Logan said it was an accident, and he could see how it had gone down that way, but Logan was a liar, and weak. Poppy ran him like a dominatrix.

"Or what, Nigel?" Poppy asked. "Don't leave us like this."

"Please, Nigel," Derek said. "Please." He was chittering with anxiety like a squirrel.

Bateson was typing something on the keyboard. He let them wait while he considered his options. Logan had only killed the maid, which made things a lot easier than if it were the daughter. She was probably an illegal. Who would miss an illegal? He got up out of his chair, turned around and looked at the two of them outside, making up his mind. He pulled a pair of disposable gloves out of a drawer and put them on.

"You have to do exactly what I tell you."

Poppy rubbed her face with her hands. "Thank you, Nigel. Thank you. I knew I could count on you. What are you going to do?"

He didn't answer. He headed back to the dead body at the graveside. "It's going to be daylight before long. Get busy."

"Can you help? Please. I need gloves," Derek complained. "I've got blisters."

"Don't be such a baby." Bateson leaned against a tree, watching. After Derek dug the grave to a depth that suited him, and a cleanup job that made the recently dug earth less obvious, he pushed them before him into the house.

He stood by while they mopped down the blood spatter on the wall, threw away the bed coverings spotted with blood, and pulled up the carpet and the under pad on the floor of the maid's room. Everything that could have had DNA traces were removed. By this time they had quit complaining and moved dully doing whatever he told them.

Bateson knew Celia slightly, the household worker with the sunny smile and hilarious English. She brought them iced tea and cookies on really hot days when the AC crapped out in the security kiosk. Security work was boring, watching screens twelve hours a day. Admitting the UPS guy was a highlight. Little things about the guy you worked with got annoying in close quarters. Seeing the girl come out with a tray of drinks lifted the mood. If anybody was going to be dead, he wished it were the cook/housekeeper, who begrudged every mouthful his guys ate as though it cost *her* money.

Sinclair and Logan bagged up their clothes, the bed covers, and the digging equipment in black plastic garbage bags and placed them in the back of Derek's Hummer, stuffing the mattress in on the side. They quit trying to engage Bateson in speculation. Bateson knew the value of silence. Derek driving, Bateson in the passenger seat, and Poppy silent in the back seat, they drove north on the 405 Freeway to take an exit in Sylmar as the first purple streaks of dawn pinkened the sky. Raising a hand, he pointed at an exit that led off into a low-income, Latino part of the San Fernando Valley. As full daylight broke on what promised to be a fine day, they flung the last of the bags into dumpsters behind apartment buildings and low-rent storefronts.

It wasn't over yet. Bateson gave them orders to get the girl's room painted, flooring and carpet replaced. This morning.

✦

Chapter Four

Derek came down hard, reality settling over him like a shroud. He and Poppy were back in the master bedroom suite, divided into his and hers bedrooms, exhausted. Bateson said he would dig up the body when it was safe, and bury it somewhere else. It was safer for the meantime to leave it where it was. The twins and Megan had slept through it all. Jake, Derek's son by his first marriage, was at his mother's. All they had to do now was get through the day as though everything was normal. Both consulted their iPads. What did they have to do today? What could be canceled?

Derek raked his fingernails through wet hair, his mouth set into a groove of dull belligerence. Poppy watched him, the critical bitch never giving him credit for doing anything right.

"Stop scratching your head. You'll make your hair fall out worse than it is now."

"It's isn't falling out," Derek said, darting back into the bathroom to peer at himself in the mirror. "Nigel could be with the cops right now," he said, paranoia flaring over him in waves.

Poppy came into the bathroom, yanking a skein of toilet paper off the roll and blowing her nose. "It's our word against his. Look who we are. Who he is."

"All he needs to say is go look there and dig up the body. I need a little toot, baby." He headed toward a chest of drawers that had a secret compartment. But Poppy had emptied it last night along with any other pharmaceuticals she could find. She gave him a shove, and he landed on the bed.

"Ah, baby, I need it," he said.

"Forget that. You need to concentrate. We have to keep it together."

Derek slumped on the edge of the bed. "I'm so tired. We've been up all night. Look at my hands. All blistered. What are we going to tell the help? They'll want to know where she went. Lupe? Especially the kids. She and Megan were tight …"

Poppy was moving around her bedroom, in and out of her room-sized closet, choosing and discarding outfits, jewelry. "Act surprised. Say she ran off with her boyfriend. I know. She left a mess, and we had to replace the carpet and the bed. She left a note, but we threw it out. Yeah, we threw it out. Do the whole room over. Lupe won't be home for a couple of days."

Derek considered all this. "He told us to redo this room as well. She might have leaked."

"I'll get my assistant on it."

"Lupe will be suspicious. So will Megan. What are you going to tell them?" Logan's handsome face fell into lines of worry and despair.

"I don't know. Lupe doesn't matter. She's with us no matter what if she wants citizenship. Say the girl never came home last night. She just left. I don't know. When we looked in her room, there was this big dirty mess. So we had to throw out all the bedclothes, rip up the carpet. Say she must have had a dog in there and the dog shit all over everything. You'll have to convince Megan," she said, brightening.

"Me?" Derek's mouth was tight, ready for a fight. "Why not you?"

"Was last night one of Celia's ESL classes at Ste. Anne's?"

"I don't know. How would you expect me to know that?"

"What about the kids?" Poppy said, pacing, smoothing lotion onto her perfect limbs. "The twins liked her. So did Megan. That girl. I don't know what to do with her lately."

"They're all like that." Derek looked unconvinced. "All those little bitches." He jumped to his feet, the towel falling off him revealing a slight paunch.

"You're getting fat," Poppy said with a sneer.

He looked at his wife, not even hearing her. He had slipped another mental disc. Drugs had shut his wife's opinions out long ago. A new high zinged around like a ping pong ball in his brain. He was too smart to get caught, he assured himself.

"It's going to be okay," he said. "Isn't it?" "We don't know what Bateson's going to do. That didn't get settled last night."

"He said he'd move the body. He will."

♪

"Where's Celia?" Megan demanded. The 15-year-old girl called her mother on the kitchen intercom, chin jutted out, purpose in every line of her body.

"Don't scream at me. I'm coming down."

Megan twitched until her mother arrived. She watched Lupe slicing and toasting bread that no one would ever eat. Megan and her mother confronted each other across a granite counter expanse in the sunny kitchen of the mansion on Woodlawn Drive. Megan found her stash of Pop Tarts and stuck two in the toaster.

"Pop Tarts? Oh, Megan, really," Poppy said with disdain.

"Where did Celia go?" her daughter demanded. "What happened to her? Lupe says she's gone."

"I get home. Celia, she's not here," Lupe confirmed with a series of nods.

"Celia? Oh, her," her mother said, taking her time about accepting a cup of coffee from Lupe

"She's gone. Left us a note saying she was sorry her room was such a mess and that she had another job." Poppy stared hard at her daughter.

"Where's the note? I want to see it."

Her mother clucked her tongue. "It was illiterate. I threw it away," her mother said with the authority that made audiences believe she was a Supreme Court lawyer, a prairie housewife, an assassin, and a 1940s dance hall girl. Her personality was vacant, which allowed her to pour out one identity after a movie and fill herself up with someone new.

"You're lying," Megan said.

"Megan. If you ever want to leave this house where you think you're treated so badly, let us have some peace about Celia. We were good to her, and she just took off, leaving behind a big mess, I might add. Why does she get to have time off for ESL classes and Lupe doesn't? You insisted till we gave in."

"Lupe doesn't need ESL classes."

"Hey, I like time off too," Lupe said, switching on the overhead fan above the stove. Poppy couldn't stand cooking smells. "You think of that?"

"She wouldn't just leave. I know her." Megan set her

face in a hard frown.

"Is she going to run to the *Enquirer* and tell big stories about us now? Maybe that's why she left. The *Enquirer* paid her to spy on us." Poppy looked to Lupe for confirmation, while Lupe scrambled egg whites.

"You know, Megan, every time we bring in some new worker, we open ourselves up to somebody making up stories about us."

"Making up stories? Like my father hitting on all my friends?"

"You shut your mouth about that. Do you want to go to that fat camp in Wyoming?"

"You make Celia come back."

"Oh, don't be so ridiculous, Megan. We can't make people want to work here."

"Yes, you can. Something must have happened to her. Look for her. It's not too late. You know people."

"She must have wanted to go. We didn't make her. Why do you care so much anyway?"

"We were friends."

Lupe slapped a plate of scrambled eggs and toast down in front of Megan and shook her head at her, frowning. Megan's eyes never left her mother.

"Oh, come on, Megan. Friends?"

"She must have left me a note. I'm going to check her room."

Her mother forced her way in front of her.

"You just stay here. I've got workers coming in to clean. Now just forget her. Honestly, you make a fuss about the silliest things."

Megan flung her plate of eggs at her.

Sinclair ducked her head, and the plate smashed against the white cabinets, eggs drooling down the walls. "You little bitch."

Lupe huffed and grabbed a rag to clean up, maneuvering around Poppy.

"You don't care about her, but I did."

"Why would you care about her? A maid. You should talk to your therapist about that."

"I hate her. I'm never going back. You can't make me."

Derek Logan slouched into the room, red-eyed, moving like an old man. He stuck a coffee pod into the Keurig and opened a kitchen cupboard door, as though he expected to find an answer there.

"Look at him," Megan said, flouncing over to drop her laptop on the kitchen table where she did her homework. "He's wasted again. I wish all the people who think he's so freakin' wonderful could see him now."

Her father's only response was to sigh.

"I'm really tired, Megan. Can't you see that? Have a little sympathy."

Poppy ignored that, turning from her daughter to her housekeeper. "I'm sorry, Lupe. I'll get my PA on this today and find someone new to help you." She picked up her coffee cup off the counter and headed upstairs where she could take a pill and finally sleep. "There'll be a raise for you, Lupe. I know this is hard."

The housekeeper shrugged her shoulders, satisfied. She kept her opinions to herself.

"Hey, wait a minute," Megan said. "Celia can't have gone just like that. Why didn't she tell me?"

"Why would she tell you, Megan?" Her mother paused at the door, taking in the girl's ordinary face and body.

"She just would. She was nice to me. She's the only one who cared whether I lived or died," her eyes filling with tears.

"Oh, for heaven's sake, Megan. Grow up." Her mother flounced out of the room. Lupe turned and walked away. Megan was left standing in the kitchen, all her unbearable emotions on show.

She ate the two Pop Tarts and put two more in the toaster. Celia was the only reason she felt like coming home after school to this immaculate, beautiful house. Celia was often in the twin's play room upstairs, and they would talk, really talk. Celia didn't think she was fat. She was fun. There was no status competition or mean-girl stuff with her.

Celia was her friend. She knew how it felt when her father, the great Derek Logan, hit on her so-called friends at her birthday parties. They had plans, once Celia's English was better. Celia was studying, serious for the first time.

Defeat showed in every movement of Megan's body as she trudged out of the kitchen, crossed the great room to the stairs, using the banister to haul herself up to the sanctuary of her room.

At fifteen she couldn't fight them. Celia had betrayed her too. She must have followed that guy Jacinto to Colorado.

♆

Nigel Bateson watched the gravesite from a distance with narrowed eyes. Different security services patrolled customers up and down Woodland Drive, one driving by on an average of every half hour of the day and night. Instead of a bored rent-a-cop, the one assigned to the lot next door where the body of Celia Talaveras still lay seemed to take his job seriously. He worked double shifts, lingering at the gate to fill out paperwork, taking a coffee break at the site, a couple of times getting out to walk around.

Maybe the night guy would be a little less diligent. He wasn't. Bateson waited. He figured he could get in and out in a few unpleasant hours.

Days passed, then weeks, while he lay in wait for an opportunity to move the body. He knew one of his celebrity employers would fuck up sooner or later. The danger increased. Logan would tell somebody. He would have to babble. If he could get the body out of there, and clean it up so that no forensic hotshot could make his reputation based on DNA findings, he'd be home free. Bateson had insulated himself carefully from any of the consequences of helping them. He had set up maximum deniability. In the meantime, he too was also being paid, paid well. He had his own dreams of retirement.

It made sense when Bateson caught the flash of sunlight off a long camera lens. The rent-a-cops knew who lived next door and were hoping for that unguarded moment when either Poppy or Derek could be caught on camera. The *Enquirer* paid, paid well.

Nigel Bateson had his own problems, which came first. He could only do what he could do. He convinced himself he still had time.

Somebody always fucked up.

🜨

Four months later

Mason drove the black Crown Vic from the station. A contractor reported uncovering a grave on a construction site along one of the short curving roads off San Vicente in the high-end real estate section of Santa Monica. Mason and his partner, Art Delgado, were doing the preliminary on the dead body found in the grave.

Turning off San Vicente Boulevard onto Woodland Drive, Delgado twisted his heavy body in his seat, looking around. "I've never been on a call up here? You?"

"Domestic violence," Mason grunted. He felt old and used up at thirty-eight. His eyes felt sandpapered with lack of sleep, his head thick and stupid. "Old lady was beating up on one of the home help."

"Wonder what these places sell for?" Delgado said. "San Vicente Boulevard looks pricey enough, and then you turn off to this little dinky short street overlooking Rustic Canyon and it's a whole league more expensive. Lot of construction. Renovations to perfectly good houses. Look at that."

"We just drove through Good, Better, and Best Santa Monica, Delgado," Mason said, feeling light-headed and a little goofy. "This street is the pinnacle everybody wants to climb to. The megastar achievers. Everybody comes to Hollywood thinking they're the next Brad Pitt and ends up working for Tires R Us."

"This is where people who handle money live," Delgado said, his eyes puffy from lack of sleep. His big lumpy head sat squarely on meaty shoulders, short silver bristles of hair buzz cut. Steady brown eyes that could halt a fleeing shoplifter. "The bastards."

Mason turned to look at him. "I'm not sure my condo at Seventh and San Vicente would count. I'm only hanging onto the edges of Good Santa Monica."

"Would you step it up?" Delgado said. "You drive

like my grandmother."

A few workers were standing around when Mason arrived, having a tailgate, early burrito lunch. The radio played *ranchera*. A few melted back into the shadows seeing the SMPD vehicle.

The contractor named Jim Prewitt walked over to Mason, talking on his cell phone as Mason got out of the car. A brown dog of undistinguished parentage shambled along beside him. Mason knelt to scratch the dog's ears.

"Yeah, like my guys were putting in the footings for an irrigation system. See over here?"

Prewitt led them toward the edge of a property which would boast a McMansion built out nearly to the street, with a probable seven-thousand-square-foot footprint. Prewitt rocked back and forth on his heels. Just another single-family home. People here thought you couldn't raise a child decently in less than five thousand square feet.

What a dog of a case, Mason thought to himself, following the contractor along a gouge in the earth made by an orange Kubota. Unidentified body found in a grave.

"We stopped when we saw the hair and the forehead. And that part of a hand. That's a hand, isn't it?"

Mason looked down. "That's a hand." He hunkered down beside the ditch and regarded the hand with natural fingernails painted bubblegum pink, a dirt and blood-covered forehead and long black hair. He was no coroner's office guy who could size up bones and decomposed flesh to identify where the occupant had grown up, his diet and condition, then grow all cagey when he fished for particulars. He and Delgado looked at each other across from the opened grave. Mason took a few steps back from the stench of the grave and turned to take a deep breath.

"I'll get going on the calls," Mason said. No use

getting excited until he had some date parameters and hard information—ideally an ID. "You start on the neighbors. Okay?"

"Fredericks coming?" Fredericks was assigned to Mason and Delgado when they got a dead body. Otherwise, she worked property crime.

"Yeah, I ducked out so she wouldn't ride with us. The mouth, you know? The mouth?"

"Yeah, I know. There's only so many houses on the street, and probably everybody's out making money. I'll take the houses to the right. Fredericks can start going that way," he pointed to the other side of the street, "once she gets here."

"I've got nothing to do with this. You know that, don't you?" Prewitt said, following Mason. "We got a performance bond here. When can we get back to work?"

"It'll be a while."

"Cut me a break, will'ya? How about we start the footings, say around the corner of the house. We won't get in your way. You won't even see us."

"You know that's not how it's gonna work, Mr. Prewitt."

"Aw, shit."

Mason got no pleasure out of saying no to people who had to work for a living. He was on autopilot, trying to keep his mind on the body in the grave. He needed a name, a family context to put the body into to charge him up and make him care. Until then it was just a body. Another thing: was it the only grave on the site? They'd need ground penetrating radar to go over the whole area to make sure.

The contractor walked away, slapping his leg. His dog followed him, giving Mason the stink eye over his shoulder. Mason got down the basics, did the paper on the case, emailed it off to the boss and negotiated a few hours' sleep. He'd meet the coroner's deputy, Dr. Audrey Moon, at noon. That would give her time to get her setup started.

Delgado nodded at the contractor and headed off down the leafy street, shot through with bands of sunlight. It was a fine California day to find a grave.

♋

Mason found himself thinking about the weekend visit with his daughter while he caught up with his other cases by phone and email. Ginger had passes to the Los Angeles Chocolate and Pastry Exhibition. He'd never met a pastry, or for that matter a carbohydrate, he didn't like. He left a message for his father back in Grand Rapids, Michigan to call him back. Some months ago he'd gone flying with a pal who worked Vice and fallen in love with the sky. Saturday was always the highlight of his week: a flying lesson and a chance to hang with the instructors and ask questions, to be around people who did what he dreamed of doing. He was getting closer to enrolling in the accelerated program to get his license, but it would mean taking vacation time and laying real money down on the line.

The first job today was to make a preliminary assessment of death, get the body out of the ground, pass it off to somebody else, and try to make an identification—if possible. Hearing the pleasant chirp of squirrels and birds overhead, he looked around. He paused in the quiet to savor the bird song, standing far enough away from the grave to breathe in the soft green air.

He took a call from the Coroner's deputy, a Dr. Audrey Moon. She owned the body. "Come back at noon," she said. "I don't want you getting in my way."

"Okay," Mason said, not wanting to get into an

argument with her so soon. Delgado was getting in the car to go back to the station, yanking at his tie, stuffing his paunch behind the wheel. He was determined to drive, which made Mason uneasy.

"Why would you bury a body here?" Mason said. "I mean it makes sense to come up here where there's no neighbors…"

Delgado turned onto San Vicente Boulevard where the joggers veered around huge roots of the coral trees that ran down the grassy median strip.

They argued whether the body could be a local. Plenty of attractive, well-cared for Latinas lived in Santa Monica.

Delgado stopped listening. He checked his phone. His wife's mother who had dementia was living with them again, and they had to watch her. She wandered.

"Why here?" Mason said to him. "Only eight properties, big houses with landscaping, walls, all of them dropping off in the back to the Riviera Country Club. There's gotta be urban wildlife here, possums, raccoons, coyotes. Surprising the body hasn't been dug up and chewed on some, don't you think? The smell would have alerted the animals long before the contractors turned it up. I think it's funny."

Delgado didn't answer and Mason lost himself in the dream of having his own plane and flying up to Santa Barbara for the weekend with Ginger and Haley. How excited his daughter would be. Himself at the controls. An older Cessna 172. He'd priced them. Ah, he sighed. A Piper Cherokee. Hard but doable.

The moment of peace and reflection changed when they got back to the station and their cubicles. The Lieutenant of Operations, Lt. Larry Vargas, wanted frequent written updates, which took time and effort away from actually doing things. Lt. Vargas was learning his new job, trying out who he was in the command staff. Vargas liked to collect people in his office to listen to him make phone calls while they sat on their asses and waited for him. He liked to show how important he was, and how many people he got to boss around. Vargas had too many training courses and not enough street experience. When he realized he didn't know what he was doing, he was liable to go junkyard dog on somebody, filled with the thrill of new command. Mason hoped it wouldn't be him today.

Detectives working major cases now could call on a Sheriff's Department's crime lab criminologist who worked under contract for the SMPD, one of only a handful of police agencies in Los Angeles County with the same arrangement. Before that, they submitted evidence to the sheriff's crime lab in competition with other agencies. Sometimes they were lined up in the queue from three to six months to get results back. Evidence submitted to the criminologist now was processed and returned to the SMPD in six to seven weeks, not great, but a whole lot better. They had other cases to work in the meantime.

Mason had never been part of the coterie around the Sarge and Lieutenant Vargas. He couldn't figure out why Vargas seemed to dislike him particularly. But he did.

Chapter Five

Since the night their security chief helped them bury the body, Bateson's billings had tripled. The current billing added an extra surcharge.

"Nigel wants more money now," Poppy Sinclair said, storming into the home gym where Derek was doing occasional bench presses. He was listening to G-War, watching himself in the mirrors, and playing their video.

"What?"

"Turn that racket off."

Derek reached for the remote control, taking his time about it. He took the billing statement from her and glanced at it. Poppy crossed her arms and glared.

"Blackmail," she said. "We're always going to have him on our backs."

A small frown pinched Derek's perfect forehead. Tilting his head down caused the thinning hair on his scalp to gleam under the high intensity lights.

Poppy snapped her finger at his head. "Spray it. Stop with the French fries. Go vegan."

"Fuh fur french fries don't make your hair fall out," Derek said, wincing away from her. "What else can we do? We need him. Have you talked to him lately about anything?"

"Why should it be me? I didn't kill her."

"Nuh nuh nobody killed her. It was an accident."

Poppy was pacing around the gym, looking for dust, a film of sweat on the machines, something to find fault with. "I haven't talked to him. He told Lupe yesterday he was taking the room next to hers in the staff wing. He didn't even ask me. I had to find it out from her. He's taking over our home now."

"What did you say to Lupe?" Derek asked, worrying now.

"I told her we'd had a few credible threats. We wanted live-in security. What else could I say? He caught me by surprise."

"If he just wants money …" Derek said, hope in his face.

"We have to talk to him," Poppy said, "Get this out in the open. Blackmailers never quit."

"If it's only money …"

"It will never only be about money," Poppy snapped, squinching up her pretty white Anglo-Saxon Protestant face. "I hate you."

"I hate you back," Derek said, grinning. "There. Happy?"

♆

Chapter Six

Back at the gravesite, Mason's first step was to see the body disinterred and try to make an ID. The victim could be local. It wasn't likely that bangers from South LA or the eastside drove up here to dump a body. Somebody had to have noticed construction had stopped here. It wasn't a well-traveled street with a lot of traffic, except for the help that arrived in these big homes daily. Several of the properties were under renovation. There was a shifting population of construction workers. They'd have to check every single one.

The coroner's deputy had dug in with her people. Mason looked around: two large houses on either side of the construction lot, a double lot across the street, half of it a screened tennis court. He heard the thwack of tennis balls.

♫

Dr. Audrey Moon, the Coroner's deputy, was a short Asian woman with a bossy manner. She was dressed in camo cargo pants and black T-shirt and smelled of cigarettes and mosquito repellent. Off-handedly she introduced him to graduate students there to assist her in the painstaking work of disinterring the body and transporting it back to the coroner's lab facilities. They had set up privacy screens around the site.

She glared at him as he came up to introduce himself. "Don't ask me any questions," she snarled. "I'm busy."

Mason held up his hands and tried his best grin on her without much effect. "So you can't make a guess, give me a range of times for how long the victim's been in the ground at least?"

Dr. Moon ignored him, instead snapping off commands to a frowsy-looking assistant who came over with a packet of short stakes. Another helper produced balls of twine. The body was owned by the coroner. She directed the search for more bodies using a ground radar detecting device. Mason stood far enough back not to challenge her and stay out of the range of the smell.

Before her team got any nearer the grave, they would dress in protective clothing. As he watched, they laid out a grid on a perimeter at a distance from the site to document anything found near and in the grave.

Detective Laura Fredericks was assigned to him and Delgado when they had a rare homicide. Santa Monica wasn't the murder capital of the world, but they had their share of whodunits from time to time. Up here in the high-income end of town, this particular victim was unlikely to be one of the homeless people who enraged homeowners and spoiled the look of the city. But you never know. He saw Fredericks arrive, park, and march over.

"You couldn't wait for me? You couldn't wait five fucking minutes, sir?" Everything Fredericks said was at top volume. She claimed she talked so loud because she'd grown up with five brothers and had to fight to get heard.

"Fredericks, the mouth on you. I didn't know how long you'd be."

Fredericks went storming off to intimidate the grave

diggers. He'd seen her in workout clothes beating up on the krav maga instructor, and didn't like her when she had to run her mouth afterward in full braggart mode. Several distinct and separate people lived inside Fredericks, and some he liked better than others. What propelled these various incarnations of Fredericks was mysterious. She was probably the most complex cop he had ever known. He also knew she would be good at forming a relationship with the coroner's deputy who would be crucial to their case. He noted everything carefully, knowing he might have to stand up in court a year from now and have his account picked at by some asshole defense attorney. He drifted back to Dr. Moon and her merry little band after he'd sketched the scene for his own purposes.

They watched the tedious process of disinterring the body, ignoring them, until Mason approached her for an update. She chased them off.

"What? There's nothing you can do here. Go bother somebody else."

Okay. Plenty of good restaurants on Montana Avenue, another one of the city's pricey shopping districts. There was even a store on Montana that sold nothing but socks. Socks. Didn't Jerry Lewis only wear his socks once?

Fredericks took a phone call, walking toward Mason. She handed him a fresh pile of bureaucracy to deal with, then grinned. He looked up. She pressed her iPhone to the side of her head like a surgical device holding her face together.

"Well, fuck me with a phone pole!" Fredericks swiped the phone closed and looked at it as though it could tell her more.

"What?" Mason said.

"Know who lives next door?"

"I got it somewhere here." He spun his finger down email messages on his phone. "I got it here somewhere. I haven't had time to look. Who?"

"Mr. and Mrs. Hollywood America. Derek Logan and Poppy Sinclair."

Mason's heart leaped up. He'd lusted after Poppy Sinclair since he'd been fifteen years old.

"Well, she's a lesbian."

"Poppy Sinclair is not a lesbian," Mason said, slapping the top down on his laptop. He didn't want to hear it, knowing he was being ridiculous. Fredericks looked up at him.

"Yeah, well, she is. You never heard that story?"

"What story?" Mason said, giving in, and willing to listen. He scowled at Fredericks. Maybe he had been a little enthusiastic talking about Sinclair's last movie.

"Gotcha, didn't I? Delgado told me you had the hots for her." She danced in her seat, making jabbing pokes at him with her finger.

"How in hell would he know that? Fake news, Fredericks. Fake news."

"Oh ho! No really, it's true. Poppy's a lesbian."

"Why don't you just Foxtrot Oscar off, Fredericks?" Mason said.

But he couldn't stop her telling him that for years rumors circulated about Poppy Sinclair's *close* women friends. Somebody had died at the Logan-Sinclair house only six months ago. Not Mason's case, but everybody who read *People* magazine and the *LA Times* knew about it, the way they knew about Phil Spector and OJ, all the rap stars, and the Kardashians. He remembered now reading about it, then had forgotten.

"Well, turns out Poppy and her girlfriend got wasted in her rooftop Jacuzzi next door. Poppy leaves to get a drink and decides to check her Facebook page. Initially, she insists she's only gone ten minutes. But Twitter and Instagram show she's gone for more than an hour and a half. She goes back and finds her friend underwater, drowned. Pharmaceuticals on board. Took their publicist's best efforts to spin the story."

"Any charges?" Mason asked.

"Nah. Seems like her girlfriend was a Carrie Fisher type person, off again, on again sobriety. Nobody was surprised she'd accidentally drowned."

Mason checked out the story himself, reading the comments below the stories, where most of the juicy tidbits were found. Some readers insisted Poppy Sinclair was a cold-hearted bitch, but millions of people loved her in all those Disney movies. The star had done a great deal of public suffering, setting up a college fund for her friend's thirteen-year-old daughter, positioning herself as having suffered a tragic loss. Nearing the dangerous age of forty when the good roles stopped coming, Sinclair was also setting up a production company.

There'd been a buzz about charging her with manslaughter, but a phalanx of attorneys arranged to let the charge on the case dissolve. A faint stain clung to Poppy despite her people's spin that she was the victim of a tragedy. It was hinted Poppy had a string of girlfriends, but nobody came forward. A happy, happy marriage to Derek Logan comforted her in her grief. So the media said.

A feeling of wild hilarity sprang up in Mason's chest. He wanted a reason to see Poppy Sinclair, see her for himself, maybe even get close to her, talk to her.

She couldn't be a lesbian.

Fredericks seemed to have a hate-on for attractive women, especially the ones who helped nature along. She got her share of male attention. Then when her ballbreaker side revealed itself, the attention cooled. Mason knew it hurt her, but he was the last one to comment. Diamonds glittered on her fingers as she hammered away at her keyboard. Fredericks had a little jewelry-buying problem at one time. Mason hoped these weren't new diamonds. Worst of all would be an engagement ring, but then who in hell would have her bossy little self? He was stuck with her and her long-term crush on him, knowing she still hoped Ginger would die.

♌

The pleasant day got hotter, the miasma from the grave stronger. Mason stayed well away from the choking drift of decomposition, only nearing the short Asian woman when she beckoned to him. Dr. Moon said over her shoulder, as she was punching keys on her phone. "Okay, cop. I can at least tell you it's been more than a month or two."

"Like up to six months?"

"Not that long."

"Cause of death?"

She just glared at him. "Anything else?"

"Can't you tell me anything?"

"No. I've got to transport the body first and put her back together."

"Female then? What else can you tell me? How old? What's all that around her eye?"

She glared at him and marched off.

Fredericks, who was standing next to him grinned, watching Moon. "I just love her," she said.

Mason took his time getting back to the car. Nobody could expect much this soon in the process. He'd had one case like this before and everything took time. He tried to call his Dad back in Grand Rapids. Busy. Mailbox was full. It was useless emailing him. He sat in the car and called his daughter, Haley, out in Rancho Cucamonga, far away in the Greater Los Angeles urban sprawl. "Hey, babe, how are you?"

"Oh, Daddy, it's you. Are you okay?"

"'Course I'm okay." He looked at himself in the mirror, not always liking what he saw. But he still had his thick black hair, and his gut didn't hang over his belt. "I don't have a job where I get shot at a lot."

She made a noise. "I'm ten now. You can't lie to me anymore. Somebody got shot over one of those Bird scooter things."

"I was miles away when that happened, pussycat."

"Oh. Me and mom watch all these cop shows. She says that's not really what it's like. But I know."

"Oh? So you know, do you? How do you know?"

"I just do. I'm smart, you know."

Mason had to laugh. "Well, your poor old Dad isn't that dumb. We're pretty careful, you know."

"But you could get shot."

He made his tone serious. This wasn't the first time his daughter had shared her fears about him getting shot. Her mother was taking these fears seriously.

"Listen, cuddle-bunny, I'm not in as much danger as you think. The TV people make everything worse than it is."

"That's what Mom and Harvey the Garvey say."

He swiped the phone closed after she'd told him a long, giggling story about her friend who had a new puppy that pooped in her bed. He knew when he was being played. Ginger wanted a dog too.

☙

PART II

Chapter Seven

The memory of the night Celia died faded into the past into the never-happened, must-have-been-a-dream realm for Poppy Sinclair and Derek Logan. Their focus had narrowed onto beating each other out in forming a production company and acquiring a hot musical property. By the time four months had passed, Logan and Sinclair relaxed. Derek and Poppy didn't have relationships with their neighbors, but Lupe Garcia, the major domo of the household, gossiped with the help in the nearby houses and the construction workers. The police were asking questions at every house on the street. Had anybody seen anything? Any unusual activity at that property? It caused a ruffle of alarm among the undocumented.

Lupe mentioned the news of a body found in a grave next door, while Poppy was pouring cereal into a bowl at breakfast. Poppy went white. She tore up the stairs and into Derek's bedroom next to hers. He was in bed with a script, running his lines. He leaped to his feet and peered out the window. A pair of detectives were sitting in a black Crown Vic parked across the street talking to each other.

"W-wha-what do they want? Are they coming here? Do they know? Oh, God. How did they find out? I can't stand this. I can't stand it. What are we going to do?"

Derek said, in a panic.

"Nothing. Calm down."

"B but but they're all over this." He tried to hug his wife.

"Stop mauling me, Derek. They're going to find out. Nigel promised us we were okay." "What are we gonna do? What are we gonna do?"

"Nothing. Those dozy cops couldn't find their ass with a GPS. Pull yourself together."

"Nuh nuh Nigel said no one would ever find her."

Bateson was elusive and hard to find even though he occupied a room in their home. Poppy was careful to keep her voice light and pleasant, requesting they meet to discuss the discovery of the body. He had become the master, and they were the employees. After several days, he still hadn't returned her repeated calls and hadn't been seen at the house. Another security operative now manned the gates. In frustration, she set a meeting time, and Bateson didn't show up. Twice this happened. They watched for his Range Rover that he parked now in the four-car garage beneath the mansion. Finally Poppy and Derek went to his room at midnight when a crack of light appeared beneath the door. He opened at Derek's firm knock.

"Yes?" Bateson's face was stern. He wore a white terry cloth robe, his hair wet.

"We want to talk to you," Derek said. He moved jerkily, like a twitchy junkie.

"Can it wait? I'm very tired."

"No, it can't. We feel like we've had to stalk you in our own home. You're here. We're here. Let's talk now."

"This room is secure. Come in."

Derek sidled past him and looked around the room where his life had changed. Beige carpet, white walls, taupe bedspread and pillow cases, a toilet kit visible on the sink, the smell of a fresh shower with expensive soaps.

"You told us you had removed the body and buried it somewhere else. You assured us she would never be found. Now the police are all over this."

Nigel shook his head. "I never said that. You may have heard that, but it's not what I said."

Derek and Poppy exchanged a look. "No, that's what you said," Poppy spluttered.

Nigel stood up. "I said things would be okay and if you keep your heads, they will be."

Their eyes followed him into the bathroom. He returned with a towel and nonchalantly dried his hair, saying nothing. He stood in front of the mirror over the chest of drawers, and combed his thinning hair, then smoothed on moisturizer.

Poppy attacked when attacked. How could he do this to her? "The police are all over us. They found her body. How did that happen?"

"If you do everything I tell you, it's going to be alright. This room was thoroughly cleaned. Nothing remains. Relax."

"Relax?" Derek shrieked. "They found her body."

Bateson slapped the palm of his hand flat on the tabletop so hard his desk top computer rattled. Poppy and Derek jumped.

"I told you. Relax."

"Megan's never bought it that Celia just took off. They had some kind of friendship going, based on what I can't imagine," Poppy said, positioning herself in front of the mirror and examining herself. "Sometimes I think even Lupe knows."

"What can she know?" Bateson said. "Nothing. Megan's your department. You keep her under control."

"Precisely how, Nigel? How? She's a teenager."

He shrugged and walked over to the door, opening it. "Keep her under control."

Poppy and Derek spent the night in Poppy's bed, not having sex, not even touching. Just occasional bursts of whispering in the darkness. They'd forgotten the skill of talking over the years, and it had to be relearned. Turning to each other for comfort was like going to the Post Office to buy a loaf of bread.

"You'll see," Derek said, "It's gonna be alright."

Poppy's heart gave a tiny jolt of hope that made her want to slap it.

"You know the police found a body next door, Megan," Poppy said.

Megan was playing with her phone at the table in the kitchen where she spent a lot of time. Lupe was unloading bags of groceries delivered from Whole Foods. Megan didn't look up at her mother's words. She was depressed, and her lank hair and stolid affect showed it.

"Megan?" Poppy said.

"What? I know that."

"People might be saying things, the kids at school. You know the media gets hold of things, and they just go from A-Z about us even though there's no connection."

"You think I don't know that? Living here with you and him?"

Derek sauntered in and sat at the end of the table, flopping down a script he was studying. "Can I have some of that wheatgrass stuff you make, Lupe, *querida*?"

"It might be a little worse this time because of—you

know—Grace drowning."

"Yeah, you're still mourning her I can tell."

"There's no need to be sarcastic. I set it up for her daughter to get a free ride at whatever college she wants."

"I'm sure that's a big consolation to her."

Derek huffed from the end of the table. Poppy shot a glance at him. *Say something,* she mouthed.

"Megan, why are you being such a bitch?" Derek said. "You know your nice life depends on your mother and me getting work. If we get slammed in the media, all of that might go away. Would you like living in an apartment in the Valley?"

Megan looked up at the ceiling, closed one eye and considered. "You know, that might not be so bad. I'll take the twins, and you can have Jake and each other."

"You little bitch!" her father shouted.

"If you need some pointers on how to handle people, you can talk to Binky, our publicist. That's her job, to protect us," Poppy said, avoiding looking at her daughter. She had made it plain long ago that the sight of her daughter caused her pain.

♫

Chapter Eight

*B*ody *found in a grave next door to America's Sweethearts Poppy and Derek* the headlines read in the celebrity press. Cop shops leaked like a colander. Soon a pack of hyenas was lying in wait on the street. The media created a memorable traffic jam on Woodland Drive in a city already choking on cars and tourists.

The next day Mason and Delgado continued the knock and talks on the houses on Woodland one by one, keeping the home of Poppy Sinclair and Derek Logan in sight. Mason admitted to himself he would love to have a glimpse of her first, even though he knew it was stupid to think she'd be outside trimming the topiary or looking over the high stone walls. They were saving the Sinclair-Logan house for later this morning. Some properties on the narrow winding street dated back to the 1920s and were modest by today's standards. Others boasted wealth and contemporary tastes. He parked and got out in front of a place the record said was built in the 50s. If there were anything left of 50s construction, it was hard to see from the street.

On Citydata.com Mason found a listing of all eight houses with dizzyingly high property valuations on Woodland Drive, a short street ending in a cul de sac off

San Vicente Boulevard. The houses were situated on the brow of Rustic Canyon, which looked down onto the smooth green expanse of the exclusive Riviera Country Club. Most of the properties were held in trust. One eye-popping house was for sale for more than eight million dollars with an estimated monthly mortgage of forty-three thousand dollars. Nope, he'd have to pass on that one.

The door knocking was like working the gang area of Santa Monica. Nobody saw nuthin'. Nobody heard nuthin'. Here it was unlikely they were protecting fellow gang members and fearing retaliation. Yes, Santa Monica had a small gang territory in the southeastern part of the city. In this part of town, nobody was home because they were out long hours making the monthly mortgage of forty-three thousand. Houses where the doors were answered by a Latina: "*El Señor no está aqui.*"

At one address where Mason finally tracked down the owner, he waited for the personal assistant to connect him on the phone. No, *El Señor* hadn't noticed anything unusual and when was SMPD going to do something about the deadlocked traffic getting in and out of the city, thanks to the new light rail line to the ocean. The white shoe downtown lawyer enjoyed the opportunity to chew the ear off Mason about the traffic.

Did they think cops got through the traffic any easier? Or first response vehicles?

The next house to cover was a yellow stucco, a red-tiled-roof mansion with an old movie star look to it. Mature palms and landscaping, which didn't look as if it had been rolled out last Wednesday. No gated entrance to this one so they walked a curving path to what looked like the front door in an alcove shaded from the sun. The entryway was filled with birds of paradise bobbing in the balmy breeze. Mason banged hard on the wrought-iron knocker.

Before they'd come, they'd run backgrounders on homeowners on the street. A Mrs. Amelia Jackson owned the home. Aged seventy-seven.

The door was opened by a stooped old woman with a head tremor. With effort she twisted her head sideways to look up at them. Mason handed her his card, and she crumpled it in an age-spotted hand and groaned.

"Oh, no." She leaned against a heavy, carved table in the entryway, looking as if she would faint. "Not this again."

Delgado stepped forward to grab her, maneuvering her towards a straight-backed chair. "Ma'am, are you alright? Put your head between your knees."

That didn't look to be a movement possible for the old woman. Mason knelt next to her to make sure she didn't slide off the chair. Delgado went down the silent hall hollering, "Anybody there? We need some help."

A heavily-muscled Filipino man in a health care worker uniform barreled out of a closed door towards him. He shoved Mason aside.

"What did you do to her?" he said, not looking at him.

Mason stood up. "We're police officers. We're here to ask for information about an incident down the street."

The man circled the old woman's shoulders with a thick arm and heaved her to her feet.

"This is routine police business," Mason called after him.

With his shoulder, the attendant shoved the door closed with them on the outside. "Not now."

"Nobody likes cops anymore," Delgado said.

"Big surprise, huh?" Mason said. He was thinking about his daughter and her fears of him getting shot. Not that he never thought about it. His father. Their telephone tag calls back and forth had stopped. His father had quit calling back. When he got this case moving forward, he'd sit down and make sure he got hold of him.

They hit the next house and encountered a household where a middle-aged couple of Middle-Eastern appearance spoke something other than English. They didn't welcome their visit. He made a note to send a translator later.

Nobody home at the next property, the farthest one away from the Sinclair-Logan home. Mason nodded at the contractor driving down the street at the same time as they passed.

The contractor lifted a finger in a half-hearted wave.

🜨

Chapter Nine

Mason approached the home Derek Logan and Poppy Sinclair shared, finishing up the knock and talks on Woodland Drive. Celebrities in Santa Monica paid taxes and contributed to the hot buzz of the city. They lived in the fine homes in the section called "North of Montana Avenue," with coral trees, magnolias, and jacarandas shading the wide, quiet streets. They bitched about traffic like everyone else, but their street lighting was better. So was their response time. After the contractors, landscapers, caterers, and maids had parked their old beaters for the day, there were few parking spaces left. Construction had resumed next door.

Mason looked over at Delgado, his usual, unflappable self, pecking away with one finger sending a text. Delgado had a cigarette reek about him today. The current quit hadn't lasted long. Besides the usual stress of a cop's life, his mother-in-law who had dementia was currently living with them. He thought of his own parent's tense marriage. Running a neighborhood hardware store put a lot of strain on his father. They'd recently sold the store to the Ace Hardware chain. He and Delgado sat a moment, running the information they had put together so far doing up and down Woodland Drive.

Only on the rack would Mason admit he'd had a

crush on Poppy Sinclair since his teens. In the illusion movies and social media offered, he felt he'd grown up with her, well, along with her at least. They both lived in the same megalopolis after all. She breathed LA smog just like he did, only one zip code over. Like all moviegoers, he had the conviction he knew her.

Whenever he saw her image on a magazine while he was checking out at the market, he'd choose the longest line so he had a moment to read the trash tabloids. She'd married Derek Logan, another star, years ago and they were still married as far as he knew. Logan was a player, caught from time to time with a new starlet. Poppy forgave him apparently. She had her good causes, Megan and the twins, and Jake, Derek's son who lived with them part-time. He'd seen most of Sinclair's movies and hoped he wouldn't make a drooling fool of himself when he was face to face with her.

A guy working security, wearing the black workout clothes and sunglasses, monitored an electric gate. Mason recognized a for-real-security-operative, not a rent-a-cop. He nosed the police vehicle close to the gate and waited.

"Good morning, sir," a fit man in his forties said in an indeterminate English accent. "Do you have an appointment?"

"Are the people home here?" Mason said through the open window.

"Do you have an appointment?" the security operative repeated.

"No, I don't, and I don't need one. We're investigating an incident on the street here." He waited.

"Yes, sir, let me make a call."

He looked over at Delgado who curled his lip.

"Asshole," Delgado said.

"Doing his job." Mason took in the expensive

landscaping on the rest of the street, tall eucalyptus trees standing straight by the curbs, pines, pampas grass, and elephant ear cactus. Discreet solar lighting. Probably beautiful at Christmas time. The gate slid open. The rest of the house appeared in front of them. Three stories, golden stone, sweeping lines, arched windows in front, four columns set in the front next to ceiling-high windows reflecting the cheerful morning California sunlight. Cameras placed unobtrusively.

Delgado rang the doorbell. Mason took a step back when the door was yanked open by a young girl. He looked past the girl, and was given a one-second video on paradise defined by Santa Monica real estate developers. Through the great room windows easily forty feet away from him, he saw a downward sloping expanse of green lawn, across the canyon behind Woodland Drive, through Rustic Canyon. The city of Pacific Palisades rose in an escarpment of white houses and a skyline of blue above. An eyeful of scenery.

He introduced himself and Delgado and asked to see her parents. The young girl looked at the card Mason handed her. From the back of the house came the whine of a vacuum cleaner. Then the click of dogs nails on the hardwood floors. A Benjie dog and a big black poodle.

Incoming. Furious warning barks. Enemy at the gate.

"Police? Really?" She grinned. "Real police?"

They lunged for Mason who stepped back, one foot raised to fend them off and hang onto his dignity. The Benjie dog hung on his pant leg, unshakeable. Delgado ruffled ears and gave the poodle butt scratches. The girl whirled and grabbed the dogs, sinking on the floor with them.

"Can I see your badge? Have you got a gun?" Standing up, she said a sharp word, and the dogs instantly went to their beds in the kitchen.

"Are your parents' home?" Mason said, stone-faced.

"You mean Derek and Poppy?" She just missed being a pretty teenager and was a little on the plump side. He'd bet she was made to suffer for those five or ten extra pounds.

"Your parents?" he repeated. He couldn't help noticing his heart beating a little faster thinking of Poppy's, sensing she was close.

"Surprised? I don't look like them, do I? I'm Megan, their daughter."

"Is she home? Is Mr. Logan?" Delgado was taking a look around. His memory was by no means photographic, but he didn't miss much.

"I donno. She's probably out saving the world."

"Oh. When will she be home? When the world is saved?"

She glanced over her shoulder. "Probably not even then. Hey, here she is now." She led them into the sunny kitchen.

As she spoke, Poppy Sinclair sailed in with a fresh breeze of energy. She had a white workout towel over her shoulder and her top had a tail of sweat over the considerable chest which had gone a long way to making her career. The low cut top was filled to the brim and overflowing with creamy white breasts retaining a sheen of perspiration. A piece of lean male flesh who could only be a personal trainer came in laughing, until he saw Mason and Delgado.

Mason was no stranger to celebrities. The city was dotted with Industry people. There were far more unrecognizable behind-the-camera celebrities, not to mention the rich and young techies who had given rise to Santa Monica's new moniker of Silicon Beach. In person,

Poppy Sinclair was a somewhat faded version of her persona on screen. But she still had the dazzle that lifted the usual beautiful woman into a megastar. Her face darkened seeing her daughter with visitors. The girl slouched over and handed her mother Mason's card. When Sinclair took Mason's card from her daughter, her face lost its color. It lasted only a second, then she regained both color and composure.

"Megan?" she said, scowling at her daughter with a glare that had the force of an open-handed slap. "You have fitness classes. Get ready."

"Yeah, yeah, I'm going." The girl turned on her heel and bolted upstairs.

The personal trainer was at the Keurig machine making himself a cup of coffee. He opened a cupboard door and peered inside, obviously no stranger to this house.

"Detective Mason?" Sinclair tilted an eyebrow at him and dabbed at her nose with a pretty handkerchief.

Delgado strolled across the expanse of the kitchen that was a homeowner's dream and gave her his card.

"Detective Delgado? What can I do for you, gentlemen?" She leaned back against the counter and glanced at the hunky trainer pouring cream into his coffee. "Carlos, we're done today."

"Can I drink my coffee?"

"Take it with you. We're done."

Carlos set his full cup down, picked up his gym bag, and nonchalantly headed for the door.

"We've just got a few questions," Mason said.

"I need to take care of something. Please, give me a minute," Poppy said to him with the attitude of someone used to giving orders which were carried out instantly.

Mason's eyes drank Sinclair in as she moved about in

the sunny kitchen which seemed familiar from the *House Beautiful* magazines Ginger sometimes left at his condo. A hipster wearing square black glasses breezed in from a hallway where the personal trainer had disappeared. She carried an iPad and stood hip-shot in front of Poppy, ignoring the two detectives. Poppy issued a series of orders: cancel the closet organizer, reschedule the facial, check on the work on the Aspen house. Confirm the dogs' play date. She flung her hands up to indicate complete exasperation. "And call my publicist to find out why our interview with *People* hasn't appeared."

A dumpy woman with Indian features stood at the counter, listening, in a passive- aggressive attitude, peeling potatoes. There was a lazy, rolling sashay to her walk as she moved out of the way of Poppy Sinclair, steaming past her to get a bottle of chilled water out of the refrigerator.

She whirled to include Mason and Delgado, waving a hand to indicate they were to follow her into the living room with its blue and gray palette and a constellation of couches and chairs forming conversational groups. None of the furniture looked particularly comfortable until Mason sat in one of the chairs and felt its luxurious embrace. He leaned forward when Poppy Sinclair crossed long legs and looked up at him from below her eyebrows. Mason knew he wasn't that hard to look at. Enough women had told him that.

"Sorry to bother you, Ms. Sinclair, but there's been an incident in the neighborhood ...

Since your property is one of the homes close to where we discovered a victim, it's routine to be asking the neighbors..." he began.

Two small children, obvious twins, burst in the front door, and ran straight to the blue leather couches in a TV alcove off the great room, grabbing up the remote controls.

A boy and a girl, black curly hair, cocoa-colored skin.
They ignored Poppy who glanced after them, sniffed, and
prettily dabbed at her nose. These must be the two orphan
children Sinclair and Logan had adopted from some
Central America slum. A hard blast of kid's cartoon music
filled the huge rooms. A homely Latina followed them in,
flopping down on the sofa next to them. The little girl
burrowed into the circle of her arms. Ah, the nanny. These
people would have a household staff. Yes, a cook, of
course. That must be the dumpy woman in the kitchen.
Cleaners. Someone for the children. Gardeners. The pool
guy. How many kids were there if each of the couple's
public marriages had produced children? Each of the
residents of this house was a potential witness.

Someone might have seen something. He hoped.

The house filled up with bustle, more people arriving.
Derek Logan strolled into the living room, big, powerful,
active, and talking fast and hard over his shoulder to a
skinny assistant with a man bun, making notes, punching
the keys with his thumbs on a smartphone. Logan had
played a bullfighter, a test pilot, behind-the-lines spy; a
man of action roles. Hot-blooded, aggressive roles. A real
man. Logan glanced in, then ignored the scene in the
living room, the two detectives, the blaring TV, his wife
and kids. He turned back into the kitchen, the assistant
close on his heels. Poppy issued another set of orders to
her personal assistant: she hated the changes the
webmaster had made on her site. Make sure the jet was
available if they wanted to spend the weekend at the
Aspen house.

Mason had a side angle view into the huge, sunny
kitchen. Logan moved aside the cook working at the sink
by placing his hands on her hips. She grinned over her
shoulder at him and said something to him in Spanish.

Mason watched the Logan-Sinclair show, certain it was meant for them. Poppy was now dictating tasks to her helper, ignoring her husband.

"Read it back to me," Logan shouted at the hipster who had allowed his laptop case to slide off his shoulder onto the kitchen table. Before the assistant got a whole sentence out, Logan interrupted him, waving his hands.

"No, no, that's not it." Striding around the kitchen, his hands on his hips, he looked at Mason and Delgado and gave them a big, actor's smile. Lots of white, shining teeth, squared chin, good hair.

"Police," Poppy said to him after a moment, getting to her feet with the grace of a panther. "Police, Derek."

Was there a word of warning in this, Mason wondered? Everybody had done something they didn't want to come to light.

"They're asking about that body the contractors dug up next door."

"Oh?" he whirled around to take the whistling tea kettle off the stove. "Lupe, make me a pot of rooibos tea, would you? Kid, wait for me in the office. Bring the tea. Type up what I've got so far. Poppy, have we got anything on tonight?" There was a hesitation in his speech, Lupe came out Luh, Luh, Lupe.

Mason walked into the kitchen, introduced himself, and held out his card. Poppy and Delgado followed him in. Derek took it, casting a glance over it. "So you're one of the Santa Monica boys. I know the chief. We made a big donation for equipment you guys needed."

"Thanks, we appreciate it," Mason said. "Sit down with us a minute. It'll only take a minute. We're talking to all the neighbors trying to get a fix on what might have happened next door." Delgado leaned against the kitchen table, giving Logan his thousand-yard stare.

"Yeah, we huh huh heard about it. Yeah. Weird, huh?" Logan's attention seemed to drift. He pulled out his phone and was about to make a call when Mason held out a warning hand

"Give us a moment here, would you? How about you, Ms. Sinclair? Anything stick in your mind you saw that might be unusual next door?"

She gave him a pretty look. "There's a bamboo hedge between us as you can see. I'd probably call you if I saw somebody burying a body." She laughed with a trill of merriment as distinctive as Goldie Hahn's giggle.

"You must be able to see into the property from upstairs, though," Mason said

"Did you see anything, Derek?" she said turning to her husband. She sniffed with a bubbling liquid sound. Allergies or she had a bad cold.

"When?"

Mason hated to say four months ago. Nobody remembered anything odd that long ago.

He tried, though. "Recently?'

"Nose, Poppy, blow your nose. Nope. Thuh, thuh, things to do. Things to do. Ask Poppy about the weirdo down the street. He's got chickens and that rooster. What the hell? Chickens." His smile said this was the most bizarre thing in the world, one of those who believed that chickens grew on Styrofoam trays in the back of the supermarket. "Rooster crows at dawn."

"What weirdo?" Delgado asked, riveting their attention. A long-ago bout of throat cancer had left him with a raspy voice, which sounded as if it was strained through gravel.

"Love your voice," Polly said, giving Delgado a long look. "Like Joe Cocker. You ever do voice over?"

Mason stifled a smile, imagining Delgado in a sound

booth, or taking part in any Industry endeavor. Delgado was about as cop as cops got. Straight as a yardstick, he and his large family lived out in the police enclave in Simi Valley, a hellish freeway commute into Santa Monica day and night.

"Do something about that rooster, would you?" Logan said, interrupting his wife. "Wakes me up. Goddamned thing."

"So you two haven't got anything to add then?" Delgado asked.

"The old lady died and then the family did a teardown," Logan said. "Construction started and we figured, oh shit, noise, and all that. The whole city's under construction," he smiled.

"Yeah, I've noticed that," Mason said.

"How long has that thing—that grave—been there?" Poppy said, taking a step forward into Mason's sacred space. He edged away from the powerful force field cast by celebrity. She gave a liquid sniff and dabbed at her nose.

"Hard to say. That will take a while to determine."

"Creepy," Poppy said. "A dead body next door to us all that time." She whirled again with another set of orders to the girl who had set up her laptop on the kitchen table: arrange the delivery of her sides, the twins' kickboxing session, a birthday card and present to her makeup girl's daughter, fix a flickering overhead light in the house's underground garage.

"So, you see anything? Hear anything?"

The two beautiful people glanced back and forth at each other. "No," they said together.

"Are you aware of anyone in the neighborhood who has gone missing lately?"

Logan screwed up his face in an expression of

bafflement.

"There's been nothing over there to see for so long. Why would we look?" Poppy said, looking up at Mason sloe-eyed.

Of all the ridiculous things, Mason felt himself blush and remembered who he was. And who she was.

"Mind if we talk to your household staff?" Delgado asked.

"Why would you want to talk to them?" Poppy said.

People like this worried about the tabloids, the paparazzi, constantly looking for a chance to catch a cinema idol in his pajamas pushing a bin of garbage to the curb. Each of them was married to someone millions of people believed themselves to be in love with. It wasn't a matter if your partner would be unfaithful, but when, and how public? That was the issue for people like them. How public.

"I see you have security people. They may have seen something that would help us. Do you have security cameras outside your house?"

"You must know the Bateson Agency? Nigel Bateson, the head of the agency is my personal bodyguard," Derek said with a lift of his head.

Mason and Delgado were familiar with the agencies from liaising with personal security accompanying celebrities to events in Los Angeles and Santa Monica. Most of them were ex-law enforcement or military, self-important, big swinging dicks who assumed the celebrity status of their clients.

"Pleased to hear that, Mr. Logan. What kind of schedule is he on with your family?"

"He's outside. Talk to him," Poppy said.

Logan was still standing at the door listening. "Hey, I've got meetings this evening, places to go, people to charm. Poppy, I need you at 8:00 at Michael's. I've got a dining room reserved for my people."

"You need me? I get to hear about your little company thing? Little me?"

Derek shot her a pained look. "Hey, for once ..."

"She wants to be in my musical," he grinned and said to Mason. "Sings like a duck with a tracheotomy."

The cruelty of the remark took Mason's breath away. Sinclair's face flamed.

She turned aside to mutter to her husband. "And what flavor of kink will the after party be tonight?"

Mason had good ears. Sinclair arranged a smile on her face and barked another order at her skinny PA with the square black glasses and ragged-looking haircut.

"Let's go back to your security detail, Mr. Logan. They with you twenty-four hours a day?" Mason asked.

"Look, detective, this is the burden of fame," Logan grinned. "It's stupid, but that's the way it is. We get stalkers, both of us, crazed fans, paparazzi. Our whole life isn't in front of the camera, though it seems that way, doesn't it, hon?"

As the endearment fell from his lips, Mason saw Poppy Sinclair's lip curl.

"We need protection from the people who want to make money off us, or love us so much they want to tear pieces off us to sell on eBay. We have to be careful. Especially with the kids."

"We understand that, sir. More than you think. But here's this unidentified body, and we're asking questions of everybody on the street. That's just what happens. So we need a list of who lives here, staff who work here, previous staff, along with contact information. We've got other houses to visit still, so tomorrow would be fine. Email it to me, would you? Along with the schedule of your security detail, etc., etc."

"I'll get somebody on it. Now I gotta go. Gotta go. Thu-thu-things to do. Things to do." Mason had read that Logan's stutter was occasional and never when the cameras were on. The studios had spent a fortune with speech therapists. The dogs started barking. Playfully Logan ran from the kitchen into the great room with a staircase that led up to second floor of the house, waving his hands, the dogs chasing him, barking.

Mason and Poppy Sinclair rose at the same time, her long, lithe body registering a hot presence in his personal space. Her eyes met his for a moment, and Mason sensed her. Her eyes registered the inert flatness of the parade of psychopaths and society's deviants who filled his life. Then it was as if she caught herself, and slid in a nictitating membrane which indicated interest and engagement. Actor.

"So you will let us know what you learn about...that unpleasantness next door," she said, walking him to the front door. In the kitchen, the dishwasher started up.

"If we're in any danger … Maybe you should talk to Nigel Bateson, our security chief."

"We will. Mind if we take a look outside, do a walk around your property, look at the fence?"

"No, no, help yourself. I'll get my PA on the information you want, Detective Mason. You'll hear from me." Sinclair pushed the mute button on her internal remote, distancing herself, already gone, shielded.

Ginger would emasculate him if she knew the thoughts that flooded his mind.

♆

Chapter Ten

The minute the cops left, Poppy and Derek went at each other in the kitchen like savage dogs fighting over a rat.

"Can you go somewhere else and fight? I've got homework," Megan said, from the kitchen table where she had placed her laptop and a textbook. The housekeeper set a sandwich on a plate down next to her. She reached for it. Her mother snatched away half of it. They glared at each other.

"You watch your mouth," Derek barked at her. "When you can afford to pay the bills in this house, you get to say what goes on here ..."

Sinclair and Logan treated the household help as if they were deaf and stupid. The nanny fled with the twins to their wing on the second floor. The big poodle and little Benjie dog slunk away. Lupe Garcia, the major domo of the household, went to her room off the kitchen and turned up a telenovela loud.

Poppy grabbed her husband by the arm. She dragged him out on the patio, down the stairs to the edge of the glittering pool, into the cabana and slammed the door. A fresh pile of towels sat on the bench inside the changing room. She went to the small fridge and got a bottle of water, shaking one of her pills into her hand and bolting it down. Her mind boiled with catastrophe. She beat herself up, knowing that instead of going to the police with the maid's dead body and an explanation, she'd colluded with him. Now it was too late. The police. Nigel. Could he be trusted? She had let Derek talk her into the stupid idea of burying the girl next door. But Nigel had been so convincing. The body would never be found.

After all, she wasn't the one who killed Celia Talaveras. She knew better than to count on Derek. The idea of them being a team had vaporized years ago. Why should she protect him? She couldn't predict what he would do in any situation. And she was afraid to take a chance. The drugs and the Maker's Mark shored him up for now, but if they ever pinned him down and were determined to break him, he would fold.

"I told them what you told me to say. What else could I do?" Derek said.

"You need to convince them."

"Huh huh how?"

"Don't talk so much. You don't have to explain everything you say."

"They're going around to all the neighbors, even the ones up the street."

"That's what they do. You watch those stupid cop shows on TV. You should know that."

"Those shows relax me."

"We can't afford to have the cops here," she said. Her face without the smile that lighted up the screen was flat. The fine scars by her ears were highlighted in the pitiless sun.

"Man, you can turn it on and off, can't you? And they say you can't act. You with that cop. I saw you." He sank down in one of the chairs by the pool. She stood over him.

"Whatever I am, we have to stick together on this.

Call Nate. That's what we pay him for. To get us out of things like this."

"Look, we just told the cops we didn't even know her."

"I know, and I'm thinking now that was stupid. They'll be back. They always are."

"You should know." Between them was the memory of the police investigation involving the accidental death of Poppy's girlfriend.

"That's why you need to talk to Nate." Poppy said.

"Why me?"

"Because you're the one who killed her, dumb shit. Not me. I had nothing to do with her. Unless somebody knew you were fucking her."

"I wasn't," he said. "The whole thing was an accident like I said. I can't stand Nate. Sanctimonious Jew."

"Your mother was a Jew ..."

"We were deli, not synagogue Jews. There's lots more Jewishy Jews than we were.

"Besides, think of all the things I could tell about you," he said, with a flash of warning.

"Call Nate," she insisted.

"Yeah, yeah. Quit nagging. Fuck off, will you?" he said moodily, Googling himself on his phone.

🜊

Megan got up from the kitchen table and looked out the window to watch her parents coming out of the cabana, their voices like knives. They hated each other. So what? It didn't matter. The sharpened edge of Celia's abandoning her had dulled. Celia wasn't coming back. She must have been too embarrassed about taking off with Jacinto. What Celia saw in him, Megan couldn't imagine. Megan's face turned sour. She was stupid to believe that their plans could have worked out. With her name and the help of the mother of one of her friends, they could have got jobs, though. It could have worked. Who wouldn't want to get away from this house as fast as she could? These weirdos?

Poppy was right. She was fat.

Nobody could love her.

♏

Poppy was alone in a way she'd never been since growing up in Visalia, California. There was no one she could tell, or share her fears with. Only Derek. In those last years when her father was dying, her mother spent every cent they had to keep him alive, at a time when cancer was a whispered sentence of death. If only he'd die, Poppy screamed into her pillow when her mother rushed back to the hospital for one more crisis. Die, damn you. It cost her precious energy to put the right emotions on her face when anyone was around and she was supposed to care.

She got out of Visalia when she was eighteen, a friend of her father's driving her to Los Angeles and paying two month's rent on a studio apartment in Hollywood, in return for pawing her body. She'd paid her Harvey Weinstein dues to relatively few men because she had a ruthless drive, and walking over somebody else didn't bother her. Then she met Derek at a party, and recognizing something in each other, they formed a marriage of cynical mutual gain. She tried to be a good mother because it was good for her image.

She tried. Nobody could say she didn't try. But children were such an effort.

♏

Mason and Delgado were dismissed, the door to the

Sinclair-Logan mansion snicking shut behind them. It took Mason a moment to stuff his thoughts away and slap his cop face on.

Delgado was laughing. "Mason, your tongue was hanging out."

Mason busied himself by putting his tablet on the top of a wrought-iron sculpture by the doorway next to one of the columns which disappeared up into the third story of the house. He turned his face away, ignoring Delgado.

"Let's take a look-see around the place. Talk to security. I want to check my email."

"Sure, whatever," Delgado said, laughing. They knew each other so well they could finish each other's sentences, even before the thought began to form. Once a sergeant and briefly Mason's field training officer, Delgado's alcoholism got the best of him. He was sidelined for a year or so and then came flaming back, his problems under control, ready to take the detective's exam.

Logan had made an impression on Mason. He looked like the confident kind of guy who disregarded anything said to him. He already knew what he needed to know. He knew guys like this, like the Lieutenant who commanded Operations. They demanded you pay them attention, then decided you were weak for groveling. Everybody was either a toady, or somebody who needed something. What was it like to live in this kind of world, Mason wondered.

⚱

A fit-looking man in his fifties wearing sunglasses and sports clothes leaned against a Range Rover parked in the driveway behind Logan's Hummer. Their observer took off his sunglasses, revealing eyes with a crosshatch of sun-faded wrinkles, which had nothing to do with good humor or smiling. The eyes behind the sunglasses were deeply set and intelligent beneath a heavy brow ridge: the nose and lips were narrow, a face like a raptor. The kind you see on the Wall Street guys who make billions. He had a long head with short hair growing on it like an animal's pelt.

"Nigel Bateson?" Mason said. "You run security here?"

"Yeah, I'm Bateson." He gestured with his chin. "Expected you before this."

"Yeah, well, we've been busy. We could use your help on this business next door," Delgado said, blowing his nose on a big white handkerchief he'd taken out of his pocket.

"Who are you looking at?" Bateson asked in an accent hard to identify.

Mason figured South African of some kind. "Everybody on the street for a start. You probably know how it goes. What kind of security you got here?"

"You see our setup there in the security room?" He pointed at the stone kiosk by the gate matching the house. "We've got exterior and interior sound cameras in most of the rooms of the house. Including the kid's bedrooms. Not the master bedrooms. They're erased every forty-eight hours. Otherwise, there'd be too much data piling up. I observed a mountain lion the other night strolling down the middle of the street."

Mason laughed. "I've seen coyotes, deer up here. True."

"Well, deer would bring in a lion," Bateson said. "There's two of us here on the house all the time." Bateson pushed off from the car and led the walk-through around the home of Poppy Sinclair and Derek Logan, pointing out unobtrusive camera locations.

The eight-bedroom mansion on the three-acre property left room for a pool, a cabana, the security kiosk near the gate. The trees planted in the front courtyard were mostly palms and looked as if they'd been trucked in and planted full-grown. If any feature of the landscape wilted or died, it was immediately replaced. The expensive landscaping still left enough room around the house for a sweeping expanse of lawn.

An eleven-foot-high chain link fence surrounded the property and was obscured behind stands of bamboo and other exotic greenery. The home was well-defended without looking as though it were under the threat of siege. Strolling along the side of the house which bounded on the property where the body had been found, Mason came to a stop when he encountered a nearly invisible gate shrouded by greenery. A large padlock hung on the hasp. Here was an entry into the lot next door.

"Who has keys to this?" he said to Bateson.

"My detail. Me. The owners." Bateson kept walking.

"Who has access to the property?"

"Just security and the family. Anybody else needs in like UPS or the pool guy, gardeners, people like that, we open the gates for them. It's all recorded."

"What kind of schedule are you on here?" Delgado asked, checking the lock.

"I've got two guys on Poppy—twelve-hour shifts when she's off the property. I'm taking Logan myself for the moment, with one other gal. They get threats. I've got a guy who looks young enough to be one of their friends if Jake or Megan go out at night. The twins and the nanny have a driver who doubles as a bodyguard. Jason lives with his mother half time. Megan, you probably met."

Mason added it up in his head. That was quite a nut to make every week. The expense must be deductible anyway. Poppy had starred in a Disney cult space epic that sold so much merchandise that money might still be rolling in. These were people way out of a cop's league. He turned suddenly and caught Bateson studying him with a speculative eye.

"So what's your background?" Mason asked with a friendly smile.

"Military. Special Forces. NYPD. You interested in security work?"

"Hey, I'm not old enough to retire. What about you, Delgado?"

"Might be. Might be," Delgado said easily.

Mason knew he wasn't. His retirement eligibility had come and gone. When his wife's mother had needed twenty-four-hour, locked ward Alzheimer's care, Maria's seven brothers and sisters hadn't stepped up much to help cover the costs. Now they had her at home. Nobody said it out loud, but the old lady wouldn't be mourned if she died soon.

Bateson got a phone call. "Lady Gaga," he announced. "I gotta take this call. She likes one of my guys a little too much, and I have to tell her I'm taking him off her detail. She won't like it."

Mason nodded. He caught a glimpse of Megan, the fifteen-year-old daughter, listening to their conversation. She had a backpack over her shoulder, and stood hipshot, scratching her arm. He walked over to her.

"Hi, there," he said. Maybe the daughter would have something to say. Bateson followed him.

"So how come you're here?" the girl said.

Mason wondered how much to tell her.

"We uncovered a body next door," he said.

"Shallow grave, huh?" She grinned. "Just like in the movies."

This confirmed Mason's experience that kids knew a lot. It frightened him how much his ten-year-old daughter knew about the world.

"You going out?" Bateson said, stepping forward to speak to Megan. "Where's Edmund? He'll take you."

"I don't need him. I'm going to Starbucks. Somebody's picking me up."

"Which Starbucks?" Bateson asked. Santa Monica had twenty-six Starbucks in an eight- square-mile city.

"The one over on San Vicente," Megan told him with a defiant tilt of her head.

"Who's picking you up?"

"A friend."

Bateson looked skeptical about Megan's having a friend. "What friend? You going to that one where all those girls fanned your father?"

"It's so disgusting. This girl my age," she said, turning to Mason, "she had Derek's first name tattooed all down her arm and wanted to show him the tattoo of his middle name on her butt."

"Yeah, fame," Mason said as if he knew all about it. He knew the reason she was wearing a white, long-sleeved T-shirt on a California summer day. He recognized the angry roughness of eczema at her wrists because his ex-wife was plagued with eczema.

He and Delgado pushed on, leaving Megan arguing with Nigel Bateson. He noticed Megan faced them head-on, but talked to Bateson a quarter-turn away from him, her voice argumentative.

It would have been interesting to hear more, but they had other houses to cover. Particularly the "weirdo" down the street, the one who had the rooster which bothered Derek Logan.

§

In her room that night Megan let herself open the gallery

of photos on her phone. Nothing said that the body next door was Celia. It might be stupid even to think that, but so many improbable things happened around her daily, it flew into her mind and stuck. She worried at it like a sore tooth.

It hurt to look through the hundreds of selfies of herself and Celia goofing around in her room with the twins. Times at the beach, security in the background. Celia studying. Disneyland. Universal City. This grave next door? No. It couldn't be her. It could be anybody.

But maybe Celia hadn't dumped her to run off with Jacinto? She thought Celia had set her sights way higher than Jacinto, who was just a boy from her home town. She didn't want to go back and live the life her parents and brother had decided for her. Or marry the old, fat lawyer with a hairy back she was engaged to. Megan understood that. But Celia never texted, never called. She was just gone. It was hard for Megan to believe the girl she thought would be her BFF would dump her. Plenty of girls wanted to be around her to get close to her parents, but she knew immediately who they were and blew them off. Celia wasn't like that. Maybe it was what she deserved, being ordinary in a world of the extraordinary. What Megan deserved for being fat and uncool.

Celia wasn't ordinary. Her mother saw her as a useful pair of hands. Her father? He saw Celia the way he saw all women. Sniff. Sniff. The scent of estrogen lit him up.

Celia had taught her how to say she was sorry, not something she had ever seen anyone do at home. She had taught her that you didn't just blow people off, that you did the hard thing and talked a disagreement through — transformative experiences for Megan.

Celia knew who she was. She was a maid playing with kids all day, speaking halting English, but she thought she was important. Her parents wouldn't even give her the dignity of calling her the nanny because they'd have to pay her more, and Celia wouldn't pass scrutiny with the press. Celia told Megan she was important too—even without them. If it ever came to them carrying out the threat to send her to the fat camp in Wyoming, she and Celia had a plan.

But just before she disappeared, Megan began to be afraid for her sake. The twins had begun picking up her accent.

Derek heard them say "J'ou" instead of "You" as Spanish-speakers did. Megan saw him exchange a glance with Poppy. They couldn't have their kids speaking English like the maid. Every day the pressure increased.

For a long time after she was gone, Megan imagined they'd paid Celia off and sent her away with a contract never to see her again.

Could they do that? They could have.

It was a consolation thinking that Celia hadn't just abandoned her.

It never occurred to Megan they would kill her. They didn't need to kill people. They could just cripple and ruin them so that they were no good to themselves or anyone else. She'd seen them do it to other employees and friends.

Like they'd done to her.

Taking a break from writing reports back at the station, Mason typed in Nigel Bateson and his security company name in a law enforcement database.

He sat back and scratched his head hard as he read. Bad things seemed to follow Bateson around. A client died on his watch, and there was an investigation, which he beat. In another incident, a client sued him because a fan ran up to his wife and snatched a diamond bracelet off her wrist. The guy on watch had failed to run him down. The insurance paid, but there was a buzz that Bateson over-committed himself, and bad things happened.

But what did any of this mean?

♏

Chapter Eleven

Although TV and social media made it seem that homicides were solved by the astonishing deductive powers of the sleuth along with high-tech forensics, Mason knew the truth was simpler. Most cases moved by somebody diming somebody else out for a reason no more basic than *I'm gonna get him before he gets me*. The story of the body in the grave had gone out the way it usually did, creating a few headlines in the Santa Monica online papers, but nothing kept it alive. Other than a desultory inquiry or two to the Public Information Officer.

With the link to Derek Logan and Poppy Sinclair, the discovery of the body was news, whatever *news* meant nowadays. Murder at a good address would always be the stuff of headlines. Poppy Sinclair and Derek Logan reigned in the Hollywood firmament of celebrities in the tradition of the former Brangelina that stretched back to Bacall and Bogart, Clark Gable and Carol Lombard.

A pack of hyenas now lay in wait on Woodland Drive for a glimpse of Poppy or Derek. A lineup of satellite TV trucks with broadcast antennas, guys with huge cameras that looked like guns over their shoulders, chittering on-air talent waiting for an opportunity to do their standup. A buzz of excitement shimmered in the air. Mason spotted three photographers adjusting their lenses. He had Woodland Drive blocked off. Still, San Vicente Boulevard was clogged for blocks in either direction around the power couple's home. He couldn't prevent the media and fans from walking in and forming a pack behind police lines across the street. The fact that there was nothing to see didn't stop people.

Statements by Derek's and Poppy's separate publicists saying there was no connection to them fanned the flames. *People* and *Us* magazine badgered them with requests. Anyone who had any tenuous link to the power couple grabbed for the mic. The studios they had projects with had a comment. Other actors. Hangers-on. Everybody had something to say—about nothing. The news beast must be fed.

Mason scratched his head, following all this. He didn't need to be told this was already a celebrity case, no matter who the body turned out to be.

🦂

Ginger had a glass of wine in front of her on the coffee table, a question on her face when Mason got home that night.

"So what's he like? Derek?"

"An asshole. Think Alec Baldwin," he said, ripping his tie off and throwing it over the back of a chair. He got a beer out of the fridge and slumped down next to her on the leather couch, nuzzling her shoulder.

"And her? I loved that movie about her and the dog." Ginger turned toward him. "C'mon. Tell me." Her eyes were shining.

"Down, fangirl. Down. Look, they're movie people. They're like your big donors you talk about, full of themselves." He waved at the paperwork Ginger had spread out on the table, writing an annual report for the do-gooder nonprofit she worked for. "You know what they're like."

"Why would they kill her?"

It was a good question. Mason had worked a few cases of sex play gone wrong and read about a lot more. Logan was the likely one involved in something like this. He hoped Poppy wasn't involved. Could the pathologist find evidence of rough sex after the body had been in the ground so long? He knew it was too soon to link them up anyway without some kind of proof.

"You got any dinner going?"

"Is it dinner time?" Ginger said. "I lost track. Let's go out."

She chatted away happily while she got ready, telling him about her day. Ginger could make a good story about anything and the tensions of the day faded while he listened to her. She was the leavening in Mason's life, the reason to come home at night after his face had been pressed close to the slimy underbelly of day-to-day policing in Santa Monica. Her father and brother were Sheriff's deputies, so she knew the life. She had her own demons. Everybody in his life told him to marry her before she got away. Trouble was, she didn't want to marry him. Or anybody, so she said. So he took what he could get. He read PoliceOne.com. She read Margaret Atwood. He loved her too much.

He took off his good grey suit and put on a black polo shirt and khakis, and tore a hunk off a loaf of bread to last him until dinner. Ginger slung a red mohair scarf around her neck and bounced down the stairs beside him. A journalist Mason recognized lurked at the bottom of the stairs. Mason put Ginger behind him automatically to protect her.

"Comment on Poppy and Derek?" the reporter asked.

Mason pushed past him.

"Hey, be a pal."

"You're not my pal. Talk to the PIO. You know I'm not going to tell you anything."

Mason ignored the hissed "asshole" aimed at his back. He was used to it.

♫

The station was full of loud voices, heavy boots, ringing phones, shouts over cubicle walls, laughter, and the clatter of keyboards. A call came in from the coroner's deputy who smelled of mosquito repellent and cigarettes. Mason heard Fredericks chatting up her new BFF Dr. Audrey Moon, another Alpha Ball Buster woman.

"Somebody's on the ball over there at the coroner's office," Fredericks said swiping the phone closed. She skidded her chair over to sit beside him. Fredericks smelled like something sharp, something that reminded him of eucalyptus trees.

"You know that little pin thing they found under the body?"

Mason nodded.

"One of Audrey's assistants identified it as a charm for one of those Disney character charm bracelets. Lots of women like them. Ick. Too girly-girly," Fredericks said, shaking her wrist, which was encircled by a wide silver bracelet with blue stones in it. Around her neck, she wore a necklace that looked like it matched. It set off the frizz of her red curls and freckled square face.

"Right. Disney, huh?" Mason said. He typed in *Disney charm bracelets* on Google, hoping against hope it might be a limited edition. He turned his laptop screen toward Fredericks. She had another call and jumped up to take it.

"Damn." Anybody could buy Disney charms for a bracelet. Here was a 37-character bracelet for $199.00. He could see his daughter being enchanted but knew if he sprang for it, she'd only lose it. Things didn't stick to Haley, and he wasn't much better, he acknowledged, thinking of the many times he'd lost his keys.

The Disney charm found with the body didn't get them much further down the road. But it was something. They had identified the scrap of fabric found under the body as coming from a very limited edition of fabric run-up as a line of Disney pajamas.

Lots of people liked Disney memorabilia. He wished he had a direct link from Disney to Poppy, who had made a handful of films with Disney.

"Keep on them for an estimate of how long she's been in the ground," Mason said as he passed her on the way out.

"Yup, doing that. Doing that. Audrey's leaning toward her being Latina, but not from around here."

"They can tell that, huh?"

"Oh yeah."

♌

"You want to go with me to the building department about that property up on Woodland?" Mason asked Delgado, driving out of the high-end wooded enclave.

His partner mulled it over, twisting his face into a question. "Nah, you go. I still got a report to finish for the good Lieutenant."

The building department, next door to the Public Safety Facility in City Hall, had a few answers. He learned a Greek family did the teardown of the previous mansion built in 1967. Some kind of family fight, maybe a divorce, had stalled the construction of the new house, and the work had been idle for nine months. Mason took the documents the patient clerk printed out for him and went back to the station, marveling at the bright blue sky and sunshine which had brought the tourists for more than a century. Santa Monica had been built out to the edges. Not enough space for the developers to rake off a profit, so now the buildings were going up and up, defying a long-standing policy of smart growth. Automatically he checked the sky for aircraft, wishing he was up there.

Development politics were a blood sport in the city. And Ginger was usually in the thick of it somewhere, she and her community activist pals.

When he got back, Delgado tossed him a copy of Dr. Moon's preliminary report. Female, approximately 115 pounds, five feet three inches tall, late teens, Latina, well-nourished, cause of death exsanguination. The forensic odontologist narrowed down her geographic origin to Central America. Didn't tell him much. The typical Juana Doe.

🐾

The case moved forward with a call on his unidentified body from the gal working Missing Persons.

"I might have something for you, sir, on that body up on Woodland."

"Great. I'll be right there."

A few minutes later he stood behind Meredith Taylor who was part of the rubber gun squad. Taylor had frozen in the parking lot of the Panera store on Wilshire Boulevard when shots were fired on a burglary alarm call. Only by luck had her partner, who was a little badge heavy, survived. The circumstances remained murky. Taylor was working hard to make up for that moment of paralysis which would mark her career forever.

Much mumbling to herself, she flipped screen after screen in the Missing and Unidentified Persons Unit in the California Department of Justice website. Taylor lined up seven missing Latinas where the reporting party identified a Santa Monica connection. Three were too old; one was too short, now only three left. One had been missing too long. Mason spent a moment looking at each of their photos.

"I've got a guess from what you tell me about the body," Taylor said. "But this one," she pointed, "could be her. See, she was hit by a car in the intersection at Fourth and Colorado last year during the Christmas shopping season. I swear somebody tried to kill me in the Trader Joe's parking lot at Christmas last year. You believe that? People! She had ID with her so we know who she is, but it was fake. Driver's license you could buy at the curb downtown in McArthur Park. Nobody ever came forward to claim her, though. Sad, huh? Nope, she was too short. Here's the last one. You'd be lucky if it was her."

A photograph posted on the site showed a sweet-faced woman with creamy caramel skin, long, silky black hair, and an eager expression. Looked like a studio portrait of a pretty girl. Accompanying it was a whole body shot: feathered earrings, sparkly eyes, and high-heeled ankle boots. Media would be all over this one. Oh yes.

"Why would I be lucky?"

"You got people caring about her. I've got a file on her."

"Show me."

"I don't know if this makes it easier or harder," she said with a smile. She found a file on her desk without looking very hard and handed it to Mason. "Had another call from him last week. He flew up here a while ago and made my life miserable. I'm not going to have to be the one to tell him, am I?"

Mason sat down and became absorbed in the file she gave him. "No, no, that's my job."

The file told him Celia Talaveras had a brother named Jorge who had been dogging both SMPD and LAPD for information on his sister, who had gone silent after regular communications with her family until four months ago. A lawyer in corporate practice in Guatemala City, Jorge Talaveras made several visits to prod anybody in California law enforcement to help to find his sister. Mason scanned through the file, not looking forward to relating news of his sister's death to a brother who apparently cared a great deal what happened to her.

"I'll need to give this to the Public Information guy to get things going," Mason said, staring at the wall behind Taylor, trying not to catch the eye of any of the array of missing persons posted there. "Get her picture out there. Someone has to notice a girl this pretty."

The height, age, and weight from the pathology report matched. The next step was dental records. They had an answer in a couple of days, thanks to Jorge Talaveras' thoroughness on behalf of his sister. A match. Mason was already drafting the report to pass up the chain of command.

Celia Talaveras. That was her name.

Mason called his missing persons LAPD contact before he called the brother. "I told him there was no report filed in Santa Monica for someone like his sister, but he keeps coming back. Even calls me from Guatemala City. Pain in the ass. Glad to know you got her."

✠

Chapter Twelve

Mason and Delgado took their case to the Sarge.

"Tell me what you've got on this body up on Woodland," Sgt. Bud York said, reaching behind him for a bottle of Tums on the bookcase filled with procedure manuals and bowling trophies.

"Actually, we've got a lot," Delgado said, leaning forward. "An ID of the body and a name and a family. Guatemalan female. Outstayed her visa, then dropped out of sight four months ago. We've got the brother, a lawyer, who's been dogging Taylor in Missing Persons. Coroner's office matches it up with the dental records from the body."

"Hmmph." York looked over Mason's shoulder at the whiteboard with its daily coded To Do list.

"Got a theory of the case yet?"

Mason shrugged. "No. Seems like the deceased's last known address was somewhere in Santa Monica. The family didn't have an exact address. We're looking at the neighboring properties to the place where she was dumped, doing knock and talks at places with kids who'd employ a nanny. We still got a few more properties to go. One of them is Poppy Sinclair's place. She's married to Derek Logan."

The Sarge's eyebrows shot up at the name. "Shit," he

said, flinging a memo onto a pile of paperwork. He slumped at his desk, fingers massaging his forehead.

"Yup. My feelings exactly," Mason said.

Everything went sideways once a celebrity was involved. The rich Muslim girl in the car arson death had almost split Mason and Ginger up a year ago. Routinely, celebrities, big and little, current and has been, attracted notice at the Concerts on the Pier and the celebrity eateries on Montana and Ocean Avenue. They liked to be looked at and written about as they paraded themselves on the Third Street Promenade. The reality stars were getting the big attention now. The worse they behaved in public, the more publicity they got. And the bigger their paychecks grew. What this said about the appetite of the public Mason didn't like to think about.

"The pair of them had nothing to add. Didn't recognize her, showed them the photo, chatted them up. Nobody at the house said they knew her."

"That's something at least. I'll be taking this to the LT. He's gonna want updates," York said. "Written reports."

Mason grinned. "Does he ever read them? Word is he doesn't."

Sgt. York gave Mason a bitter smile. Once Sarge York's dirt bike buddy, Vargas had been promoted to a job that station consensus said should be York's. Lotta talk about it in the locker room. The Sarge had kept his dignity. Vargas was a schmoozer, a golfer. York wasn't. Being able to chat it up with the command staff made a difference, the same as it did in every workplace.

When Vargas wasn't busy working his superiors, he was angry and pissed off, shoulders hunched, arms swinging, brow furled, lips pursed. A big guy, he looked like somebody on a wanted poster. He was full of ugliness about the vicious ex-wives who'd taken him to the cleaners. He had an eye for the women, especially the civilians in the station. So far he'd kept his hands and his mean mouth to himself.

The Sarge was bald and fit. Vargas wore his hair gelled and long, and his gut was edging over his belt. Bud York was closer to the street and the memory of being grabbed by the hair by some dirtwad.

There was always the chance the Lieutenant would get shot in the line of duty. But that was unlikely.

♏

The department kept a clamp on the victim's probable identity, but they couldn't tamp it down for long. Celebrity involvement automatically created leaks. A body in a grave found on the lot next to Logan and Sinclair's home was grist for headlines.

Poppy and Derek living in fear of their lives. Will they be next?

Mason busted out laughing when he read this, slapping his desk. He flipped through the *Enquirer* to keep up. Tabloid reporters were spinning rumor and innuendo, making Olympian leaps involving so-called secret sources and conspiracy theories. Sidebars to the Celia Talaveras story came from people claiming to be close friends of Logan and Sinclair.

The Lieutenant of Operations, Larry Vargas, howled about confidentiality but the Public Information Officer had to give them something.

♏

Now they had an identification, Mason had a procedural path to follow. First, get hold of the victim's brother. He dreaded notification calls. He put it off, thinking about going up to sit on the roof of the station looking out over the old downtown: palm trees, wide streets, and mountains, the ocean, new high-priced condo complexes, ah, the smell of money. Up there doing something about crime looked as if it might be possible. But then he'd catch the hot, dry wind of pollution and see the dirty brown rim of smog on the horizon. Watching the activity in homeless encampments below him made him realize it wouldn't ever be possible.

Nobody could predict how a close relative would take news of the death of a loved one. Even though months had passed since his sister had dropped out of sight, Mason knew her family hoped against all the odds that Celia Talaveras had lost her memory and had been taken in by some kind soul just like in the movies. Mason scanned through the file, not looking forward to relating news of his sister's death. He debated giving the hated notification task to Delgado to do in Spanish, but this one was his. Jorge Talaveras spoke good English.

After the shift change, when most of the detective teams were out in the field, he called Talaveras in Guatemala. The receptionist switched from Spanish to English hearing his accent and put him through to Celia Talaveras' brother.

The silence at the other end of the phone was so long after Mason delivered the news he wondered if he'd been cut off. "Mr. Talaveras? Are you there?"

"Yes, yes." A pause. "We knew she was dead. She would never let us worry about her." He made an awkward gulping noise of grief, and Mason had to grip the phone hard.

"She was so young. We couldn't keep her once she got the *El Norte* bug. I came up to bring her home, and she wouldn't let me see where she is working, what she is doing. What happened to her? When can I see her?"

"The investigation is ongoing," Mason said, falling back into cop clichés, hoping to rob the moment of emotion, fearing Talaveras would cry. It was hard enough to get through these calls in person. A phone call to a foreign country when he couldn't observe the caller's facial reactions made it worse. Or was it better?

"We're calling it a homicide. Her body was uncovered by construction workers here in Santa Monica."

"Homicide …who killed her? How did she die? We want to know."

"We're not there yet, Mr. Talaveras…"

Talaveras interrupted him with urgent words. "We thought she would marry Antonio, her *novio*. His heart is broken."

Ah, an Antonio. He got the details. Antonio was an older lawyer who worked in her brother's firm. So they had Celia's future all worked out for her. And she had plans of her own.

"I come this weekend. I want to see her. So will my parents."

"No, please don't do that, sir. Remember her the way she was. We have no idea yet when we can release her body. Please don't come. Please. You can't see her."

🐾

Chapter Thirteen

The photo of Celia Talaveras posted by the Public Information Officer got attention. An anonymous male caller called the We-Tip line to report Celia Talaveras used to work at the Miramar Hotel in downtown Santa Monica. The caller had recognized her photo. How much was the reward? Antonio, Celia's fiancé, had put up a $25,000 reward.

So she outstayed her visa, her money had run out, and she'd found a job. Was her brother aware she was a hotel worker, which was a pretty good immigrant entry job for somebody with limited English?

Mason's spirits soared when he got the word from We-Tip line. He called the Chief of Personnel at the Fairmont Miramar to make an appointment. Overlooking the ocean, the hotel and its thirty-two bungalows had been a luxury haven for celebrity guests, drawing business to the downtown since the 1920s. Employees had to have papers to work at the Miramar. But a lot of those papers were bogus. The hotel would run a match with Social Security numbers and give employees a couple of months to straighten it out if it didn't link to a valid Social Security number. Then the employees had a chance to buy new paper and start all over again. It was a game that big employers of service workers played.

If all the immigrants stayed home, Mason wondered, who would do the work in the fields or the tourist industry?

The Fairmont Miramar had been at the center of union politics for years. Ginger was involved with the social justice community group supporting the union and had lectured him on the machinations of the union-busting firm management hired to beat them. For years marches and delegations and demonstrations tied up the police monitoring demonstrations and delegations to management. Resentments lingered. In the end, the union won.

Mason walked through the Third Street Promenade, a hugely successful outdoor, blocks-long mall, wondering why anybody would come from Japan or Europe to shop here. The old hotel was a block or so north. Geared to tourists and teenagers, the Promenade was anchored by multiplex movie theaters and retail stores seen everywhere in the world. He'd been told you could see the same stores in Dubai or Berlin or Tokyo. Homeless people with all their baggage occupied the benches, providing an unsightly contrast to shoppers in their urban best. He was grateful Ginger did her shopping online and didn't make him wait for her in stores.

The head of Human Resources met him in the lobby. He got a cool, aloof reception from the tall woman with a tight blonde chignon and charcoal suit. Diamonds in her ears. Yes, she admitted, after taking him to her fine office to consult her records. Celia Talaveras had worked for the Miramar on the housekeeping staff for a short time. They had no forwarding address for her.

"Give me what you've got on her," Mason insisted.

She tried to stare him down, then relented. "Our records are confidential."

"Yes, I know that. So is my homicide investigation. You never know where an investigation will lead, though, once you start digging," he hinted. He saw alarm in her demeanor at the prospect of workforce disruption. "I'll need to speak with your housekeepers now. Will you arrange that for me?"

Her bright, thin smile faded. She led him from the slick corporate offices of the hotel to the bowels of the old hotel with quick, determined steps, asking for assurance Mason wouldn't keep the staff longer than necessary. The housekeepers had rooms to do. Delgado had driven over to the hotel and joined him. One by one he and Delgado interviewed a file of workers, bellmen, housekeepers, bar backs, and front desk staff. The Human Resources boss got bored finally hearing the same questions and the same answer. She left them alone, tapping away to the elevators on kitten heels.

Talaveras had only been at the Fairmont Miramar a short time and had a hard time meeting her room quota because she liked to chat and fool around. But people liked her sunny disposition and optimism. She left the hotel, telling her friends she had a job in a private home. Nobody had an address, other than that it was in Santa Monica.

♏

Rosa Becerra, one of the housekeepers, answered Mason's question with her head averted toward the cement-walled break room the Human Resources director had given them to talk to people. She whispered answers, denying she knew the victim. Mason knew everybody lied to him. He was used to that. The shift of her narrow shoulders away from him, and his experience told him she had known Celia Talaveras better than she was admitting to. For another thing, her English had to be better than this. After he'd wound up the interview, she skidded past him while he stood talking to the Human Resources director in the hall. His eye followed her down the echoing corridor. Becerra was small and slight, slight enough that he wondered how she could do the heavy work hotel housekeeping demanded.

Mason's Spanish was rudimentary. He muttered a sidelong comment to Delgado and gestured toward Becerra who looked careworn and anxious. Printing her name in his notepad, he drew a question mark, tilting it so Delgado could see. Rosa Becerra. He gestured to Delgado to come with him. Delgado caught up to Becerra as she was getting her lunch out of her locker.

Delgado put on a smile and started a conversation. Mason caught a word or two here and there in their conversation. His brain in Spanish had to catch up after it had recognized a word or phrase, and by then, another thousand words flew past.

At first, Rosa Becerra hid her face behind the door of her locker, but Mason could see Delgado was winning her confidence. Getting answers. She shut the locker door, and the conversation was at an end. Delgado and Mason walked down a long hallway filled with air conditioning, electrical wiring, and heating ducts the guests never saw. A set of stairs led to the street level at the employee entrance at the back of the hotel. Delgado seemed pleased.

Mason paused on the sidewalk. "So?"

"They did their training together. The victim couch-surfed with her for a couple of days till she moved in with a Lupe Garcia."

"Who's Garcia? I don't remember her."

"She left too at the same time. This girl says Lupe got Talaveras the job. They were going to be working in a private house here in the city."

A home employing two household workers was bound to be a big one with children. People remembered Lupe Garcia worked with a caterer and bragged about being a good cook.

"Any idea where?"

"Nope. None of the housekeepers heard from either of them again. I'll run down Garcia."

"Good luck. How you gonna do that if the hotel doesn't have a forwarding address?" Mason asked, eyeing a mangy looking couple slouching away from them. He knew them from past arrests. Shoplifters. Seeing him, they turned and walked the other way.

"Let's hope she's somewhere in the system. Work the street, I guess."

"Yeah, maybe. Wouldn't it be nice if people filed with worker's comp and all that when they hired household help?"

"Instead of trying to do it on the cheap," Delgado said. "You think they get rich by throwing it away on big salaries and benefits for the workers?" He waved a hand at passing traffic, which included a Porsche Carrera and a mini Mercedes. At the shop on the corner, they could buy pots and pans and dishes which cost more than a week's salary.

Two blocks north on a side street off Wilshire Boulevard, they found Delgado's Crown Vic. Delgado huffed and puffed beside him, complaining about the city's parking problem the whole way. He could have walked from the station to the hotel in fifteen minutes. It took longer than that to drive and park.

Delgado didn't walk unless he was forced. As for being one of those guys out there runnin' and gunnin', that was sure a thing of the past.

⚘

Mason had a lead from another worker he had yet to chase down. A hefty woman, with the texturized eyebrows that were so fashionable now, went shifty-eyed. "I used to see Celia with that union guy," she said.

"Oh yeah? The hospitality worker union, huh?" Mason said.

The union had been in the news in Santa Monica since the nineties. He knew where the union hall was from Ginger. The rent control and living wage people she volunteered for used the union hall on Colorado for phone banking at election time. Ginger got herself mixed up in all that, no matter what he said.

Mason and Delgado thumped down the stairs into the parking area below the station, kicking around the day at the end of the shift. Delgado drove a big white family van and was examining it for dents. His sixteen-year-old daughter just got her license. Mason looked over his old Jeep. If Haley and her mother were actually going to move back into Los Angeles from where God lost his shoes way out there in the urban sprawl, he might get a few more miles out of it. New car or flying lessons? Flying lessons won out. He couldn't explain the soaring peace and excitement he felt when he was in the air high over Santa Monica, the Pier tilting below him, the ocean spreading out, pushing away from the continent. He daydreamed about would it would be like when he could fly solo.

"So we update the Sarge tomorrow. What's still hanging?" Delgado asked, his keys in his hand.

"I'm planning to sniff around the union guy. I heard from some of these people Talaveras was tilting towards the union."

Mason hailed the PIO who was leaving the station at

the same time. "Hey, Mike, you know this guy. Brian Anderson? The union organizer for the hospitality industry?"

"Yeah, he comes in to get a permit for any kind of march they want to do. Demonstrations, that kind of thing."

"Is he credible?"

"Yeah, he's okay, but all those organizers are crazy. They're tough, though."

♪

The next morning Mason walked to the union hall about six blocks away, across the bridge spanning the Santa Monica Freeway before the first glimpse of the Pacific Ocean. Sandy beaches, the Pier, Pacific Coast Highway curling around the Bay to Malibu and beyond. He banged on the glass door of a one-story stucco building with two front entrances. Facing the street in one office was an elongated brass sculpture against a scarlet wall. A thick black rug carpeted the stone floor. A gorgeous redhead smiled out at him from behind a glass desk. Something told Mason this wasn't a union hall. On the glass door of the next building entrance, a sheet of copy paper was taped, on which Local 15 was scrawled with a Sharpie. Locked. Mason banged on the door, and after a minute, a fast-moving young guy already losing his hair, came forward to answer it.

Mason held his badge up to the glass.

"We keep it locked because we get a lot of homeless people coming in," he said. "I'm Brian Anderson. Come on in. You called about Celia."

He led Mason through a large open room, the walls papered with homemade slogans, meeting notices, election and union posters. *Si se puede.* Banged up wooden desks hosting old computers lined the perimeter.

The news she was dead troubled Anderson. He looked away, and his eyes were shiny when he looked back. "How did she die?"

"It was a homicide, sir."

"You won't tell me?"

"We're not releasing the details yet."

"Was she raped? Hurt that way?"

"Not that we could tell." Lying in a dirt grave for months hardly made it easy. "We're not releasing anything official yet."

"Then how did she die?"

"Head injury," Mason said, looking down at his notes. "How well did you know her, Mr. Anderson?"

Anderson didn't answer. Instead, he got up from behind his desk and took a sheaf of paper from the printer, tapped the edges even, and stapled it together without looking at it. Mason swiveled around to watch him, waiting.

"The union is always on the lookout for leadership potential. Like everywhere, I guess. Celia came to a meeting and we spotted something in her. A woman from my team followed up with her, just for coffee. She gave her the assignment to talk to one of the other housekeepers who was scared to come out for the union. Celia was just supposed to talk to her, feel her out, no heavy recruiting. The next meeting Celia shows up with this woman and has another one in tow as well. That got noticed. We went out for coffee a couple of times and talked. I got her story. Then she disappeared, quit coming to meetings, answering her phone. Her texts stopped." He paused and looked up at the ceiling. "She was different in lots of ways."

"How so?"

"Had more family resources than many of the others.

Brother was a lawyer. Did you know that?"

Mason nodded. "You know anybody else who was friendly with her?"

He shrugged. "Not really. She was outgoing, friendly with everybody. She was taking ESL classes at St. Anne's, though. You could ask around there."

Mason knew St. Anne's. People called it the Mexican Catholic church. Father Mike was fiercely protective of his parishioners. Mason knew of one or two police chases into the parking lot where Father Mike had all but invoked sanctuary.

Brian Anderson raised a hand to his face and pinched the bridge of his nose as if to stave off a headache. "The last time I saw Celia she told me she got a job in Las Vegas. I thought it was a little fishy. I called the local over there and she wasn't listed."

"So what did you do?"

Anderson gave a huge shrug. "What could I do? I asked around about her. Tried to find out where she'd gone. Then I forgot her. So many bad things could have happened to her out there in Vegas."

"She have a man in her life? Anybody you ever hear of?"

He looked away. "Maybe. I had my doubts. I asked her but she denied it."

"So just coffee with her? You ever want more?"

"Sure. But that's a no no in my job."

He was finished here. "My job too, but it happens. You know a Lupe Garcia?"

"Which one? It's a common name."

"She worked at the Miramar with Celia."

"No. Don't remember her."

Mason stood up; then his phone vibrated on his belt. He took a look at the incoming call. His *father*? Again.

His Dad never called him on his cell. He could barely remember a time when his father had called him at home on his landline. Maybe his sister had emerged from the world of drugs she lived in and was calling his parents for money again.

Maybe his mother had finally reached her limit with her. A whole lot of maybes.

🐜

Chapter Fourteen

Mason caught up with Talaveras' ESL teacher in a classroom at St. Anne's church. The sun blistered the asphalt in the huge parking lot outside the classroom buildings next to an outdoor chapel and the church itself. After the day students wearing St. Anne's uniforms cleared out, the school turned into an immigration counseling and ESL center. Mason found the classroom and Alejandro Morales, the teacher. Late in the afternoon, other students began filing in, students of all ages, many Latino, but not all. Most of them wore uniforms and joined the cheerful conversations around the microwave. They heated up homemade dinners to eat during class, then headed off to the second job in the evening.

Mason shoved the studio portrait of the victim across the teacher's cluttered desk. Morales looked at it a long moment, then raised troubled brown eyes to Mason's.

"That poor girl. Too many of them die. She missed a lot because her employers kept her late, even though they knew she had classes. But she tried. Nice girl. I remember her."

Mason looked around as the classroom filled up. "You didn't know her well, then?"

"She wasn't around long enough to know well. Ask

some of the other students." He pointed.

Mason walked over to a group of older Latino women who fell silent at his approach. He had cop written all over him in his bearing, the haircut, the gun at his waist. Worse, maybe Immigration. He didn't even try to do the interview in his horrible Spanish.

"I'm looking for somebody who might have known this girl," he began.

They passed the photo around. "What happened to her?" one of them asked. She wore a McDonald's uniform and a name tag reading Alicia.

"She was murdered," he said. "Can you help me? She's got people who loved her, who want to know what happened to her. Her brother, he comes to the US to ask about her. Her parents care. We care. We want to find out who killed her."

Alicia crossed herself. "*Dios mio.*"

There was a buzz of conversation among them. Mason heard the name *Lupe* mentioned more than once, and looks back and forth –"*la amiga de Lupe.*" There was no way he could catch what was going on. Delgado should be the one doing this interview, not him. He kicked himself for being so stupid. But Delgado was up to his ears dogging the forensics people. They had other cases as well, though this was the highest priority.

One of the women, braver than the others, handed the photo back to him. "She was friends with this girl Lupe. She liked that guy. The union guy."

"What guy?"

She screwed up her face. "Anderson? Maybe he knows."

"You have a last name for Lupe?"

That started the buzz up again. "Ask the teacher."

Lupe Garcia. Anderson had lied about knowing her.

♨

Mason stopped for a corn dog and a Coke at the 7-Eleven on Wilshire Boulevard because he saw a parking place, and he'd learned to eat when he had a chance. He hoped nobody saw him buying what Ginger called trash food. Yeah, yeah. Sure it was trash food, but he liked corn dogs once in a while. On the way out he spotted a tabloid with a photo of Derek Logan and Poppy Sinclair emerging from a high-priced restaurant in Santa Monica holding hands. Wasn't that sweet?

Logan liked to be recognized in Santa Monica riding his bike. He would pause to pose at the crosswalks, hoping to be noticed. Just one of the people: that was Logan. He had spurts of fiscal piety and was photographed shopping at the 99 Cent Store at a location which bordered Santa Monica and Venice, one city to the south. Mason read everything he came upon mentioning Poppy and picked up a lot about Derek as well. Logan came from small-town Indiana, and waved off his success as luck, though Mason figured he secretly believed he was the greatest actor since Olivier. Poppy came from small-town California and soared to the top with one lucky Disney movie, the one about the dog. They had roughly similar backgrounds: lower middle class. They had one of the few long-term Hollywood marriages.

No matter how ferociously station personnel was told to keep their mouths shut, somebody told a girlfriend. Somebody tipped the tabloids. It wasn't long before the *Enquirer* led with the story that finding a body next door to the Logan-Sinclair household had led to their children being traumatized. The accidental drowning of Poppy's publicist was rehashed at length.

Death Visits the Sinclair-Logan Home Again.

Parents Anguished by Tragic Death

Mason now had a Google alert on Sinclair-Logan. He skimmed an online gossip magazine reporting Santa Monica police had identified the body in the grave next door to their place. They were withholding any information on the victim as part of an ongoing investigation. Ooooh, conspiracy. That was more than enough to get the motors going at one of the many fake celebrity news sites.

The machine of celebrity creation had to be fueled with tidbits gleaned from a stable of PR hacks and inventive writers who simply made things up if it was a slow news cycle.

Did anybody really believe Hillary Clinton had an alien baby? He scratched his head, listening to Fredericks' raucous honk of a voice talking on her cell phone next to him. Yeah, they did.

♌

The media coverage suggesting a link to the Sinclair-Logan establishment was more than enough to get Jorge Talaveras to call again. "We don't know yet that she worked in their home, Mr. Talaveras," Mason said. "They said they don't recognize her photo. We don't have any link to them. And I can't tell you any more than that."

"But can't you at least go and see if they have a children's swing in their backyard? You remember that photo I sent you? There's a photo of a swing set."

"Half the backyards in Santa Monica have a swing set, sir. I can't do that. You're a lawyer. You know that. We have to have a reason to go on people's property. I'm sure there's something like that in Guatemala."

"Yes, but ..." His control broke, and there was a flood of impassioned Spanish. Mason's Spanish wasn't up to this. He looked around for Delgado and found him spreading cream cheese on a bagel at his desk and reading a memo. The tentacles of Talaveras' grief and anger reached to grip Mason through the phone.

"I will contact you the minute there's more to tell you. I can't say any more right now. I'm sorry. I have to go now."

Shit. Of course, he'd studied the photo. Grass. Trees. A swing set, a wall, Celia smiling at the camera. It could be anywhere. He wasn't psychic.

In the meantime, he'd been angling for a trip to Guatemala to interview Celia's fiancé. Fat bloody likely. Maybe he could get something from the locals. Did anybody he knew know anybody in lawyer circles in Quetzaltenango, Guatemala?

※

Mason caught up with Brian Anderson as he was leaving the union hall on Colorado Avenue. Anderson had the hatchback up on an old red Prius and was stacking boxes of flyers onto a dolly. He jerked back when he saw Mason. His face went pale and wary.

"Afternoon, Mr. Anderson. You didn't return my call."

"I meant to call you. You're on my To Do list today, to tell you the truth."

Anybody who said "to tell you the truth" Mason discounted as a people-pleasing liar. He chased the skepticism off his face and leaned against the car. "See, I heard you didn't exactly tell me the truth about Celia Talaveras."

Anderson's face went rigid. "Yeah?"

"One of her friends told me you were real friendly with her."

Anderson tilted the dolly back that held the two boxes from a printer. "Let's go inside. It's hot out here." He looked around as though there might be some opportune interruption but they were alone in the parking lot. Mason followed him into the building, through the big room filled with beat-up desks, shift schedules, and union propaganda on the walls.

Anderson set his cell phone on his desk, and Mason sank into the chair with the busted leg propped up on a telephone book. He let the silence cook as he got out his tablet as though he intended to record everything Anderson said. That usually got people going.

"So tell me the truth this time. You knew her better than you told me."

"Well, maybe a little. I worried about her. That's all."

"Worried about her? You do this for all the women you run into around here?"

That didn't even get an answer from Anderson. He took a box cutter from his pocket and sliced into the box, pulling out the top flyer. He ran his eyes over it, checking for accuracy and seemed satisfied. "I asked around where Lupe got the job and got a number for her. I called her and she admitted Celia worked there too until she'd taken off one night."

"And you went there? To the house? To do what?"

"See if she knew anything."

"And you lied to me about Lupe Garcia. You knew her."

"Yeah, I know."

"Did you talk to Lupe?"

"Yeah."

"So tell me. When you got to the house…"

"Poppy Sinclair met me at the door and told me Celia went back to Guatemala. I knew she came from

Quetzaltenango because I went to language school there to learn Spanish. That was a tie between me and Celia."

Mason noticed a weak chin and his darting eyes as Anderson tilted his head to the side. "Did you believe her? Sinclair?"

"Yeah." He sank his head in his hands. "I made a real fool of myself over her."

"Yeah?"

"I left my wife, told her we needed a separation. Broke her heart, especially because we had our little girl."

He looked up at Mason expecting sympathy. Mason had sympathy in short supply. He saved it for the real victims.

"So when was all this?"

"Back in June. I stopped paying my guy in Quetzaltenango to look for her in September. I guess she was dead long before that."

"Let's go back to your visit to the house. Start there. You talked to Sinclair?"

"Yeah, but before that, I had to talk to their security guy. He was a cold son-of-a-bitch hard-ass, but I eventually got in to see Poppy. I told the security guy I'd go to the press if he didn't let me see her."

"And what did she say? Tell me again."

"That Celia had a boyfriend back in Guatemala. That she'd gone back. Sinclair stood in the doorway and didn't even really look at me. I got like thirty seconds of her time. But Lupe saw me and she sneaked down the street after me when I left. She didn't know either where Celia had gone. But she did say that Celia was afraid of Derek. He used to get wasted and chase the workers around the house. Poppy didn't even seem to care. Weird, huh? You think he killed her?"

"We're thinking a whole lot of things. So why didn't

you come to us with this information? I thought you cared about her."

"I know it makes me look bad. When I heard she was dead, it all roared back in my mind. I was creeping around trying to keep my wife happy. I didn't want to upset her again. Besides at that point, what good would it do? Celia was already dead. Here I thought she had just been avoiding me."

"So there was nothing going on between you and her?"

"In my head, maybe."

That was it.

Mason waited in a line of cars, tapping the steering wheel with a finger, and trying to tamp down his frustration. He waited through three long lights to turn left on Fourth Street to get back to the station. People weren't all that complicated at their essence, at least most of the ones he met. You tried to figure out what motivated them and play on that. There was usually a reason for the way they acted—even if it was plain stupidity and panic. And then there was craziness, which was its own special deal.

Chapter Fifteen

Nigel Bateson was working the gate at the mansion on Woodland when Mason and Fredericks arrived for follow-up questioning. Bateson glared at Mason who slid down the window as he pulled up to the gate on the long, curving street ending in a cul-de-sac. The house seemed to be inspired by 18th-century French romantic architecture, or so Mason had heard from a stocky African-American woman who worked in the planning department. Inspired by, but only realized in a few incongruous details. Otherwise, it was a hodgepodge of different construction materials and time periods. The Logan-Sinclair enterprise was thoroughly hated in the city offices, as well as by their neighbors. They were said to be trying to buy up adjacent properties to privatize the street. They had also submitted plans to excavate beneath the underground parking garage to create a theater and entertainment room.

A flash of light glinted off a long-lens camera. Mason spotted photographers adjusting lenses, dying for the shot which would pay the rent this month. Mason wondered why Bateson was working a shift here himself when he had a company to run. Was he required to keep back the ghouls and looky-loos who lined the sidewalk across the street as though there was something to see?

"Yes?" Bateson asked stone-faced.

"We need to see both Mr. Logan and Ms. Sinclair. Is either one of them at home?"

"What kind of questions?" he asked.

Mason laughed. "Just open the gates."

Bateson shrugged and gestured to another operative who had appeared out of the shadows and slid the gate open. The house glowed golden in the late afternoon sun. The magnolia trees were in full bloom, blossoms big as plates. Curving paths in the courtyard led through small hills with ponds and stands of foliage hiding the back of the property. Mason drove in and parked in a circular gravel path behind a Range Rover and a slinky grey Maserati. Fredericks was all eyes.

"The way some people live," she said, envy sharpening her voice.

Mason pressed the bell, and Lupe Garcia came to the door wiping her hands dry on a kitchen towel. The two dogs, the Benjie dog, and the big poodle roared out of the kitchen with enthusiasm at a new visitor. Mason tried to shoo them away, but they continued to bark and hump his leg, while he tried to maintain his dignity. Lupe ignored them.

"Where is Detective Delgado?" she said, her face flirty. "I made my green chili sauce for him."

"I'll take it to him," Mason said. "Can you get the dogs off me?"

"Oh, they bothering you?" She grabbed them by the collars and stuffed them into a room off the entryway where they continued to bark.

"I give it to him. Tell Detective Delgado. You tell him."

"I will. We need to see Mr. Logan and Ms. Sinclair now," Mason said as the barking died down. The house smelled like baking bread. How many people in this house would be vegan and gluten-free?

"Come in. Come in."

Mason figured her employers wouldn't be pleased about her inviting them in, but Garcia was all smiles and goodwill. Megan, the fifteen-year-old daughter, glided down the stairs and into the room and stood watching them. She hadn't inherited the best features of either of her parents. She might have been ordinarily a nice-looking young girl a little on the plump side, but not with that glare on her face, the pouty lips, and crossed arms in long sleeves.

"So are they home?"

Lupe grinned. "You should make appointment." She pulled the apron off and stuffed it in the pocket of her black rayon pants.

Megan slid forward. "Have you found out anything yet about Celia?"

Mason turned to face her. "We could use your help."

Lupe was giving Megan dark looks and seemed about to grab her by the arm. Mason handed his card to Megan, lifting his eyebrows, hoping she would get the hint to call him. Instead, Lupe grabbed the card from Megan's hand.

Megan twisted away and ran for the stairs, shouting at Lupe over her shoulder. "You can't stop me."

Mason jingled his keys, watching her disappear, and then stuffed them back in his pockets. What he wouldn't give right now to get that girl into an interview room. He reminded himself to show her the photo.

Lupe Garcia. A common name, Anderson had said.

"The union, huh," he said to her.

"Yeah, what about it?"

"You know this Anderson guy? You ever work at the Miramar?"

"Maybe a little," she said. "This better job."

He brought out Celia Talaveras' photo and handed it to her.

"Do you know this woman?"

Lupe gave the photo a long look. "Yeah, that's Celia. She was working here. What happened to her?"

"She was murdered, Ms. Garcia. That's her body they found next door."

Lupe crossed herself. "*Dios mio. La pobre chica.*"

Mason gave it a moment to sink in. Fredericks was roaming around the living room checking things out.

"Let's sit down," he said.

Garcia busied herself, insisting on making coffee while Mason and Fredericks watched her as they sat at the kitchen table.

"You sure it's her?" she said finally when she put cups down in front of them and then returned with the coffee pot. She pulled out a chair and sat down, her hands on her knees.

"It's her. What can you tell me about her? When did you last see her?"

"I come home from visiting my daughter in Pacoima. She's not here. Megan's all upset and everything's crazy."

"What was the date?" Fredericks interjected.

"I don't know. I could look it up."

"Do that, would you?"

Garcia got up heavily and went into the back of the house returning with a cell phone. She scrolled through to her Events and clicked on June 9th.

At this point, Mason wanted Garcia on record, Sinclair and Logan in the station. They'd lied not knowing Celia, not recognizing her photo, and he wanted to know why.

✠

He and Fredericks got back to the vehicle and nosed out on the street. Bateson opened the gate without looking at them. A row of media trucks lined the curb, engines humming in hopes of action. Antennas spiked from their roofs and wires spilled down the side. So-called reporters were coiffing their hair and powdering their noses. Maybe they figured he would bring Sinclair and Logan out the door, their heads covered by coats, in a perp walk.

Mason ignored them. Sorry, no perp walk.

✠

Fredericks swung into the bullpen, high-fiving other detectives and probation officers along the way. Mason gathered she'd won another martial arts tournament. He'd hear about it from her. All about it. He reminded himself how good she was at ferreting out the critical piece of information when he got annoyed with her popping bubble wrap at her desk. And fast. A lot of people annoyed him. He would grumble to Ginger, "People. That's what's wrong with the world." One time she said back to him, "And that's right with the world." He was still thinking about that.

"Hey, boss, our guy Talaveras?" Fredericks said.

"Yeah, what about him?"

"Private security reported he tried to force his way into Poppy Sinclair's place. They warned him off but he's still up there now, hanging around."

"I knew that guy was trouble. I didn't tell him there was a link to them."

"He got that on his own," Fredericks said. "The whole world knows we're looking at them. It's all over the Internet. Buckle up, buttercup. We're in for a real ride on this one."

Jorge Talaveras wouldn't let his sister's murder go. He tried to lose himself in the crowd of people hanging on the curb together opposite the gravesite watching the construction workers. The body had been gone for a week. What the hell was there to see?

The TV crews were long gone, leaving the ghouls. A few Asian tourists there with long-lensed cameras. Packs of teenage girls. Boys shoving each other. Must be hard on the daughter. Megan.

And Talaveras. He started talking about his sister and showing the photo around. The TV crews came back fast. Then he became a nuisance. He was in the back of a police unit when Mason got up to Woodland. And not happy about it. He banged on the closed window when he saw Mason drive in. The officer walked over to Mason as he got out of the vehicle. She was short, her black hair up in a stiff French braid, wiry and snapping with energy.

"He says he knows you, sir."

"Yeah. I know him. What did he do?"

"He was acting like a 5150 wack job and insisted the security people ring up to the house. He wants to see Sinclair. Yeah, well, does he think he's the only guy in the world with a hard-on for Poppy?"

Mason twitched uncomfortably.

"What do you want me to do with him?"

"Let him go," Mason said. "I'll handle him. It's his sister they pulled out of the grave next door. He's not right in the head at this point."

"He thinks that pair had something to do with it. Really?" Mason saw an *Enquirer* folded on the seat next to the patrol officer. Everybody was a fan.

"Like I said… let him out."

Talaveras shot out the back door of the vehicle when

it was unlocked, slamming it hard behind him. He headed toward Mason, his face a mask of bitterness.

"C'mon, Mr. Talaveras. Let this go. Can I call you Jorge?"

"But she worked there. You know that. People knew her. I want to talk to them," he shouted.

Mason held up his hands. "Yeah, I know, but you can't go busting in like this. They don't have to talk to you. You don't even know they're home."

"She must have left things behind. Where is her phone?"

He was standing way too close to Mason, a bead of sweat forming on his brow.

"What did those people do with her things?" he said, winding down.

Mason felt sorry for the guy. The uniform was watching them. "C'mon, let me buy you a coffee? We'll get you on the way home back to your family. There's nothing you can do here."

Protesting, Talaveras let himself be led to Mason's vehicle. Mason had no intention of buying him a coffee. He had things to do. Talaveras slumped in the passenger seat, all the fight gone out of him. He was glum and silent for the ride back downtown. Mason pushed through the traffic back to the DoubleTree on Fourth Street opposite the Public Safety building to let him off in front. He put a hand on the sleeve of Talaveras' jacket before he got out.

"Hey, man. I know this has gotta be hard, but you can't be harassing those people."

"Harassing? I want justice for my sister."

Ah, justice. Mason didn't have an answer for that. Not a quick one anyway. "We'll be in touch immediately when there's something to say."

Talaveras didn't answer. He pushed the door closed

and Mason watched the bellman come out with a hospitality worker smile and speak to him. Talaveras pushed past him.

✠

Chapter Sixteen

In frustration, Jorge Talaveras contacted one of the online tabloids, and in a flash, he and his beautiful sister and her story were all over social media. He was charging an SMPD cover-up to protect his sister's celebrity couple employers. Talaveras was handsome and photogenic, a tall, exotic Latino lawyer who spoke good English and teared up talking about his sister. Dynamite. Mason groaned when an email from Fredericks gave him a link to *Access Hollywood*. Then, he skimmed one of the Santa Monica Facebook pages law enforcement monitored.

Mike Rosen, the media manager at the station, was tearing his hair out. Mason's private opinion was that Rosen was a little too excitable for the Public Information Officer job, but nobody asked his opinion. Rosen was waiting for him when he got in early the next morning.

"Do you know how many video files I've got in my email box about this, Mason?" Rosen's breath was already rancid with cigarettes and coffee.

Mason leaned away from him. "Hey man, I'm just doing my job. Your job is handling media."

Rosen sank on a chair, his head in his hands. "This morning I've got three hundred and eighty video clips, and it's probably more now. God knows what's on them. We tell people 'See something. Say something,' but this is beyond ridiculous," he complained. "Now it's send something ... anything. I get all this shit. Videos of the windows at Logan's house, and the guy sending it is telling me to look at the ghost in the window. That's the killer. It's clear as day to him."

Mason laughed.

Rosen followed Mason over to the coffee station and shook his head, rubbing his stomach at his offer of coffee. "God no, my stomach. Look, crowdsourcing is a great solution--especially when the community is outraged at what's taking place like they had in Boston with that bomber."

"Hey, it helped in the Las Vegas shooting too," Mason reminded him.

"All these video ghouls want to get involved in Poppy and Derek's life and feel close to them."

"I don't think we've got a ghost killer, Rosen. Suck it up."

Rosen took a call, swiped the phone closed and with a loud belch, left.

Mason skimmed the bio on Derek Logan's website. Logan grew up poor, a factoid he always got around to mentioning in every interview. It wasn't strictly true. His father worked for the phone company. Logan was a good interview, a good talker, and schmoozer. With a wry grin, he acknowledged his failings, his worst excesses before Megan was born. He liked women and confessed to a series of hookups before he stopped using drugs, some of his indiscretions while he was married to Poppy. At present, he was reading scripts and preparing for his next movie shoot in Morocco. The public gave him a lot of sympathy over his hard work to conquer his stammer.

Hinted at, but managed and papered over by his

lawyers, personal assistants, and publicists were lots of drugs, blowouts, lies, and meltdowns. He went on drug-fueled talking jags. They tried to keep him away from Twitter and Facebook and giving impromptu interviews on the street.

Mason laughed at the mention that Logan was writing his memoir. A studio publicist was lining him up to sound like Hemingway.

Mason found the private number of a Hollywood insider he'd had a minor involvement with when he investigated a murder in the Pico neighborhood. He confirmed Derek's reputation as a womanizer, Poppy's rages to contain him, epic fights. Maybe Derek was on steroids. He was another celebrity who didn't allow anyone to photograph him, fearing a bad angle. Stars who were way worse than Logan.

Celia Talaveras lingered as an active malignant presence in the house, souring the air, thickening the atmosphere. Derek and Poppy now talked to each other more than they had in years. Routine existence, and there never had been a routine in their life, demanded an effort both of them found hard to maintain. Poppy blamed Derek. Derek fueled his denial of reality with an increased appetite for mind-numbing drugs and dreams of a Broadway hit. Lovely drugs. In the beginning of their picture-perfect marriage, they'd been happy enough, floating on a cloud of public admiration and hit movies. The wisps of desire they'd felt for each other had long ago drifted away. The jolts of testosterone Derek projected on screen and in public appearances seemed to disappear in the bed they shared. His wife suffered from irritable bowel syndrome, and the brown cloud of farts and her bathroom fixation lessened the appeal of her smooth pale body. Logan found comfort elsewhere, and as long as he was not publicly photographed committing bestiality, Poppy didn't care. Now she found everything about him distasteful. Even the way he breathed annoyed her. They'd worked out a way to project contentment in public, and that was all either of them needed.

There was no call from Sinclair or Logan by afternoon of the next day. Mason knew he hadn't handled his time at the house well. He came back, his groin tugging at him as he imagined himself close to Poppy Sinclair again. The idea of her, even thinking about her, was ridiculous. But he couldn't help it. He reminded himself he was there to do a job and strengthen the links between Celia Talaveras and the Logan-Sinclair household. He wasn't there to drool over some movie star, ducking his head and blushing like some fourteen-year-old altar boy.

The circular driveway in front of the house was clear, except for a big Mercedes. Which one of the superstars drove that? There were a few old beaters on the street outside the house.

"These probably belong to the maid and the gardeners," Delgado said, looking around.

Lupe Garcia answered the door and said Poppy couldn't be disturbed. She gave Delgado a long look. The Señor wasn't home. Delgado insisted Lupe call Poppy. Lupe went into the kitchen and made a call on the intercom. Delgado followed her into the kitchen and struck up a conversation in Spanish. Mason remained in the hall, examining the paintings, the weavings, the sculpture. Hard to tell children lived here it was so neat and uncluttered.

Poppy made an entrance down the stairs buttoning the

cuff of a red business suit made of a fabric that clung to her. She flung a brochure and program at him.

"I'm the main speaker at a fund-raising lunch downtown today. I can give you five minutes." No pretty smiles of welcome. All business and in a hurry.

She beckoned them into a room off the foyer which looked like the room where the lady of the house met with tradesmen. They sat down on opposite couches, Poppy fussing at something glittery around her neck.

Mason came at her with the first question, not allowing himself to linger on thoughts of her. "We've learned the woman whose body was found next door worked in your house. Do you recall I showed you her photo when I was here before?"

He passed her the same photo he'd shown her before. "Her name was Celia Talaveras. And you didn't recognize her?"

"Oh really? Celia Talaveras. Hmmmmm. Didn't she have a big mole on her chin?"

"I don't think so."

"No, I don't remember her. Dozens of people have worked in our house, Detective. You may not know how difficult it is to keep good help. And there's no longer any such thing as loyalty."

Mason figured if you paid people enough and treated them well, they would put up with an amazing amount of shit. "Who does the hiring and firing?"

"I do. I deal with the house and the children."

"Big responsibility," Mason said, looking up from his notes, flicking his glance away from her breasts. "And your husband?"

"He does what he does," she said. "So you say she worked here. I don't remember her," she said, rising. "People come in our home, and they see things they want, and they take them and sell them on eBay."

"That was your experience with Celia Talaveras?"

"I didn't say that. I don't really remember her well. Perhaps, now that I look at her photo again. I was away two months last year shooting in Canada."

Mason made a note to check that. "She was here six months. Did she have a relationship with Ms. Garcia?"

"Lupe would have been her boss. I suppose they must have had some sort of relationship." Her tone grew waspish and impatient.

"And you and Ms. Garcia didn't think to file a missing person's report?"

"You know these women…" she said.

"Well, no, I don't. That's why I'm asking you." Mason kept his eyes level, his tone flat. "Did you mention her leaving to your security people?"

"Why would I do that? They didn't have any interaction with her. Their job is to keep people away from Derek and I and the children."

"See, nobody else recognized her name when I was first here. She lived in this house, didn't she? I can understand you might not have known her, but six months here and nobody knew her name? That seems odd."

"They change names to avoid Immigration. It's not all that odd to me. I've told you many people come and go here. I can't help that."

Mason took another tack. "Her brother filed the missing person's report. He's been up here in the US several times trying to find her. He didn't know she was working for you. She'd been very cagey in communications with her family about where she worked. Why would that be?"

Poppy sighed and tilted her head back in impatience. "Our lawyer and business manager drew up non-disclosure agreements for household staff. We're in the public eye for heaven's sake. The last thing we want is for some worker here talking about what kind of toilet paper we use and that Derek and I sometimes fight. Are you surprised Derek and I sometimes fight? Are you married, Detective Mason?"

"I know married people fight, Ms. Sinclair," he said, evading her question. Ginger and marriage was a complicated subject.

"We also established a connection to you from a hotel worker union official who knew she worked here. He says he came to the door and talked to you about her. And also from the priest at St. Anne's. It seems a lot of people knew she worked for your family." That was enlarging the truth a little.

This didn't appear to faze Sinclair. She was poking a diamond earring into a hole in her ear.

"And you had no memory of her when I first showed you her photo?"

She made a pretty frown and continued poking at the hole in her ear, then shrugged.

"Nobody said anything to you?" He waved around at the rest of the house, taking in the household staff, indicating his growing suspicion. "I showed that photo to everyone on staff here. They must have recognized her."

Megan, the 15-year-old daughter, appeared in the doorway, dressed in a private school uniform. "We knew who she was, but they told us not to say anything."

"Who do you mean *they*?" Mason said, swiveling.

Megan pointed at her mother. "And Derek. Celia was nice. She was fun." She edged into the room.

"Megan, you hardly knew her," her mother said in a strangled voice.

"Yes, I did. I did so."

Mason looked back and forth between them, letting the tension between them cook.

Poppy stood up. "I absolutely must leave now. This is a very important engagement for me. I take my charity work seriously."

"I'll be calling you into the station then to make a formal statement. And we may have other questions."

A look of displeasure swept across Sinclair's expressive face.

"Where is your husband, Ms. Sinclair? We need to talk to him as well," Mason said, pretending to consult his notes.

"I really don't know. Maybe he had an early call. Between the two of us, it's hard to keep track of anything. That's why I hardly recognized this Celia person."

"Don't you have help with keeping track of things?"

"Certainly. But with all the PAs I've hired, it still seems I'm still the one keeping track."

"You never let anyone help you," her daughter said, making it sound like an accusation. "And you're not nice to them."

Her mother didn't answer, raised her eyebrows, and smiled the Poppy Sinclair smile.

"How long did Celia Talaveras work for you?" Mason asked. "Do you remember now?"

"How can I say? I'm very busy, you know."

"Mom, you did so know her. She worked here for six months. She was the one you gave the halter top to and then you took it back."

"Oh." Poppy covered a small silence by crossing her legs. Mason lifted his eyes to the ceiling. White crown molding against taupe walls.

Megan leaned against the couch, scratching the reddened back of her neck. "She used to tell me stories about her family and all the fun they had when they were little."

"It couldn't have been all that much fun, Megan. Guatemala is a horrible country," Poppy snapped.

"It is not."

"Isn't it time for you to go to your spin class?"

"I still have time." Megan wasn't budging.

"Where are your employment records? It could help us pin down the date when she was killed," Mason said to Poppy as the silence fell with mother and daughter glaring at each other.

"Well, not here. Our business manager, Jay Stone, does all that." Sinclair reached for a card file that lay on the glass coffee table between them and handed one to him. Mason noted the address: Century City, a business, financial, legal address in the middle of Los Angeles. Traffic. Inwardly he sighed. It would take at least a couple of hours to get there and back.

"I really must go now," Poppy said, rising. "They've sold 600 tickets for this luncheon, and I told you I'm the main speaker." She smoothed her hands down her long, slender thighs. She made a great fuss over when she would and would not be available for interviews.

"Let's make it simple, Ms. Sinclair. You and your husband come to the station tomorrow at 9 o'clock in the morning." She stood up with shrieks of protest which he ignored.

"Since you have to leave now, I'll talk to your household staff."

"Don't you need a warrant to talk to them?" she said, looking down at him.

Mason laughed and stood up. "No, I'm not going to interrogate them. They're not in custody. I'm looking for information about the victim. Any lead is a big help to us."

She turned away.

"You get going," Poppy Sinclair said to Megan, grabbing her by the shoulder. "You're going to be late. Don't you want to lose weight?"

♌

Delgado was in the kitchen where Mason joined him. The mood there was easy and convivial, unlike the snapping tension between mother and daughter. A radio played softly and a telenovela was playing without sound on a small TV on the expansive granite counter. Lupe Garcia, Celia Talaveras' former boss, brought Mason a cup of coffee along with a lot of cheery chat about the weather and the dogs, who kept running in and out, barking and jumping up on his legs. He ruffled the ears of the tall black poodle with the intelligent eyes. The Benjie dog jumped up on his lap and he let it stay, getting a bead on the housekeeper. Delgado was leaning back at the kitchen table where Lupe Garcia peeled carrots.

"So I heard from a guy over at the union office you used to work at the Miramar," Mason said, stirring his coffee.

"This is better job. Hotel work breaks your back. Those big duvets on the beds? They weigh thirty-five pounds. J'ou try making beds all day."

"I know it's hard work," Mason acknowledged. Ginger had been involved marginally in the hotel worker unionizing campaigns which had kept the hotels frantic for a couple of decades now.

"How do you think she died? Did she have enemies?"

Garcia shrugged that off. "She's too young to have enemies." Garcia herself looked like a good hater with black eyes that had violence etched in them.

"She wanted this job instead?"

"Sure. Her own bed. A room to stay. Good pay. Sure she wants to come here."

"Brian Anderson told me you got her the job here."

"Who?" Her heavy face lifted in puzzlement.

"Brian Anderson. The guy at the union."

"Oh, yeah, he likes Celia. He likes her a lot. He wants her for the union. Yeah." Lupe was grinning. "The men like her. The outside guys?" She pointed out the windows toward the security kiosk at the gate.

"You mean the security staff?"

"Sure. I like her too. She is fun. I cried for her. I prayed for her soul."

"So Anderson, the union guy. Was it all business between him and Celia?"

Lupe rolled her eyes. "He called her. At first, she had no phone, so he calls her on mine asking her out places. I tell her, girl, get your head on straight. He's married with a little baby. She say no."

"So what happened?"

"He came here one time. Tried to get her to go outside and see him."

"Did she go out with him?"

"Maybe on the street. But not go out, go out. Celia likes the boy who tutors the kids here. Sometimes he helped her with her ESL homework, all flirty. But that's all. Just flirt. You know? She was a good girl," she said, looking across the table at Delgado.

Mason realized with a start that Lupe Garcia found Delgado attractive. Good Lord, Delgado?

"She ever flirt with the security guys?"

Lupe turned down her mouth and shook her head. "Not them. We don't like them. They're mean."

"What about Bateson? The boss?"

She gave a shudder. "We're scared of him. So is the

Lady and the Man."

"You mean Ms. Sinclair and Mr. Logan."

"Yeah. He has room here now."

"In the house?"

"Yeah, Celia's old room. Next to mine."

Interesting.

♏

Mason was going through a pile of takeout menus at his desk at the station, thinking about lunch. Delgado looking bemused, swiped his phone shut and yanked at the knot in his tie. "That was the housekeeper. Lupe Garcia?"

"Oh, yeah?" Mason said, noticing he was flushed.

"She knows something about a boyfriend the victim mentioned a few times. His name was Jacinto. That's not a common name."

"That's all you got?" Mason asked. "You were on the phone with her for five minutes."

"Look, Mason, I'm working it. I'm working it." His heavy face flushed. "His name was Jacinto. No last name. Lupe's brother knew him. She says she'll ask the brother. This Jacinto may have moved to Colorado. There was work there in the mushroom plants."

Mason noted it, but it was a real long shot finding the guy. An undocumented worker could fall back into the shadows for years at a time. He had ICE contacts and would go through the motions, but he wasn't putting a lot of hope into this lead.

♏

Poppy called their lawyer, Nate Silverstein when the detectives left. Derek had dragged his feet, making excuse after excuse about getting in touch with him. So she had to do it. Derek lied a lot, and Poppy was never sure what he was up to in his unaccounted for absences and side life sexual adventures he thought she didn't know about. Nate Silverstein assured her the conversation would fall under attorney client privilege. Derek had nothing to worry about. Moving a dead body would fall under California Penal Code § Section 152 Active Concealment of Accidental Death. A misdemeanor. Poppy was stunned to hear that. Unpleasant dealing with the police to be sure, but it could all be managed, and Nate said there was no risk of jail time. That is if it were truly an accident. Poppy didn't leap to Derek's defense, insisting that it was. She wasn't sure herself.

"I don't know, Nate. What if the cops say Derek was trying to rape her? She's got a brother who's a lawyer and he's all over this. He's working with the cops too. This happened in her bedroom."

"Oh." A silence.

"Yeah. Oh. And you know Derek."

"Who else knows about this besides you and Derek?"

"The chief of our security. He helped us bury her next door. Nate, he promised the body would never be found. He promised." Her voice rose, trying to make it truer. An anguished wail, then a flood of heart-rending tears.

Nate Silverstein was used to this. Lots of similarities between big actors, rock stars, sports figures: big paycheck, celebrity, bigger ego. And an unwillingness to own up to anything, and realize the source of their problems was themselves. Guys like Derek Logan were always on the lookout for newer, bigger ways to spend their money and kill off brain cells. With Derek, it was high-risk women and drugs. Silverstein knew because it was his business to know, that Poppy and Derek were competing to position their new and separate production companies to buy a hot musical property while the market was hot for musicals.

Poppy was a mystery to him, a chameleon. He waited to hear from Derek. He hardly needed the billings or fresh aggravation.

And he had an ego of his own to protect. Derek could call him.

Poppy mulled it over and decided not to tell Derek what Nate had said about it being a misdemeanor charge. Let him suffer. He could have called Nate himself.

Chapter Seventeen

On the advice of their personal publicists, Poppy and Derek tried to get out in front of the story. They had been giving affecting interviews in which tears were shed, telling the story of their poor beloved nanny who was killed and buried next door. "Nanny" they always referred to her as, not kitchen maid. She might have kept bad company, they hinted. Latino could be coded to mean gangster. They screamed to the celebrity media that two incompetent detectives of the Santa Monica Police Department, namely, Dave Mason and Art Delgado, were ignoring the crazy person out there, maybe a fan who had killed their household worker who had been a valued member of the family. The answer was somewhere outside of their home and their life. It was crazy to keep harassing them. They'd given the police copies of letters from fans threatening them and their children. What were the police doing about that? They should focus on the person who had killed her. They sobbed and teared up over how much they had loved Celia Talaveras. How bereft their children were. A family in mourning who just wanted justice and to be left alone.

It appeared again on *Stars* and the other celebrity tabloids. Available on Thursday in the new edition of *Enquirer*. *The House of Tragedy* story got rehashed, a reminder of the accidental drowning of Poppy's lover. As a scandal, it had all the delicious components.

Jorge Talaveras came along in the same week's edition with the counter story. He scoffed that the celebrity couple had never filed a missing person report or contacted the family. The story gained traction. They loved him on TV with his Antonio Banderas good looks.

Watching social media and monitoring Facebook on the Logan-Sinclair case had become a legitimate, and almost overwhelming use of time for the team. They linked articles for the file, and when that grew onerous, the PIO assigned one of his team to assist. Mason fanned through the *Enquirer* Fredericks left at his desk. The gossip magazines rehashed the whole story: *Power Couple Fear for their Lives. Who* is *Threatening Them?* The story implied Poppy and Derek were being held captive in their home by Islamic terrorists.

"Just when you thought *The Enquirer* had hit bottom, they find a new low," he said to Delgado, who was clipping off a snag on the cuff of his frayed navy blazer. With a pale yellow shirt and a tie with a forgettable pattern, Delgado sat down hard in his chair and humphed a breath out as his stomach hit his belt line.

"See this?" Fredericks crowed. News of an overnight burglary flashed through the station. She turned her laptop toward him, and Mason saw the files of a local plastic surgeon had been stolen from his office on Wilshire. Patients of the prominent face-maker were probably cowering at home, waiting for the spotlight of the media to descend on them.

Mason had to laugh. "Ah, confirmation. Who's had work done? Who hasn't? One thing, though," he said, gulping down a cold Starbucks which tasted good even cold. "Logan and Sinclair aren't the lead story. See how it's pushed the story about how incompetent SMPD is off the front page?"

He glanced over and saw Fredericks at her desk, her bright red frizz of hair bent over a pile of documents.

Sinclair and Logan were the obvious persons of interest. But the obvious wasn't always the right course. He typed out a list of questions and next steps for discussion with the Sarge. The Lieutenant of Operations had scheduled them in for an update on the case. Some of it was waiting: waiting for the final pathology report, toxicology, trace analysis. Waiting for backgrounds on other people of interest on Woodland: the new mother married to the dentist at the end of the street; the autistic kid and his grandmother; the union organizer; the young male ESL teacher. All the construction workers on the street.

First, though, were Sinclair and Logan.

Maybe the interviews scheduled for the next day at 9:00 a.m. would rattle some kind of truth out of them. Mason snapped a rubber band at the wastebasket and missed. Ah, truth, he thought. Who believes in truth anymore?

♌

The news that Derek Logan and Poppy Sinclair arrived for interviews spread. The air in the station was charged the next day, like the crackling atmosphere before a thunderstorm.

Delgado waved his hand at a clipboard. "I got Interview Rooms 2 and 3 set up. You've got Poppy. I see you got eyes for her."

"Tell me you don't," Mason growled. He picked up his cup of cold coffee and downed most of it.

"I took Lupe. She can fill in a lot if I can get past her

non-disclosure agreement. She knows which side her bread is buttered on."

"But if a crime is being covered up here, that invalidates the agreements ..." Mason said. "You tell her that?"

"I did. But she's got the citizenship process going, thanks to them. She's not going to do anything that puts a crimp in that."

"Keep working on it. I think she likes you," Mason said with a grin. "You better watch yourself."

Delgado's face went sour. "You got Logan. The Lieutenant wanted to yank it away from you and do it himself, but he had to go run his mouth at a Chamber of Commerce meeting. Good luck."

Mason clattered down the stairs to the first floor of the station and called in Derek Logan, ignoring Poppy. They were on time and seated in the lobby, the airy reception space crisscrossed by civilian workers arriving for work. He glared at one Community Services officer who looked as though she was going to go all fangirl on Logan. She changed her mind.

Logan and Sinclair ignored it all, hard at their cell phones. They weren't clawing their way to the top, like everybody else in the theater and the movies. They were so big, they didn't have to care anymore.

Both of them showed up. Not alone.

Logan's lawyer, a fat cat Century City type accompanied them along with an underling. Mason recognized the lawyer's name. If a celebrity ran up against a scandal, Nate Silverstein had his name all over it. Fredericks had prepared a report on Silverstein's tactics of harassing and intimidating witnesses, lawsuits and smear campaigns, and presenting his celebrity clients as misunderstood victims. Logan was dressed for the golf course; Silverstein was dressed for court. Beautifully draped fabric disguised the lawyer's substantial paunch and broad beam. Silverstein probably had his pajamas tailored. The two made their way through the civilians in the lobby, parting the waters, like tumbling rocks breaking up a fast-moving river. Mason hadn't arranged the celebrity treatment, guiding them to the interview room, which smelled like a lockup. The underling could cool his heels outside. He gestured to Interview Room 2, a white cube with a recessed video camera. The history of the room was inside: insecticide, cleaning products, a ripe scent of fear sweat, pants which had been pissed in, then puked over.

Logan sniffed, twitching as he took his seat at the table. Mason took his time getting his chair just right, his notebook out, taking off his jacket and slinging it on the back of the chair. He rolled up the sleeves of his gray shirt and loosened the blue silk tie Ginger had given him, all the while in silence, watching Logan. He counted on his experience with liars, his eyes and ears. Everybody lies, especially in an interview room at the police station. Logan had a reputation of being difficult, which had many meanings.

This would be tricky. He couldn't go after alibis because nobody could say when Celia Talaveras had died with any certainty. They had a scrap of fabric from the Disney pajamas which could possibly link Celia to Poppy. The charm bracelet. Rumors about Logan. Whispers. All circumstantial. The most damning fact was that she had worked in their home yet they denied they knew her.

"We can give you fifteen minutes, Detective," the lawyer said, checking his very expensive watch. Mason let him talk, telling the lowly cop how the interview was going to be.

Mason smiled at that, getting a real satisfaction out of the fact they were now on his turf. Logan looked around, seemingly unconcerned, not really there, as though none of this touched him. His pupils were huge.

"We're going to take as long as it takes, Mr. Silverstein. You know without me telling you." Then he did all the protocols and turned to Logan. "So what can you tell us about Celia Talaveras, Mr. Logan?"

The actor seemed to collect himself. "Is that her name? Look, even if she worked in my house, I would hardly be aware of her. Especially if she was in the kitchen."

Mason took out a notebook and flipped through the pages as though he needed to check details in all the evidence they had collected thus far.

"She did housework as well, made up the beds, cleaned the bathrooms, watched the twins, things like that. You would have seen her around."

"Still…" Logan opened his hands and turned them over, palms up.

"She was a beautiful girl, Mr. Logan. C'mon."

"You think I don't see beautiful women all day long, Detective? You think my eyes would fall out of my head if I saw that at home? Look at who I sleep with every night. Every man in America wants Poppy."

Mason stirred uncomfortably. "So you're saying then you don't remember her at all?"

"Maybe," Logan said, switching on the liquid smile which meant so many things. "Maybe. I saw her around, I suppose. That's all I can tell you."

"So who runs the house?" Mason said. He looked down at Logan's foot thumping to a nervous rhythm, cocaine-user fast. Logan saw him looking and immediately stopped. He went sullen, pouty, and crossed his arms.

"If you're asking who cleans and cooks, well Lupe, of course. The kids like her. More important, she gets along with Poppy. Poppy does the hiring along with this agency our business manager set us up with. I stay out of things," Logan said, patting his hair.

"And Celia's job then?"

"She was with the twins most of the time, I suppose. Went with them to school and all their activities. I guess if she had time when they were in school she helped out Lupe. I don't know. I don't pay attention."

"You were never in her room then?"

"What are you saying?" Logan reared back, an expression of distaste on his face. "I had no reason to be there."

"So if I found your DNA in her room, how would you account for that?"

Silverstein drew himself from reptilian calm to interject: "It's his home, Detective. Of course, he could have been in that room at one time."

"The twins and Megan were there sometimes. I could have gone in looking for them.

If you're saying I had anything to do with that woman's death, you'd better have some proof," Logan exploded. "You should be looking at all the people she hung out with on her time off. A boyfriend. I can think of a dozen leads you could follow down if you can't."

Mason looked up from his notes and caught Logan's face going through a succession of changes from outrage to anger to what looked like apprehension. An actor's repertoire.

"Maybe I'll be back asking for your advice then. I know you played a detective in *End Notes*. Good movie."

"You aren't the first cop who's told me I got it right," Logan said, settling down and looking complacent now.

"I'll need to be talking to your business manager," Mason said, changing directions. "Give me his contact information, would you?" he said, even though he had it from Poppy. It didn't hurt to let Logan know he was checking up on him.

Silverstein immediately objected, calling this a fishing expedition. He was right but Mason still had the right to ask. After five or six thousand words out of his mouth about nothing, Silverstein took out his phone and turned his attention to that.

The request caught Logan by surprise. His face tried on attitudes, settling on a false boredom behind which Mason detected panic. "Why our business manager?"

"Because I need to talk to him. He'll have her employment records."

"What about? He's got nothing to do with this."

"His contact info?"

Logan tapped the cell phone he'd set on the table in front of him and read off a couple of phone numbers. "Look, Lupe has papers. If this Celia Talaveras worked in the house, she had papers too. Our guy insists on that. We've got too much to lose."

"Yeah, well, you won't mind me talking to him then, will you? And you never saw anything unusual going on next door?"

"Just a hole in the ground." Logan shot his cuffs and looked at his watch again, then meaningfully at Silverstein.

Mason twisted the questions about Logan's relationship with Talaveras, hitting the stone wall every time. Until they turned up something else as leverage, this was it. Unless one of the helpful citizen video idiots turned in a photo or a clip of Talaveras and Logan in some compromising situation, this line of questioning was over.

Mason stood up and held out his hand.

"Nice to see you again, Mr. Logan. Mr. Silverstein. That's all for now. Thanks for coming in."

Logan turned on the bluff charm again. "Luh luh let me know if you want tickets to the premier of the sequel to *End Notes*. These premieres are a bore, but if you're not used to them …"

He trailed off, knowing Mason was highly unlikely to have gone to enough movie premieres to be bored. It hit a condescending note which amused Mason as he led him back to the lobby of the station. Yeah, he liked Logan's movies, but he was shorter and fatter in person than he showed up on screen. He'd read in the *Enquirer* that Logan dieted before movies, then binged on M&Ms and Red Bull when the movie was shooting.

Logan looked nervous, but plenty of innocent people had sat in that chair looking guilty. Embedded in the culture was an image of interrogation in movies and TV. An interview in the station made people sweat. Still, he'd trust Logan as far as he could spit a rat.

🜂

Mason made notes and called in Poppy, telling his inner teenager to fuck off.

This was only an interview. He thought of the other interviews lined up for the day: the autistic kid down the street from Logan, the cutie new mother up the street. Follow up on the neighbors who were out of town and had since returned. Return yet another call from Jorge Talaveras. Keep working on a mention of Celia Talaveras' boyfriend, the elusive Jacinto. His daughter's birthday was coming up soon. And another call from his father. He'd call him tonight. They continued playing phone tag.

Like her husband and his pricey lawyer, Poppy

Sinclair found the smell in Interview Room 2 not to her taste. Her personal lawyer in a sharp Gloria Allred suit and stiletto heels followed her in. The attorney was attractive, but not many women shone around Poppy Sinclair. Poppy swooshed her fine leather bag with a Coach label across the chair before she sat down. Mason regarded her for a long moment and turned to his list of questions they'd devised with the LT who was fascinated with the Logan-Sinclair connection.

Poppy looked down at her lap and picked at an invisible spot on her skinny jeans, ignoring him. Her limbs were slightly too long, giving her the attenuated leggy body that was the current fashion ideal. Whether it was makeup or not, and Mason couldn't tell, her fortyish skin was clear and seemed lit from within. Did she have someone come in and do her hair beginning at dawn to give her that sunny gold mane of curls? How much time did it take someone like her to get ready to face the paparazzi who must be a constant in her life? So many questions he knew he'd never get to ask.

Poppy had admitted now to knowing Celia, which made Mason's task easier. "Your husband told us you hire people who work in the house..." he began.

"Well, I could hardly turn that over to him, could I? He makes himself useless. Derek stays as uninvolved in the household as he can, and that's fine with me."

Mason ratcheted down his speculations, made himself stop staring, squaring up his IPad on the table, pretending to review his notes.

"You knew her well then?"

"Hardly at all. I just remember a pleasant girl who did her work. Lupe never complained about her that I remember. And a great deal of time has passed since I've seen her. I have too many obligations to chat with the help."

"Did she ever talk about boyfriends?"

"I told you. We didn't have those kinds of conversations. Lupe dealt with her on a day-to-day basis to get the work done. My PA would notify Lupe about any changes in the twins' schedule, when Jake was coming, what events Derek and I would be attending, alone or together, people who would be coming to the house. Jake's Derek's son," she said to prompt Mason.

"Yes, I know. Do you and Mr. Logan do a lot of entertaining?" Mason didn't even know what that might mean to people like them. To him it was one of the guys and his wife coming over for dinner, Ginger fussing over something in the slow cooker. He brought the beer and chips.

"If you're asking whether Ms. Talaveras served and was involved in any parties, then no. I hire a caterer to do parties we're forced into having. My husband is the party guy. Not me. There are hundreds of people coming through our house every month. Any one of them might have encountered her and…"

She wanted Mason to take the bait but he refused. Her lawyer regarded Mason from across the table, and then took out her tablet and began tapping away. He ran that line of questioning into the ground, but Sinclair didn't budge. The lawyer leaned over to her once and whispered to her. Poppy batted her away. He turned to the scrap of fabric that had been blown up and was recognizable. Celia Talaveras had been wearing pajamas made of this fabric, which had been a very limited production. It wasn't much but he hoped it would rattle Poppy. She seemed unconcerned about the Disney charm bracelet.

"You can't imagine the crap the studios give out, the promotional merchandise. Derek and I have a ton of that stuff from all our movies. I haven't any idea how they came into her possession. Maybe she stole them."

"Yet you trusted her with your children …"

"These Mexican women are good with children."

"She was Guatemalan."

Sinclair waved that unimportant fact away.

"And was your husband friendly with her?"

"Derek is friendly with everyone, Detective. But it's not as if he helped clean up after parties, Detective, or hung out in the kitchen. He trots the twins out for everyone to oooh and ahh over, the group gush. And he'll introduce Jake to people who can help him in business when he's older. Megan, well."

"Megan?" Mason prompted.

"She's become a discipline problem. I'm the bad cop who has to discipline her. My husband works on his image as the family guy. He does the minimum when we're together in public of looking like we're still crazy about each other. Well, so do I," she said, smiling at her attorney, "but that's it."

"Okay." Mason held her eyes.

"We live very separate lives, Detective," she added. "Separate careers. Derek is moving into production, away from acting, a whole new circle of people. And so am I. We've both set up production companies and our interests are in musicals."

Mason had already read about this in the trades. Fredericks had also told him they were now competing for the reigning musical star and things had got ugly. Sinclair blocked every possible lead he might develop. It was--and it wasn't--like doing interviews after a gangbanger drive-by shooting. Nobody saw nothing. Nobody heard nothing. He couldn't keep her any longer. The lawyer was the first one out the door. She waited in the hall.

As Poppy Sinclair stood to leave and Mason followed her to the door, she stopped, one hand on the doorknob, turning to face him. She took a step closer, looking up. She knew he was stiffening in his pants. She knew. Her hand came up to cradle his cheek.

He'd been propositioned before, lots of times, but not by a woman who looked like this and transmitted the aura of surreal sexual promise. Still, he knew the cameras covered the doorway and he stepped back, his heart thumping.

"Sometime," she said huskily. "After this …"

He didn't trust himself to speak, knowing he'd babble like a teenager. He felt the heat of a blush. Instead, he opened the door wider and stepped through carefully in front of her, holding a file against his pants. She held the moment, a slow familiar smile crossing her face.

He'd seen it in the movies.

🌒

Chapter Eighteen

Lupe Garcia could be the lynch pin to whatever was going on in that house. Mason watched for a while through the window of the interview room along with the Sarge. Delgado was sitting across the table from Lupe Garcia, both of them looking relaxed and chatty. He tapped on the door of the interview room and beckoned Delgado outside into the hall.

"Thrill me. Tell me you've got something."

"I'm workin' her with my charms," Delgado grinned, looking pleased with himself.

That brought Mason up short, Delgado thinking he had charm. Delgado with his shit brown suit, paunch hanging over his belt, hair thinning into a V way back on his head. Attractive to a woman? He'd been married to Maria since he was seventeen.

"She's giving me her recipe for green chili sauce."

"That's all? C'mon, Delgado."

"Hey, she's not gonna trash her employers because I've got a sweet face? Little by little I'm getting stuff."

"Like what?"

"Derek Logan had eyes for our girl Celia. The kids are spoiled. They don't like fans coming up to them everywhere they go asking about Derek and Poppy."

Not much. "Surely Logan isn't going to be hitting on

the hired help in his own home," Mason reflected. But he knew some guys had to prove themselves with every woman they met to see if they could get the old vibe going. Maybe Logan felt that was safer, having the woman connected to him by a paycheck.

"The security guy. He probably sees things. I'm going to hit him harder." He made a note.

"Is Garcia legal?"

"She says she is. Says they got her papers. I'll make sure. People like Logan have ways if they really want somebody in."

"Where did Talaveras get papers?"

"C'mon, Mason. If she had them, she bought them."

"But how? That costs money."

"Lupe's not going to be telling me that, no matter how much she wants my body."

Mason snorted. "They pay Lupe good?"

"Apparently. The business manager takes care of all the household bills. She's got a credit card. They trust her."

"Hunh." Mason thought a moment. "Mind if I sit in?" he said, gesturing toward the interview room where Lupe waited.

Delgado scratched his ear and screwed up his big heavy face. "We're talking Spanish, Mason. It'll throw her off." The interview would be recorded, translated, and transcribed anyway.

"Okay." Mason walked away, jingling the change in his pocket, back down to his cubicle to start on his reports. Poppy Sinclair had hit on him. How was he going to write that up? Or was he?

Jake Logan made it clear talking to cops was a waste of his valuable time. The eighteen-year-old who lived with his mother part-time had the look of privilege, a haircut refreshed every week, the unwashed patina of brand-new clothes, a body fed on organic produce and expensive supplements. Logan the Younger argued with the parent's lawyer, insisting he didn't need either a parent present or legal representation. He had his own lawyer. The kid kept texting on his phone, paying half-assed attention to Mason until Mason reached across the table and grabbed the phone away from him and placed it on the table in the interview room next to his laptop.

"Hey!" the kid protested. "You can't do that. That's mine."

His nondescript young attorney bristled but said nothing. Had he graduated from law school last Wednesday? Mason gave him the expressionless face and flat cop eyes.

"Did you know Celia Talaveras?"

"The maid? Some wetback? Hardly."

Mason gave him a measuring look. "You ever see anything funny there next door at the abandoned construction site? Your bedroom is on that side of the house."

Jake Logan had also reached expert status in eye rolling. "Look, I've got nothing to do with those people. I hate my father. She's disgusting. Half the time I'm at my mother's place in Pacific Palisades. You heard of it?"

Mason looked up from under his eyebrows and held his eyes.

He stuck to his notes. Celia Talaveras was a beautiful girl and under Jake Logan's nose.

"You never talked to her?" He pushed the studio photo of Talaveras across the table. Logan gave the photo a glance and with the tip of his finger, pushed it back.

"What were we going to talk about? Think about it. Megan was tight with her, though. Ask her." With a shrug, he sketched out the social distance between himself and someone who might have cleaned his bathroom. "You can't even say when she was killed. For all I know I might not even have been there. And what if she was killed somewhere else and dumped next door to us?"

It was a good question, and one Mason had an answer for, but didn't feel the need to share with Jake Logan.

"We're done here," Mason said, getting up. Jake Logan flounced out of his chair. Mason held the door open for him and walked him to the elevator in silence. He'd be glad to come back on the kid, but for now, he was done, a nanosecond before he punched the snotty little shit.

🕮

The team collected in the conference room to debrief after the interviews, discouraged. Fredericks reported that Megan Logan blamed her parents for Celia's absence. But maybe Celia had left with her boyfriend, Jacinto. The girl had been sullen and unhelpful.

"Maybe the parents got her to sign a non-disclosure agreement too. I bet a lot goes on in that house," Fredericks said. "They've got something over her. The whole dynamic between them is weird."

"You get any further tracking down this Jacinto?" Mason asked.

"I'm working it," Fredericks said defensively.

Sgt. Bud York sidled in a minute or so late--a problem with SWAT. The LT sniffed, running the meeting like a bean counter. The team brought him up to date. Lieutenant Vargas had no useful suggestions. York didn't have to run his mouth, saying what the last guy just said so that it would look like he was contributing to the meeting.

"We won't be able to get at them again," Mason acknowledged. He lifted his hands a few inches and then dropped them on his laptop. "Not until we've got something new."

"You can submit questions through their lawyer," the Lieutenant said.

That would not be helpful. "Yeah, right. Like we're going to get anything out of that."

"You and Delgado were supposed to have more on the ball than this, Mason. You've had almost a week on this. And you've got nothing?"

A sneer cracked across his face. He put on his Armani sunglasses and then tipped them down to look at the two detectives revealing green eyes like boiled grapes. Flipping his keys in the air, he caught them and pushed past Delgado toward the door. "If you have any brilliant thoughts, Mason," the LT said, "I hope you'll be sharing them with us." A sardonic smile and a shake of his head from the doorway terminated the meeting.

"We gotta do something to pop it loose," Mason said, wondering how Vargas ever got promoted. He'd be there posing for the cameras, though, whoever they pulled in for this.

"You've got other leads. Work them," the Sarge said, looking seriously depressed.

"Like what?" Delgado said, combing his thick black hair.

"I'm thinking," Mason said. Silence was painful. It was not a thoughtful or contemplative pause.

"We still haven't checked the report of shots fired in the Woodland neighborhood around four months ago. That could fall within the probable range of dates for Celia Talaveras' death."

"But she wasn't killed by a gunshot," York pointed out.

"It's a possible lead, " Mason said, as York packed up his laptop to end the meeting. Mason had been in touch with the firm Celia's attorney fiancé worked for in

Guatemala. He learned that the attorney had been engaged in a long trial that kept him in the courtroom and accounted for during the entire period around Celia's death. That was as good an alibi as he was going to get. The boyfriend, Jacinto, if he even was a boyfriend would be harder to nail down.

He went back to his desk to read over Fredericks' notes about the maxilo-facial dentist's wife: 27, attractive mother of a male infant, pianist, two double lots farther up the street from the burial site. Anything involving dentistry caused the saliva of fear to collect in his mouth and made him feel dizzy if he stood up quickly. The potential witness jogged with a stroller down Woodland and was familiar to all the neighbors. Claimed she had noticed nothing suspicious. Fredericks had turned in a report with a row of question marks. Mason decided to do the follow-up interview himself.

Since they'd established the connection to Derek and Poppy, it was tempting to give the neighbor a miss. But settling too soon on a suspect led to other options snapping back with a snarl and biting somebody in the ass. Likely him. They were also working their stable of street informants about a body dump. He asked around the station about upscale drug activity in the North of Montana area. Drugs. Moneyed people found ways of connecting. Nothing came back from the street. If Logan was getting drugs, as was rumored and Mason suspected, he had private sources, which wasn't surprising.

A picture of Celia Talaveras was building in his mind. She had an ambition and the courage to work for it. Unlike most undocumented workers, she wasn't here for economic reasons. She had a good life in Guatemala, but she didn't want it. The older fiancé? He would probably never know what that arrangement was all about, and it gave Celia Talaveras a layer of mystery that all victims had. He would never know everything. From what people said about her, she was fun-loving and positive. Huggy, sweet, smart. She could have been anything she wanted. Who knows where the course of life would have blown this girl?

Maybe he'd try seeing the dentist's wife now? He thought about getting through downtown to the north part of Santa Monica, a distance of three miles, from the station and back within an hour when he had court on another case. He sniffed, turning back to his email, dismissing the idea. Since the new light rail terminal came to a halt mere blocks away from the station, nothing went fast or easy.

🜊

Mason was surprised to see Poppy Sinclair's name show up on his phone. What the hell was she calling him for? Another big lie about Celia Talaveras? How she had buried herself in the property next door? He put as much faith in what Sinclair had to say as he did in crystal balls, chicken entrails, and prayer in solving crimes.

"Yes, Ms. Sinclair. What can I do for you?"

"I was hoping to see you for an update on poor Celia's death," she said. Her voice curled around him like a wet tongue.

See him?

"Well, I'm pretty busy. Do you have something you want to tell me?"

"It would be better if we could get together."

This was as startling a prospect to Mason as if a door suddenly opened in a blank wall. He felt his cock rise like a steeple. He hesitated, knowing what was being offered.

"Well, I uh …"

"I could meet you someplace. I'm here in Santa Monica. I'm free for a couple of hours." Her words danced in the air, sparkling,

Mason slammed that door shut, like a man walking who comes to a brink. Desire for Sinclair had run its course like a long and serious illness. He had seen the ugly streak and felt the cunning in the smile which came through the telephone. Still …

"No, I don't think so. I'm too busy." He felt the urge to explain, to leave the door open. Foolish. Stupid. Stop this.

"Okay, but if you change your mind, you have my private number now. Call me anytime."

He swiped the phone closed and stared at it. It felt hot in his hand and throbbed. He needed to document this call. But it could wait until later.

Chapter Nineteen

Billy Jackson, the so-called weirdo with the rooster which bothered Derek Logan, was another loose end. He had lived with his mother in Redondo Beach, a city down the coast, where he had a police file. When Mason read the backgrounder on the 20-year-old male, he caught up with the psychologist consulting with the department. Dr. Irene Kallman was a straight-shooter.

"Autism spectrum," she said, grimacing. She skimmed over the report Mason handed her and handed it back to him, tilting her head to look up at him with a bright, inquiring look. "Terrible. Terrible. I remember a presentation about this case at a conference last year. It was a sting operation. An undercover hung out near the school, pretending to be his friend, which pleased his parents no end because he had no friends. The officer looked young and kept hounding Billy to sell him marijuana or his prescription medication. He just wanted to make a bust and gave him twenty bucks to make a buy. Billy couldn't get at his own prescription medication because his parents kept it locked up. He and the undercover hung out for a couple of weeks until the kid bought a half-joint from a homeless man, and gave it to the officer. He'd made the buy to keep the undercover as a friend. They took him in and kept him from seeing his parents until his court date two days later. The parents sued the department claiming their son was seventeen at the time and traumatized. The experience left the kid with post-traumatic stress disorder…insomnia, panic attacks, depression, paranoia, and infliction of self-injury. You tell me this is him? Connected with the body found up on Woodland?"

"The connection's pretty loose. And, of course, that would never happen here," Mason said, raising his eyebrows. "Maybe in Redondo Beach."

"Of course not," she said with a warning smile.

Now he lived with his grandmother, the old woman who had collapsed when he and Delgado had knocked on her door. What had she been afraid to hear?

🐾

Billy Jackson, the autistic keeper of chickens, was a nighttime walker. Down Woodland and turning right, down the grassy median of San Vicente Boulevard with its row of coral trees dropping red blossoms and heaving up roots to trip the joggers. Jackson walked down to Palisades Park all the way to the California Incline. Below the park lay the changing blue mystery of the ocean. In a hoodie shambling along talking to himself, Billy Jackson looked scary, not like one of the locals who lived in the pricey condos and original old homes which still survived on San Vicente Boulevard.

Maybe Jackson had seen something. They had an appointment and a lot of conversation with the psychologist on how to approach the autistic young man.

🐾

A late-model Buick was parked in the driveway and an old

beater parked next to it. Somebody was home. Mason knocked on the door. He hoped Billy Jackson's grandmother they'd scared into the hospital wasn't going to answer it. No answer. They could hear faint music from inside the house. Mason and Delgado gave each other a look and Delgado shrugged.

"Let's do it."

"What?" Mason said. "Kick in the door?"

"Yeah, right." Delgado laughed and headed out, following a path set in flagstones that led around the house. Mason followed, raising his head to sniff, puzzled by the change of the scent in the air as they rounded the back of the house. There were struggling patches of lawn, but the large enclosure was dirt-packed.

From a ramshackle structure of chicken wire, plywood, and 2 x 4s, a rooster charged out, flapping high in the air, followed by a flock of chickens. Mason gave it a glance, then turned to say something to Delgado, who took a look at the rooster and ran for the back porch on the house.

The rooster flew up in Mason's face. Startled, he swatted at it, which seemed to outrage the bird. Its head back, menace in its small eyes, it flew at him again. Ten or so chickens gathered behind the rooster, blocking Mason's path. The chickens fluttered around the rooster, clucking, like the little kids watching the bully pick on somebody in the schoolyard. Mason wasn't going to run from a rooster. He whirled in a circle, beating at it. Delgado stood on the safety of the porch jeering at him.

He faced outstretched wings, and angry caws, feathers flying in the air. The ruff around the rooster's neck was extended, its neck stretched toward him, beak snapping.

"Hey, hey, hey," Mason shouted beating his arms in

the air, running for the porch, scrambling away from his attacker without life-threatening wounds. A lumpy old pitbull shambled across the yard to Delgado. Delgado was petting the dog, almost falling over with laughter.

"Don't mess with a pissed off rooster," Delgado gasped out. "Roosters know they're the descendants of dinosaurs."

"I should take that thing next time we go into a crack house," Mason said, trying to regain his dignity. "If I hear one word about this going around …" he said to Delgado.

Delgado was shaking his head, "Angry birds, Mason. Wipe the chicken shit off your pants."

♣

They circled around the house and were met at the front door by a middle-aged man wearing a well-cut grey suit and tie. His manner was stiff and unwelcoming, as though having cops come to the door lowered his dignity. Nothing new about that reaction. He didn't seem to know about Mason's fight to the death with the rooster and the chickens in the back yard. Mason wasn't going to tell him.

"I'm Terence Jackson. Mrs. Jackson is my mother. When I heard you wanted to talk to her and to Billy, I decided to be here to greet you myself. I'm an attorney."

Oh. An attorney. And I'm a storm trooper, Mason thought.

"This is just routine, Mr. Jackson. A body has been found nearby and we're looking for witnesses."

Without comment, Jackson led them from the foyer into a living room furnished in the style of another time. Mason scuffed a toe of his shoe in the carpet, figuring it was at least three inches thick.

Terence Jackson perched on the edge of a blue brocade wing chair and gestured Mason into a chair that faced a wide picture window looking out on an overgrown garden. Delgado took a seat on a couch opposite a long-unused fireplace filled with vases of dried flowers.

"We'd like to talk with your mother," Mason said to get things started. "Sorry about the other day. She's okay now, is she? This is simply a matter of routine since a body was discovered nearby. We're looking for ..."

"Yes, I'm aware of that," Jackson interrupted. "My mother is resting and can't be disturbed. She's just been released from the hospital today."

"I'm sorry to hear that." Was Jackson going to sue the department for upsetting her? Aw, shit. He could imagine the reaming out he'd get from the Lieutenant. "We will need to speak with her, you know. You're aware a body has been discovered down the street."

The lawyer shook his head firmly. "It's impossible to talk with her right now."

"Perhaps she'd like to come into the station instead to answer some questions. We could send a car for her." Mason said it in a flat tone. An acknowledgment took place between himself and the lawyer.

"Why would you think my mother had anything to do with that? She rarely goes out, and right now she's very unsteady on her feet. Could you give her another day or so?"

"We could do that. Perhaps your nephew saw something." Mason was determined to get something out of this after his loss of dignity. "We'll need to talk to him. Do you live here as well, Mr. Jackson?"

Jackson waved that away.

"Is there anyone else who lives in the house?"

"We have cleaning people who come in on a regular basis. Someone who does the shopping and any errands. And a Filipino couple who care for my mother and whatever needs Billy has. You know about Billy and I presume that's why you're really here."

Delgado shifted in his chair. His family knew what it cost to give his wife some respite from caring for her mother. Money helped. Mason frowned, hearing the rooster crow triumphantly in the back of the house.

"Perhaps we can talk to your nephew first."

"Do you know anything about the autism spectrum? Asperger's syndrome, Detective Mason?"

Mason shrugged. "A little. And yes, we are aware of the incident in Redondo Beach and the reports of your nephew walking late at night." And the lawsuit against Redondo Beach.

Terence Jackson stood up and put his hands on the back of a brocade wing chair which matched the one Mason was sitting in. He looked toward a shadowy hallway leading to the back of the house.

Mason raised his hands. "We need to talk to him as we have done with everyone on the street. As a matter of routine," he emphasized.

"My nephew doesn't adapt to sudden change such as meeting new people. He's very inflexible. We structure his life so it's easier for all of us. He has a number of mannerisms that are unusual."

The number of mentally ill people on the streets of Santa Monica had introduced almost every variation of unusual human behavior. Mason knew what happened to people on the autism spectrum who didn't have family money. It was now law enforcement's responsibility to care for the ones who hit the streets.

"All right then. It would be best if you came with me to the kitchen, rather than asking Billy to come here. From 10 to noon, Billy works on his puzzle at the kitchen table. If he wants to talk to you he will."

"Let's do that then," Mason said, rising. He and Delgado followed Jackson back through the house to a kitchen last updated in the sixties. Ducks and chickens marched in a pattern across the wallpaper where a shaft of sunlight caught them. Billy Jackson sat, hunched over a complex puzzle at a table. The kitchen smelled of potatoes boiling in a pot on the stove.

"Billy, these people want to talk to you."

Billy didn't look up. Delgado and Mason sat down at the table in the breakfast nook under a valence-covered window. Billy hung his big head on his chest, moving the puzzle pieces. His T-shirt was too small for his big, powerful body. Thick hair sprang up from the neckline. He was doing his best to let hair cover him, a brush of thick hair hanging over his eyes. His beard was scarce; his chin covered with pimples.

"Billy," his uncle said. "This is Detective Mason and Detective Delgado," he said, pointing to each of them. Both tried to look mild and friendly.

"We just want to talk to you," Mason said.

"Not talking." He spoke in a flat, robotic kind of way. And those were the last words he spoke, no matter how they tried. From time to time he looked up at the clock on the wall.

It wasn't Mason's first brush with the autism spectrum. He'd run into individuals involved in cases who talked about themselves all the time and would zero in with exhausting intensity on a single subject, like rocks or football stats. Repeated themselves, especially on one topic. Or were silent, like Billy. Flapped a hand, shrugged, whatever. Or wouldn't look at you.

They gave up finally and left, ignoring an *I told you so* look from Jackson's uncle.

Mason put Fredericks on getting Billy Jackson to talk.

She was good with the oddballs, aggressive with men, and hard on attractive women. Fredericks began spending every spare moment she could get away in the kitchen of the house trying to get Billy Jackson to talk to her. A lot of cop time went nowhere. Billy still wouldn't look at her, but he didn't get up and leave now when she came in. She sat there reading reports and checking her email, once in a while pushing a puzzle piece toward him.

Was this a waste of time or not? She was also trying to pin down the woman with the baby up the street. "Husband stays at work late, goes in early. She says he heard nothing but I want to hear it from him. She's a pianist, says she's preparing for a big audition." Fredericks shrugged. "Her piano teacher's there every time I come. I don't know what's going on with her, but she's got liar written all over her face."

"You see the husband, the dentist yet?"

"First thing tomorrow. His office. UCLA."

She laughed and poked him in the chest. She knew Mason feared dentists so much he would probably faint at the door if he had to go into a place that smelled like dentist, much less one that offered surgery.

🜊

Lupe Garcia arrived at the station for a follow-up interview. It wasn't that Mason didn't think Delgado was a good interviewer, but the dynamics there were weird. Garcia seemed to hope this was Delgado's attempt to see her alone, and her face fell when Mason and Fredericks entered the interview room without him. She glared at them and pulled her purse off the chair next to her onto the table. She ignored them while rummaging through it. She didn't need more shiny lip gloss.

"So Ms. Garcia," Mason said while setting his folders

down and pulling out his list of questions. "Let's go over again how Ms. Talaveras came to be working in the house."

"I tole you already," she said huffily. "Where is Detective Delgado?"

"He's busy. Maybe he'll be in later."

"You call him. He wants to talk to me."

"Why are you so sure of that?" Fredericks asked. Lupe's crush on Delgado was hilarious to Fredericks. She couldn't keep her mouth shut about it, threatening to tell his wife, Maria. Delgado told her to go ahead. She wouldn't believe it.

"He likes me," Garcia said with a confident lift of her chin.

"He'll be in later," Mason said, hunching forward. "Why didn't you call the police when Celia Talaveras disappeared? You must have known something happened to her. It was a good job and she just left? That didn't seem strange to you?"

"Not so good a job. Maybe not for her. Yes, for me. I speak good English. They like my cooking. The kids like me. I organize the house." She preened, her hand on her iPhone as though it might ring at any moment with an important call. "They said Celia moved out, took all her stuff. I was mad, sure, she leff. More work for me. But what can I do? The missus, she gets somebody new from the agency. That one, she stayed a month, too far from her son. She quits. Somebody else. Megan doesn't like her. All more work for me."

"Ms. Talaveras must have had a phone. You didn't call her?"

"Sure, I did. Leff messages. Ask her to call. Nothing."

"And that was it?"

"What else can I do? The missus said she took off. I

tole you Celia, she had boyfriend. Maybe somebody else we don't know. Where is Detective Delgado? The missus, she doesn't like me to come here and waste time." She looked at her watch, a large affair which sparkled. Something Poppy was tired of?

"We have her party tonight. Big important people coming. *Mucho trabajo* I got still."

Mason sat back and turned Fredericks loose on Lupe Garcia. Two competent very different women, both of whom could run a multinational corporation. They stared at each other. Then Lupe grinned. Fredericks laughed her wild cackle. Some unnamed tension Mason couldn't decipher broke in the air. Would he ever understand women?

"So," Fredericks said. "Celia was very pretty. Somebody told us Mr. Logan used to bother her."

"Yeah? Somebody? No bother to her. Celia, she liked it."

"And Mrs. Logan. What did she think of that?" Fredericks said.

"Her? She don't care. She likes the women. *No importa.* I like la señora very fine. She is good for to me." Her English appeared to deteriorate talking about Derek Logan.

"How do you think Ms. Talaveras died?"

Lupe Garcia's lively face adopted the stupid mask. "Girls like her die all the time. Donchu' know that?" Her shoulders crept upward.

"But she wasn't like any other girl, was she, Ms. Garcia? She came from a well-off family in Guatemala. Her father was a successful businessman. Her brother was a lawyer. You saw him when he came to the house," Fredericks leaned back after peppering her with statements. "You talked to him. He told us that."

"So I talked to him. I can't tell him something I don't know."

Fredericks hitched herself around in her chair and consulted her notes, making Lupe wait. Garcia's eyes darted around the room in which there was nothing to look at except the two investigators. She picked at her fingernail, twisted a large garnet ring back and forth, waiting for Delgado to appear. A jar of green chili sauce sat on the table in front of her.

"Nigel Bateson, the head of security, has a room next door to yours since Celia Talaveras was killed. Why do you think that is?" Mason said.

She waved a hand in the air. "Nothing to do with me. They ask me he moves in? They tell me anything?"

"We got some information that says people are scared of him. Even Ms. Sinclair and Mr. Logan."

She looked away.

"And he has a room next door to you? Did any of the other security people ever have a room?"

She scratched her neck and looked away from him to the door, hoping Delgado might appear. No answer.

"Ms. Garcia?" A pause. "Did any of the other security people ever have a room inside the house?"

"Maybe before me. How I going to know?"

"But not while you have lived there?"

"No."

"Why do you think he's there now?"

"They say they get threats from crazy people. I know is true. I go to Whole Foods. Media people give me business cards. Tell me they pay me to talk about the family," she said with pride. "I tell them they're crazy and walk away. This is a good job. I save my money," she said self-righteously, tugging at the front of her blouse to draw it away from under the roll over her belt line.

"Didn't you care what happened to her?"

"Yes, I care. We both do."

"Both?" Fredericks looked startled. "Who's both?"

"Megan. She cry and carry on. Get depressed. Eats all the time. But she's a kid. Her and the lady fight all the time anyway. She forgets."

"Were her and Celia close?"

"I just tole you."

Fredericks stole a look at Mason. He gave her a tiny shrug.

"Nobody else pays attention to her except me and Celia. She's got no real friends. It's all the time fights in that house. Megan, she follow Celia and the twins around all the time. I tell Celia, you do your work. The lady find out your daughter likes you better than her, there's trouble."

"What kind of trouble?"

"You think Poppy kills her? Oh, c'mon," Lupe said, flushed. "She doesn't care that much. Where is Detective Delgado?" she said, half rising. "I got work to do."

Conferring later, Fredericks couldn't stop laughing about Garcia's crush on Delgado.

Then she got serious. "That non-disclosure agreement has Garcia's mouth shut tight. She's smart and you're not going to break her."

🐾

Mason reached for his phone and then set it down again on his desk. He'd put off calling his mother, certain she would call him. She was the family communicator. If there was any news, like the re-appearance of his sister, she would let him know. It had always been that way. The phone rang and rang at home in Grand Rapids. Shoving away a stack of file folders on his desk, he called

Fredericks to schedule a check-in meeting later in the day with the team.

"Fredericks, I'm seeing the security guy today."

"Hey, I'd sooner do him," Fredericks brayed into the phone.

"Hose yourself down, girl," Mason said, holding the phone away from his ear. Fredericks was a little too enthusiastic about men, with an unerring instinct for the wrong ones. She got more than her share of initial attention with her hot little body and cupcake breasts. He'd noticed Logan eyeing her with a predatory smile when they'd done the interview at his house. That would be a coup for him, nailing a cop.

𝕃

Mason drove down Ocean Avenue, past the section called Main Street, a few blocks farther into Venice looking for an address for Nigel Bateson's security company. This close to the beach, the air smelled of the ocean. Slamming the door of his Crown Vic, he noted a very good address, with uber-connected, style-savvy, momentarily rich young techies. Not so far away was Gold's Gym, a land of thick necks, turbo tans, and tattoo parlors. A line of perky, perfect soccer moms flooded into a women's workout studio from valet-parked Lexus SUVs with Pilates-toned bodies, ponytails bouncing. He moved out of the way of two skinny Asian techies coming from BuzzFeed on the electric Bird scooters. Bateson Security looked prosperous, situated in a new three-story block of ground floor offices and high-income apartments on the upper floors. A glossy receptionist looked up from a glass-topped desk and took his card.

"I can give you an application form, but Mr. Bateson is tied up right now."

"I don't need a job," Mason smiled, handing her his card, "but I'd appreciate it if you'd tell Mr. Bateson I'm here."

Maybe he did need a job, Mason thought as he settled into a comfortable chair looking around, wondering how long Bateson would keep him waiting.

Bateson opened a door at the back and motioned him in. He was in a suit today, the tie yanked off-center around his thick neck, and unsmiling.

"What more can I tell you?" he said, leading Mason into a professionally decorated office, settling himself behind a desk strewn with papers. "You got anything for me? Or do you want a job? Is that why you're here?"

"Maybe," Mason said, putting on his getting to know you face. He'd put off thinking about his future after police work until the idea of flying made him look forward to retirement.

"$600 a day to start, twelve-hour shifts, half-hour for lunch and dinner. I'd start you on corporate work. You stand around looking menacing. Think you could do that?'

"I could do that. Doesn't sound too bad."

"Then I'd move you up to celebrities. Big crowds pushing and shoving to get at your target. They're so in love with them they'd tear off their arms and legs." He grinned.

"I've done that. You ever been to one of the Concerts on the Pier? Hundred thousand people there."

"Is that why you're here?" Bateson said, canting back his chair. "You want a job?"

"I had another question. See, checking the record, we got a couple of calls reporting shots fired on June 9th on Woodland at the property where the victim was found. In that neighborhood, we take a lot of things seriously."

"Like you do every neighborhood, I'm sure," Bateson

smirked.

Mason ignored that. "We're putting together a timeline of anything out of the ordinary back four months ago. Old ladies living alone who think they hear a prowler. They call it in. All that. See, we got a couple of calls and I'd like you to check back to the logs that night and see if you've got anything. We're checking with all the neighborhood security companies."

Bateson turned to his screen. "The date again?"

Mason gave it to him and waited. Three shots fired.

"Nope, nothing."

"Who was working that night?"

Bateson tightened his eyebrows. "Look, if I tell you there's nothing on the report, then there's no point talking to anybody."

"C'mon, Bateson. You know how investigations work. What's the problem?"

"No problem." He skidded his rolling chair closer to the screen. "Oh yeah. There was a problem that night. One of the guys had a bad toothache and had to go to the ER. I came in to cover the rest of the shift. No mention of shots heard on the log. But your victim didn't die from GSW, what I heard."

"Yeah, but we check everything. You know that. Print out the page for me, will you?"

"You need a warrant for that, Mason."

Mason held back his surprise. "Can do, but why do you want to put me through all that? Why? Just give me the name of your other operative then, and some contact information. If there's nothing, there's nothing."

Bateson hesitated a moment then asked for Mason's card. "I'll email it to you."

Mason got up to go. "Why did you quit NYPD? You were doing pretty good there."

"The politics. It's a lousy job. Low pay. You can get your head shot off real easy. I hated the wrestling matches with mean drunks."

"Something happen?"

"Something always happens."

"Like what? I asked around about you. People notice things you get involved in a lot of people get hurt. Funny things."

Nigel glanced at him. "I don't remember all that many laughs."

When Bateson rose and led him out of his office, he paused at the door. "What have you got so far on this?"

"An ID. Not much beyond that," he said truthfully.

"If you need anything else, let me know," Bateson said, shutting down the nice guy face.

♌

Mason took the call from his father when he got outside on Ocean Avenue again, fighting traffic back to the station. At this time of the morning, the traffic up to the I-10 was heavy through Santa Monica, all the way through the life-shortening commute east to downtown Los Angeles. His mother always called him. If his Dad answered the phone when he called, he'd say, "Nice to talk to you, Dave. How's the Jeep running? What's the weather like in your neck of the woods?" He was a chatter and a big joker with everybody but his son. It wasn't they didn't get along. They just didn't know how to talk to each other. Then he'd say, "I'll get your Mom."

"I'm here at LAX," his father said. "Just decided to come out for a visit. I need a ride. Okay if I stay with you?"

"You are? You're here? In LA?" Mason said, not comprehending his father was at the airport wanting a ride.

His parent's visits to Los Angeles had always been proceeded by months of back and forth careful planning and getting free passes to all the attractions.

"Oh, she'll be along later… I'm on my own this time," as if his mother had gone to the store to pick up a quart of milk.

"Dad, I don't get it. Mom isn't with you? You never told me you were coming. You're here in Los Angeles?"

"Dammit, Dave, are you going to pick me up or not? I can take a taxi and stay at a hotel."

"No, no, Dad. I have to juggle a few things around, and I'll be there in an hour. That's the quickest I can make it," Mason said.

What was going on? He tried to remember what state his condo was left in this morning. Ginger refused to give up her apartment, but she more or less lived with him. Neither he nor Ginger was a fanatic neatnick. Neatness probably didn't matter a pinch of coon shit right now. His father's sudden appearance was already far out of the ordinary. His Dad could have the bedroom he kept for Haley when she stayed with him on weekends. He made a few calls, one to Fredericks to put off their meeting by a couple of hours. He checked his email and saw Bateson had sent a name and contact information for his operative.

Had his sister made a re-appearance? No, his mother would have come, not his Dad.

Fredericks picked up.

"I want you to track down this guy named Bruce Draco. He's one of Bateson's operatives and was working the night we had the report of shots fired. I'm forwarding you the contact information," Mason said. "And I'm taking a few hours off. Personal time. My Dad flew in just now."

Lincoln Boulevard linked up with the airport after

miles of small storefronts and tedious traffic. Mason hit a Starbucks on the corner of Lincoln and Ocean Park, hoping a jolt of caffeine might blast his thinking process enough to deal with whatever trouble his Dad was going to land on him. He had to admit to himself he'd been avoiding his father's calls sensing something way out of the ordinary. A rack of tabloids near the door on the way out caught his eye. This issue featured Poppy and Derek on the red carpet with the blazing headline: *Marriage in Trouble?*

He passed by the corner of Rose and Lincoln where a Whole Foods and a 99 Cent Store on the same lot showed how differently rich and poor shopped. A fresh flower shop in front of Whole Foods did a good business. A row of skinny blonds huddled over phones and tablets sitting at tables set out within inches of passing cars, which circled like sharks looking for parking. The blonds checked with their agents or booked their next Silicon Beach party, yoga mats stuffed under their chairs. Along with poor elderly whites, blacks, and Latinos, homeless guys with all their possessions tied to their bikes shopped at the 99 Cent Store.

Horrible traffic all the way to and from the airport. His father was tired and grouchy and in no mood for a chatty conversation about the weather or the traffic. Making the left turn into the alley behind his condo, a kid on an electric scooter roared, almost knocking down his father who was getting his suitcase out of the truck of the car. Damn those things. Mason held his breath, hesitating, debating if he had the energy to chase the kid down. He didn't. His energy was used up trying to pretend everything was normal with his Dad. He got him settled in at his condo, then headed back into the station to see if anything had sprung loose. A few last-minute attempts at asking him why he was there went nowhere. He'd deal with it later.

"What did you get from the woman with the baby up the street?" Mason asked Fredericks, breaking all the laws of cellphone use while driving.

"She's the second one who called in the report of the gunfire. Says it came from Logan's place. She's hiding something, but I don't know what. I keep going back, and she doesn't answer the door. I can hear the piano going, though."

"Okay," Mason said, "We're burning daylight." He looked at the incoming emails: Jorge Talaveras, the Coroner's assistant. The union organizer stuck in his mind. Talaveras rejected him. Was that enough for him to kill her?

This time when he stopped in at the union hall, another organizer, a no-nonsense woman, told him Anderson was in Cleveland working a strike. She gave him the contact number, but told him Anderson would be pretty busy. Hmmph. Like he was just sitting around reading magazines, and checking himself out on Google?

Mason called Ginger and told her about his father. Ginger was silent a moment, while he hoped she would tell him whatever needed to be done. In some ways, she had a better relationship with his parents than he did.

"Have you talked to your mother, Dave? What does she say?"

"Not yet. I keep calling, but she doesn't answer. She'll call me, I guess. Dad was dead tired. You know him. He's usually chatty." He flung the empty wrapper of a Subway sandwich on the floor of the car. "Will you come over for dinner? Please. I'll pick up something. You don't have to cook."

"I don't think so, Dave. He's your Dad. You need to talk to him. You better find out what this is all about."

"Please. We can't talk about stuff, whatever's going on. I probably don't even want to hear it. You know how it is with them. It's not like you and your Dad."

"Maybe it's time you did learn how to talk to him."

"Ginger, c'mon."

"I'm hanging up now, Dave. Man up. A big teddy bear fell out of a truck in front of me when I was on the 101, and I ran over it. I've got karma problems."

🐾

Chapter Twenty

Mason took stairs two at a time up to his second-floor condo on the noisy corner of Seventh and San Vicente when he got home that evening. ESPN was playing when he walked in.

He walked in front of the TV and yelled, "Dad? You going deaf?"

George Mason grabbed at the remote on the arm of the chair and fumbled at it until the volume was lowered. "Must've turned itself up."

"Yeah, it does that a lot," Mason said, going to the kitchen to heat the lasagna he'd bought at Ralph's on the way home. While the microwave ticked away, he got out plates and sprinkled on some chips and a few olives to represent the vegetable group, popped the caps on a couple of Dos Equis he set by the plates. He tore off a few sheets of paper towels and folded them, napkin size. They'd eat at the breakfast counter which separated the kitchen from the open living room.

Desultory conversation about the Packers vs. The Wolves. Dave followed hockey, a veteran of the beer league hockey team which played at the Culver City arena. They talked about George's hip operation, his mother's COPD, what Haley was up to. His Dad had liked Diana, Mason's ex-wife, and now that they were divorced, Mason liked her too. She had a new baby with Harvey the Comic Book artist. He got out his phone and showed his father pictures of Haley and the baby. Ginger's new job came up. She was working as a fundraiser again, work she didn't really like, but this time it was for a children's good cause. The lasagna was gone: the olives remained.

There wasn't much to clean up, but Mason dragged it out. The silence gathered. Finally, he closed the dishwasher and turned around to face his father who was still at the kitchen counter.

"So. You get a nap?"

"Yup, yup."

"Everything okay with Mom?"

"That why you think I'm here?"

"I don't know why you're here, Dad? Why don't you tell me?"

"Maybe I will have another one of those beers," his father said, pleating the paper towel napkin.

Mason took his time getting the beer, glancing at his phone which registered an incoming message from Ginger. Please, Ginger. Tell me you're on your way over here. His hand crept to his phone to call her back.

"Oh, I guess it's partly your mother," his father said, his voice harsh, almost panting. "Mostly the store. The changes they're making. Tore out my garden department, put in all these little mowers. Nobody's gonna buy them. I told that guy…"

"What guy?"

"My boss."

"You knew you'd have a boss when you sold the store, Dad," Mason said mildly, taking a swig out of his beer. Maybe if they both got drunk, this would go easier. He reached behind him to grab another beer.

"I knew, of course, I did. But that guy left, and now I

got this kid who doesn't know his ass from a hole in the ground." He looked up. "So I quit. We had words and I quit."

Mason was silent. He knew a little about getting people to talk. He shoved around the beer coaster and waited.

"Well, more than words. He pushed me, Dave. So I pushed him back. Knocked him into the counter. What a wuss. You'd think he'd busted his arm. So he bruised his elbow. God's sake."

Mason went cop. "He didn't press charges, did he?"

"I didn't stick around to find out. Guess your mother would have called if it amounted to anything. She didn't call you?"

"Nope."

"Well, there you go. It won't amount to a hill of beans." George Mason paused to scratch at his flat belly and look out the window. "She'll be all over me about the money, though."

Mason had grown up in Santa Monica, and when his parents were in their fifties, they'd sold the little bungalow on Twelfth Street for a fortune. It was his Dad's dream to go back to Grand Rapids and buy a neighborhood hardware store. His parents had always been close-mouthed about finances, but there were no big vacations, or jewelry, or obvious luxuries. The house was paid for. They shared an old Ford truck. His mom still worked around the corner in the office at the elementary school. The store did well enough to support them in middle-class, small city Michigan comfort. That is until Ace Hardware moved in on the next block. Businesses all over the downtown were hurting.

"You're 68 now, Dad. How much longer were you figuring on working?"

"I'll be working till the day I die, son. Your mother too." He was beating out rhythms on the arm of the gray recliner with fast-flicking fingers.

"What are you talking about, Dad? You must have got a good price selling the store, didn't you?"

His father got up, jammed his hands in his pants pockets and walked over to the window, which looked out on the busy intersection, joggers and bike riders coming to a stop at the light, traffic streaming one way and then the next.

"Everything we had went into keeping the store afloat. Goddamn Walmart and Home Depot gutted the business. We had to practically give it away to the buyers, inventory back to the walls. The only thing they thought was worth anything was the name and the goodwill."

Mason's shoulders slumped seeing a hard new reality.

"And your mother's been sending Stacey money for years…"

Hope flared up. "She know where Stacey is then?"

"She's got a post box up in Eureka. Way up north here in California. Let her go, Dave. She doesn't want us. The upshot is we've got no money, and I spent money on a plane ticket, and I've got no job to go back to."

Mason leaned back in his chair and stared at the ceiling. The fury came out of nowhere. He sat forward abruptly. "So you just took off and left Mom to deal with everything?"

"What was I supposed to do?"

"So you're the big victim here? You're the one who punched the guy. What if he sues you? You expect Mom to deal with that too?"

"I can't help it I'm the one who's good with customers. People like me."

"What are you going to do no? You can't hide out

here."

His father jumped out of his chair, grabbed his windbreaker off the doorknob and cried out over his shoulder as he yanked open the door. "Now I'm not even welcome in my son's home?"

"Dad, I didn't say that. Come back."

His father's steps clattered down the stairs. He didn't go after him. This was the way the family dealt with conflict—run away. In one of the few real moments he'd ever had with his sister Stacey, she'd insisted the reason she was fat was that his mother's resolution of conflict with her was to pretend nothing happened.

She'd knock on the door of her bedroom after an hour or so. "Stacey, I made a cake. Come and have some."

🜨

Another frustrating day going nowhere, a lot of it spent thinking about his dad. Mason put some time in on another case, wasted more time writing reports for the LT who probably wouldn't even read them. He brought home a meatloaf, again from the Ralph's on Wilshire. His Dad hadn't answered his cell phone all day.

His Dad wasn't there. Where could he have gone? Mason pounded into Haley's room. His suitcase was there. No note.

The meat loaf cooled on the counter. Mason watched ESPN, an episode or two of *Criminal Minds*, and went to bed tired at 11:00. He couldn't even focus on the material covering his next flying lesson, which was a first. He woke up in the middle of the night. Rain spattered against the windows sounding like the rustle of cellophane.

He didn't hear his dad come in.

What the fuck? His father was supposed to worry about him being out late, not the other way around.

Everything would turn out fine, he hoped, knowing it was amazing the lies he could tell himself, and the shit he could believe.

❧

Derek Logan edged onto the soft grey carpet of the great room that spanned the length of the house in suburban Mar Vista. He had escaped his security handler for the night, striking a deal with one of the gardener's to borrow his truck.

He watched. Cocks and tongues and flicking fingers awaiting entry, eager eyes, churning buttocks. Tears, moans, screams of delight, and from the back of the house—pain. He snickered, watching the circle around a famous star's young wife who demonstrated a remote-controlled vibrator. The elderly star could no longer perform and didn't want her to miss anything. Derek stood on the edge. He would not stay unnoticed long. Noticed, but avoided by the careful, and those who still had functioning brain cells.

His HIV status was well-known.

A B-list Disney actress, once Poppy's competitor, opened her legs for a hairy man in his 60s. Lucky for her that her new movie didn't require much acting, other than reaction shots to action sequence.

Another watcher would be sniffing around for divorce lawyers after she witnessed her husband on another coke and hooker bender.

What's done in the dark always comes to light, as Poppy was fond of chanting at him. Like a botched abortion he was still paying for. The pulsing rock came to an end with a brief silence. Nigel Bateson was at his side, his hand on his back.

"Aw, shit," Logan said, turning to look at him. The

rap music began again. "I just got here. C'mon, man."

"Let's go, Derek," he said, pulling the bill on his ball cap lower.

Chapter Twenty-One

Fredericks located Bruce Draco, the security operative, and set up an appointment with him in the station. She led him into one of the conference rooms, where Delgado and Mason waited, all her sexual innuendo tamped down. Draco was a big guy, lean, fit, and rangy with eyes that were wary and intelligent. The hair was cut tight, military. The head of the agency, Nigel Bateson, liked to hire Israelis and South Africans. Everybody on his staff had law enforcement or military experience. Mason got Draco talking about his work, just to get him relaxed.

"Nigel has us all doing CrossFit now," Draco said, skidding back in his chair at the table. "One time in Iraq I was responsible for this old fat guy, and I had to carry him out under fire. You need to be lean and whippy and on top of your conditioning all the time. The rich blacks, see, they like to hire the retired football players. Those guys might look good but they can't run."

Mason led him around to June 9th, the night gunfire was reported. It was the only incident report out of the ordinary in the month Celia Talaveras was planted. Every other report in that neighborhood had been followed up. It was tempting to go with this as the date of her death, but there was no corroboration.

"That was a long time ago," Draco shrugged. "Days are pretty much alike."

"We had more than one report of automatic weapon fire from neighbors that night. Something happened up there. That's a pretty quiet neighborhood."

Draco scratched an ear and looked away.

"C'mon," Mason said. "Neighbors heard it. You must have heard it too. How come you didn't make a note of it in the log?"

"Maybe I was inside the house."

"Aw, C'mon, Draco. I saw Bateson, just to let you know."

His face sharpened. "What did he say?"

"Tell me what you saw," Mason said with no special emphasis. Military guys were used to being shouted at. It did no good to try and intimidate them that way.

"Yeah, I remember that night. I was working with Eddie and he was bitching and carrying on. He had a bad toothache and he finally decided to go to urgent care. So I call the boss because this place is a two-man job, and Nigel comes over. These people, they're under the threat of paparazzi and some nut kidnapping their kids, so we're not alone there in case anything happens."

"And that night somebody's shooting and you hear nothing?" Mason was openly skeptical. He let the silence blister a moment. "Hey, does Logan have weapons? He does these action-adventure movies."

"Yeah, Logan's got weapons," Draco said, shifting uneasily in his chair. "But I thought the body they dug up wasn't shot? That must be why I'm here, isn't it? That body. Why are you asking about guns?"

Mason shifted focus. "Did you know the victim?" He shoved a photo across the desk, the studio portrait.

"Her English wasn't so good. Don't think I ever

talked to her, except the day of that big explosion downtown. We were at Bloomingdale's when it went off."

"Yeah, tell me about it," Mason said, interested.

Draco was a good storyteller, relating how he had led his charges out through the parking garage. Celia had held it together. Megan had fallen apart.

"So Celia and Megan—the daughter, I hear they hung out together?" Delgado interjected.

"I'd see them around. Drove them places a few times."

"What did you think when she disappeared?"

"I didn't think anything. Poppy said she just moved on." He shrugged. "I had no reason to think anything different. She was good with the little kids. One of the guys asked her out, I remember that. She said no. Said she was all involved in school, things like that."

Mason made a note. "So what's Logan like?"

"Does a little coke. Runs around naked. He's an asshole. All these HNWs are."

"HNW?"

"High net worths. That's what we call them."

"And you don't remember anything unusual that night?"

"It was the last night I worked that detail … that I remember. Nigel put me on the Kardashians for a while. Not Kim. God, not her. One of the minors. Now I'm out in Calabasas, some Saudi princess. These people are all the same, whether they're Hollywood or not."

"So you don't recall anything about that night?"

"Not really. Sorry."

"You like your job?" Mason asked.

"I like the money."

Long-time security officers got in close to their people. The story still didn't sit right with Mason. Draco knew more than he was saying. The whole security business was full of loopholes and slippery, slidy exit routes, and cut corners.

✸

Fredericks brought the billings for Nigel Bateson's security company for the Logan-Sinclair household to Mason's attention in a late afternoon briefing when they were getting caught up with each other at the station. Other detectives and the probation officers were drifting back to the barn at the end of the shift, bitching about the traffic.

"What the fuck?" Fredericks crowed, handing them over with the total circled in red pen. "That's for one week."

Mason took it from her and flipped through the pages. "The housekeeper told us he's got a room there. Is he living there full-time?"

"How would I know? Like we could get surveillance," Fredericks said, widening her eyes and tightening her lips.

Mason thought about that. "This is way off what that pair should be paying for security."

"That's what I figured."

"So?"

"So he's got something on them," Fredericks suggested.

"Blackmail? Yup. I think they might have mentioned that in detective school."

"What now, then?" she said, eyes bright.

"I might have to do something to prod this forward."

"Better check with the Lieutenant first." She looked around before she said it. "He's star-struck. He wants *to be* Derek Logan. We're going to have to pry him off the guy if we go in."

"Yeah, he likes working the street when it's celebrity stuff. The rest of the time he's hiding in his office hoping nothing big happens."

Sinclair's call to Mason was now part of the record. He hadn't ever seriously considered not reporting it. Lots of guys would consider him a fool not taking up a movie star's move on him. But he'd been around enough women to know Polly Sinclair was a sucking vortex.

Still, he could dream, couldn't he? No quick way of getting over the hots for somebody which had lasted decades.

Mason walked over to the electric car charging station behind the Public Safety Facility and called his mother in Grand Rapids. This time she answered.

"So he told you?" He heard a weariness in her voice. He saw her twining the telephone cord around her hand. An orange princess phone hung on the cheery yellow kitchen wall. He heard TV news playing in the background. The kitchen always smelled of toast and bacon.

Mason leaned against a pole and swiped his hand through his hair. "Yeah, I heard. Mom, are you coming out here? He says he doesn't want to go home. He knows you're mad at him and he's in a real funk."

"He's in a real funk when he's here too, Dave. I'm not sure I want him home."

"Mom. What am I going to do with him? I got things going on. What about this guy he punched out?"

"Oh, that's what he told you, is it? I have to go to work. Somebody's got to bring in some money around here."

"Mom? Don't hang up. I gotta know."

His central relationship had always been with his mother, his father a distant figure growing up. His father worked for the phone company back then and made himself absent from the house as much as possible to avoid the fights between Mason's sister and her mother. Mason was the buffer between the two of them. But Stacey had left the house long ago. His father had never been palsy with him. His life was outside the home.

"You do something about him," Edna Mason said, hanging up.

Chapter Twenty-Two

Mason watched Fredericks walking toward him talking on the phone, wearing one of her beige suits she thought tamed down her frizzy orange-red hair. She leaned a sinewy hip on Delgado's empty desk and grinned at him. He started listening when he realized she was talking to the coroner's office, and the look of her told him she had something. He made a whirling motion with his finger and mouthed "Speaker. Speakerphone."

"So tell me again," Fredericks said. "I got you on speaker. "One more time. C'mon."

"I already told you. I got things to do."

"C'mon. I got my boss on speaker."

Big sigh. "Okay, we've got this kid here interning. Likes the movies, all that stuff. Remember that pin we found with the design on it. We turned it up when we disinterred the body up on Woodland. The kid was going through the evidence log. It's his first disinterment, and it's got his motor going. This little pin they found under the body was part of the swag they gave out at the premiere of that movie with Poppy about the boy and the doghouse. You know the one."

Mason whistled at Fredericks who was grinning, kicking her heels back against Delgado's desk.

Mason was already googling Poppy Sinclair, and not

for the first time. The dog flick was a three-handkerchief weepy with a little boy and a dog. He swept through the site and paused when he got to the dog. The logo, or whatever it was called for the dog, was a doghouse tilted on the triangular.

He'd gone through Google images himself when the pin had first turned up. But Sinclair had made movies since and the image one was buried deeper in her website. People missed things. Even cops. Anybody could have had a Disney bracelet, but this pin and its location was unique. Unique at least to how many people who had gotten a swag bag at the premiere. Both Sinclair and Logan had been at the premiere.

It was something. Finally.

Fredericks got off the phone and high-fived Mason. "But where does it get us?"

"What're you talking about?" Mason said. "The victim took it to the grave with her. It gets us right through the front door." He said it loud, trying to convince himself he was almost there. Warrants for digging equipment, bank and telephone records, Talaveras' room. There was bound to be blood there.

It was too late in the day to talk to the Sarge, and round up Lieutenant Vargas. He put Fredericks on finding out how many of those pins were in circulation.

Fredericks had one more thing. "The female with the baby up the street? The one with the piano?"

Mason turned to look at her. A loose end they should have tied up long before. "What have you got?"

"I'm down the street calling on Billy Jackson, the walker? The autistic kid?"

"I remember, Fredericks. And what?"

Fredericks grinned. "He's always there, but this time he isn't, so I stroll up the street to call on the woman with the baby. I know she's lying about something. This time I sneak up on the deck and look in through the front window. There's her and the piano teacher lying on the couch fooling around. I knock and they jump up. The *female* piano teacher, I should mention. The baby starts crying. I go in. The pianist is not happy to see me, mmm hmmm, no. She's scared out of her wits I'll tell her husband, the dentist over at UCLA. I assure her I couldn't care less what she's doing with her piano teacher. I want to know if she's got anything to tell me about our victim. After all the tears and the long story, she's got nothing to add. She's scared of her husband leaving her if he finds out."

"And you buy it?" Mason asked, turning back to his computer screen.

"Yeah, I do."

Billy Jackson was also a loose end, and it looked as though it would stay there. Fredericks was good, but she wasn't that good. Jackson refused to talk. And Mason wasn't going back to face that rooster.

♪

Mason's mood went bleak when he opened the door of his condo that evening, slung his jacket over the back of a chair, and went to the kitchen for a Heineken. None left. He tried hard not to think about his father and whatever the hell was going on with him during the day. For the most part he succeeded, schooled long ago in family conflict avoidance. He thought of how rarely he'd been alone with his father as an adult. Since his father's retirement from the phone company and their move back to Grand Rapids, family visits had been few. He and his first wife took Haley back to see her grandparents, and the focus was on their grandchild. Ginger went with him a couple of times, and they loved her. Ginger could talk to anybody.

A message from the flight school. Where was he? He'd have to go in soon to keep up with his cohort. An ache about missing something he really cared about. No return call from his mother.

From the door of Haley's bedroom, he saw his father curled up in her twin bed, his face to the wall.

"Dad?" He walked over and looked at his father for a long moment. "Dad, you awake? You want some dinner? I got that chicken you like from the Thai place."

"I already ate, Dave. Think I'm getting a cold. Just leave me be, okay?" He snuffled a few times convincingly.

Mason noticed the wastebasket filled with used Kleenex. He sat down on the edge of the bed, preparing something to say. After a time, he heard his father's soft snoring.

♉

The next morning, excited by the discovery of the Disney pin found in the grave linking Talaveras to the Sinclair-Logan household, Mason had a strategy session with the brass. He talked hard and fast, bargaining for approval to seek a search warrant on the Woodland address and grounds.

The Public Information Officer from the station sat in the conference room with them. Mike Rosen, the station spinner, had the press contacts, and experience with smearing the shit around evenly. Mason laid out the evidence: the pin, the victim's employment in the house, and statements from the household staff that Logan had his eyes on Celia. Their denial they knew her, then later the acknowledgment she'd been with them six months. Delgado brought up the possibility their security chief Bateson might be blackmailing them, based on the huge billings. Mason pointed to each fact in Frederick's neat handwriting on the whiteboard.

The chief sat forward, elbows on her knees, studying the board. "Yeah, she worked there. They deny it, then come clean. That looks bad. Their lawyer could say they were both gone so much. Yeah, you and I would recognize somebody who worked in our house for six months, but these Hollywood people? Who knows how they think?" she said, rising to dismiss the meeting. She looked at a plain wristwatch and pursed her lips.

"Narcissism is big this year," Fredericks commented.

The chief shot her a look. The Disney pin linking the couple to Celia Talaveras was the deciding piece of evidence.

"Okay, let's see if we can even get a warrant," the chief said finally. "But kid gloves, Mason. Fredericks, you watch your mouth."

Fredericks lifted her eyebrows and made a zipping motion across her lips. Once the chief had left the room, she grinned and high-fived Mason. They went over Bateson and Draco's account. Mason figured Bateson knew as much about the household workings as Lupe Garcia. What if he knew more about Celia Talaveras as well?

Because this was a celebrity case with the potential of enormous blowback, the Assistant District Attorney sat in with Mason and Fredericks while they crafted the search warrant. The ADA scanned Mason's draft and then took off for court. They planned to hit the house at 6 a.m. Too early for the looky-loos and the cameras, early enough to catch the power couple at home and off guard.

"How do you know it was Poppy? Why not Logan?" the Assistant District Attorney with his eyes glued to his laptop asked. "Maybe it was both of them."

"I don't. Look, I can't tell you which one of them it is. That's the pisser," Mason admitted.

"Weak, Mason, weak."

"So we play them off against each other. I've got to get them in different rooms and kick the truth out of them."

"Not going to be so easy."

"Like anything is? They've stonewalled us."

"And you're so sure you're gonna turn up your evidence with a property search?"

"Yeah, I am."

"Let's hope so, Mason. You know the LT doesn't like you."

Mason tried his best not to roll his eyes. "Yeah, I know."

He knew this in his gut, but he didn't realize other people knew it as well. Fracture lines had formed around LT's promotion. Mason drank with Sgt. York once in a while at Friday night's choir practice, the informal gathering of station staff in one corner of the motor pool to have a beer and unwind. Had Vargas considered him a serious competitor on the way up the ladder?

Mason looked down at his phone vibrating on his belt. Ginger. No callback from his father. He'd asked what his Dad's plan was for the day before he'd gone to bed last night. He growled he was plain sick and wasn't planning on doing a damn thing. Okay.

"I made him some soup," Ginger said. "He's got a bad cold, but you'd think he's dying. He's just like you. Your mom's coming in today."

"Really? When? I gotta figure out how to get time off to pick her up at the airport."

"It's okay. She wants me to pick her up."

"Really?" Too much ground was shifting under his feet.

"Yeah, it's okay, Dave. I can do it. Easy peasy."

"What's going on?" He tried not to sound whiny. But dammit.

"I don't know any more than you do."

"And she wants you to pick her up? Not me."

"Don't take it personally."

"Oh, how could I? My mother likes you better than me."

Ginger just laughed at him.

He got practical. "They can't both sleep in Haley's single bed."

"She wants to stay with me."

"Oh." That was a gut punch.

"Dave, I know this is hard. I'll see you tonight. I'll get together some kind of dinner. Don't worry about it."

"Don't worry about it. Easy for you to say."

His parents argued, sure, but most of the fights between them were over his sister Stacey, the family druggie fuck up. Mason couldn't think about it now. He spent the day pulling together details on serving the search warrant, which had been approved and signed.

When Mason got home, his mother sat at the table with his father,who had his chair facing away from her, his head in his hands. Edna Mason yanked her scarf off and sat it on the table along with her purse. An overnight bag sat at her feet.

"Hi, Mom. I would have picked you up." He paused just inside the door. They weren't a huggy family.

"Oh, I know you're busy. Ginger told me." She tightened her mouth and looked at her husband, who was gazing out the window at the traffic on San Vicente

Boulevard. His shoulders slumped and he picked at his fingers, then blew his nose.

"So everything all right?" he said looking between them. It obviously wasn't. He had never been able to do anything about the tension between them, which always made him feel he was vaguely at fault. Of their two children, he was the poster boy. His sister got all the attention. He was the responsible one. The good one. Was that better or worse?

"This old fool has gone and done it this time. He tell you?"

"You know, Mom, maybe I don't need to hear this. Why don't I get you and Dad a room somewhere so you can talk things out?" He went to the cupboards and pretended to be looking for something, opening and shutting doors.

"I don't know what there is to say," she said, bitterness twisting her mouth.

"Oh, c'mon, Mom. There's always something to say. Let me make a few calls. You'll be too crowded here at my place."

"No, I'm staying with Ginger. I want to see my granddaughter while I'm here too. Ginger and I are driving out to see them tomorrow. She had to go to a meeting tonight but she'll be back any second."

"How long are you planning to stay?"

"Why? Are you trying to get rid of me already?"

"Aw geez, Mom. Gimme a hug." Edna Mason hauled herself to her feet and moved toward him. He towered over her and breathed up the smell of her shampoo and a long day traveling.

"We have to have a talk, Dave," she said, tapping her husband on the shoulder. He looked around at her, stricken. "I don't think he told you the whole story. But not now. I'm beat and Ginger will be here soon to take me to her place."

Chapter Twenty-Three

News of Celia Talaveras' death had probably reached the Gobi Desert by now. A volunteer worker, one of Frederick's confidential informants, called her up when she noticed a patch of blood on a yellow silk kimono, part of a substantial donation of clothes from Poppy Sinclair to Step Up on Second. The bags were set aside because the manager of the thrift shop figured she could get more for celebrity wear. The secondhand operation was a thrift shop for mentally ill people operated by the homeless community do-gooders. Frederick's sharp-eyed CI was working off her community service. It set Mason alight, getting the processing going on the blood sample.

It would take 24-hours to get a match on a DNA sample.

"What if the blood is Talaveras'?" Mason said to Delgado, hope in his voice.

Hardly a tight chain of custody. That was the problem. Still, a pickup request was on the record from the celebrity address. It was a link, but a weak one. Another weak one. Everything depended on the results of the search.

The rest of the day and the one following was spent preparing to serve the warrant on the celebrity household.

What would they do if either Logan or Sinclair left town suddenly? What if they shut down the Santa Monica house and decided to go to the Aspen house? Or fucked off entirely? The consensus was they weren't a flight risk. They had too much going on. Mason and Delgado would execute the warrant and supervise the search, whether they were home or not.

Mason looked around the conference room where his team was waiting for Vargas. The Assistant District Attorney was going over the affidavit. The space smelled of aftershave and cleaning solutions.

"Delgado, he's ready to sacrifice his dick to the housekeeper. She really likes him," Fredericks said, smirking. They all looked at Delgado who blew out a raspberry. Mason was the good-looking one; this was the first time a witness went for Delgado rather than Mason. Nobody mentioned Sinclair's call to Mason, though it was in the record.

"But which one of them is it? Poppy or Derek?" Fredericks said, jittery and looking as if she wanted to jump up and punch somebody.

"Or both of them. I don't know," Mason admitted. He didn't want any discussion to develop about the flying shit that would coat everybody if nothing turned up in the search of the house.

"You're taking a risk, Mason," the ADA said, not looking up from the file he was reading as they waited. "You could be sacrificing your own dick. You're opening up a real can of whoop ass here."

Mike Rosen, the fast-talking PIO, was in the hall outside the conference room waiting for Mason after the meeting broke up.

"You got all your ducks set up?" Rosen asked, sympathy in his look.

"Yeah, I think."

"I hope so, Mason. I hope so. There'll be blowback that'll set your hair on fire if you haven't."

Vargas blasted open the door and charged in as though he had discovered a secret meeting. He listened to the discussion for a moment, then snarled, "Anybody caught making us look bad by tucking some little souvenir in his pocket during the search better think about his health plan and his pension first. Got me?"

The room filled with male and female officers suddenly found their notepads and tablets urgent. It didn't need to be said. Everybody knew that. It wasn't that his officers didn't have the occasional brush with celebrity. Santa Monica had more than its share of rich and connected Industry insiders: people who fought the I-10 traffic coming home turning off at 26th Street where the Metro train crossed. Mason thought to himself, and not for the first time, that living in Santa Monica might not really be worth it anymore.

But where else would he go? He had let himself dream about being a flight instructor after retirement, buying his own aircraft. Even with the Cessna he had in mind, if he could ever afford it, he couldn't exactly fly it over the traffic to get to work. Would Ginger ever leave her father and brother behind to leave LA? They were close.

The thought led him to his father and mother, who were meeting at his condo this morning to talk. His sister Stacey had turned up with a little boy at his doorstep a few years ago. She and her boyfriend and fellow losers had been cooking up a batch of meth in her trailer when it exploded. Stacey had fled with an orphaned child, certain her brother could somehow fix things for her to keep him. She took off again when he told her what he could and couldn't do. He checked in the system often to catch her trail. Last known address was Mendocino County in Northern California. He told himself that you couldn't give up on people, that they were still capable of amazing change and surprise.

Stacey made him lose faith in that conviction.

♏

That night Mason made himself leave the station at 6:30. Ginger was making dinner at her apartment, which now felt like neutral territory. Over the years Mason's parents had come to know Ginger, and they liked her and hoped they'd get married. So did Mason. Ginger was a slow cooker cook and her small, rent-controlled apartment on Third Street near downtown Santa Monica smelled inviting. His dad was parked in front of the TV watching ESPN. Before dinner, Mason pulled Ginger into her bedroom for a restorative snuggle, arming himself to face whatever the evening would bring. They talked about the best ways to make Crock-Pot chili over dinner until they'd beat the subject to death. Ginger's old cat walked past the table, his tail high in the air, intent on cat business, ignoring them. It wasn't until dinner was finished that the subject Mason had been dreading came up.

"I don't think he told you everything," his mother said.

His father looked at her sharply and got up to take his plate to the sink.

"You. You just be quiet," Edna Mason said to him.

"What?" Something terrible was coming, and Mason wanted to run. It must be worse than decking his boss. Mason had never known his father to be violent. He'd always been an affable guy with a good story and the customers liked him.

"It was the women."

With this came a jolt of recognition. Mason stood up and jammed his hands into his jeans, a flush rising to his face. He'd been embarrassed when he was a kid to have his father sneak up behind a girlfriend he'd brought home, and put his arms around her from behind under her breasts and, all jolly, shake her back and forth. Was he rubbing an erection against her? It was the first time he'd let himself recognize it, and the words left him one by one.

"These women, Dave," his father said. "They can't take a joke. Everybody's so damn sensitive these days."

Ginger set her coffee cup down on the arm of her chair with unnecessary force.

Mason thought of all the times he'd said nothing, turned away, failed to see the look on a woman's face, ignored the vibe in the air. He didn't want to see.

It wasn't going to work this time. He had to say something because the world had changed.

"That McArdle woman? You remember her, Dave," his mother asked.

"Yeah," he said, his voice thick with new anger.

"Her daughter started working in the store and…"

"C'mon, Edna. For God's sake. He doesn't need to know that."

"No, George." She pounded her fist down on the arm of the chair. "I'm telling him. Her daughter said your dad got her on the bags of fertilizer and tried to rape her. Her mother stuck up for her."

"All blown out of proportion. She never said get your hands off me. She never said nothing."

"But she went into the breakroom where her mother and some of the others saw her blouse all ripped."

"She got it all wrong …"

"Now she wants money, plus we had to hire this

lawyer. Where we gonna get the money to pay him what he's asking?" she shrieked at her husband. "Then he gets mad at the new manager of the store and hits him … and that guy's talking about suing him too."

Mason slumped forward in his chair, his head between his knees. He looked up at his father from under his eyebrows.

"And you think this is okay, do you? You're the poor misunderstood victim here?"

"Well, no, I'm not saying that. Don't you be getting me all twisted up here, but like I said, this is all crazy. Have a heart. C'mon, Dave. You know how it is with women." He bucked forward in the recliner and put his hand out to Mason. Mason stood up and ignored it.

"How do you think it makes me feel, Dave? Everybody knows. We don't go down to the VFW anymore and I miss my friends."

"Did you ever think of Mom when you were trying to cop a feel?" Mason said. He was circling the chair he'd been sitting on, unable to sit down, wanting to run for the door so this would be over.

"I told him and told him that women don't like this, but he just says he's being friendly, that women like the attention," his mother said.

"Look at that McArdle girl," George Mason jumped in. "Nobody would give her the time of day. I just made her feel good about herself."

Ginger reached forward to place cold fingers on Mason's wrist, seeing his clenched fist and move towards his dad. "Don't," she said.

Mason looked between Ginger and his mother, swamped by an ocean of despair. How could this be happening? He walked out to the kitchen to get a beer from the fridge. Behind him the silence buzzed. The cat walked back into the room, a strip of fur raised along her back, registering the tension.

"Dad, don't you ever watch TV or read the newspaper?" he said. "Hitting on women when they don't like it has been on the news everywhere? Even in Grand Rapids. You ever hear of Harvey Weinstein?"

"Yeah, well, I don't go out looking for it."

"Are you saying these women hit on you?" Edna Mason shouted.

"No, I'm not saying that. I guess I wasn't thinking right."

"The lawyer's asking for a $25, 000 retainer that we have to pay him up front, and we just don't have it, Dave," his father said.

Mason turned away in disgust. He wanted to hit his father, but he was long used to suppressing those kind of urges. He kept his ass in the chair and his mouth closed with sheer self-discipline.

"And you're asking me to cover it for you?" he said.

"You're the only person I can ask."

Mason made himself look at the ceiling to still the eddying currents of rage, dislike, and resentment he felt for his father. He could feel the beat of his racing heart in the veins in his neck. He looked to Ginger. She wouldn't meet his eyes.

He wanted to cover his ears with his hands and howl.

♟

Driving home to his own place, Mason was in turmoil, shame and bitterness flooding through him. He'd never wanted to see why the young girls working the counter didn't want to be in the storeroom alone with his father. Or why they insisted on Dave coming with them. Why they turned away towards Mrs. Polaski who was old and fat.

She would stick up for them in court and be credible.

"Was this why my mother never wanted to work in the store?" he said, looking at Ginger as they turned right at the big Catholic Church on Seventh Street. Late in the evening, there were still basketball players shooting hoops, the ball slapping the pavement in Lincoln Park.

"I don't know, Dave."

"But she talked to you, didn't she? She told you stuff I'm never gonna hear. I know her. She'll hold it all in and take it out on him. I'm sure this doesn't come as a surprise to her."

"There's no hiding things now anyway. The paper got hold of the story."

Mason's fists curled around the steering wheel. "That McArdle bunch were never any damn good."

The brakes on his old Jeep squealed, and his mind went to his bank balance. He made a good salary for a cop, but he had child support he insisted on paying even though Harvey the Garvey, Haley's stepfather made a shitload of money illustrating comic books. He had a stiff mortgage on his condo. He still had enough working years to make up for a withdrawal from his pension fund which would be taxed heavily.

He ground his teeth until his jaw hurt.

🜨

PART III

Chapter Twenty-Four

A day had passed since the approval for the search warrant was given due to the tedious, mundane shit that just plain happened in law enforcement. Couple of crucial uniforms were on vacation. Mason had a brief court appearance and then was notified the lawyer in his case died. The chief wanted to be available for the execution of the warrant, but she had some kind of minor surgery scheduled, which they had to work around.

The team, along with Sgt. York, discussed Logan's arsenal of weapons and reputation for celebrity meltdowns. Logan made no secret of his love of guns and the NRA. That made him the first target to restrain and extract from the situation. They set up plans for removing the children and household staff. The SWAT team, headed by York, was ready to deploy, staging areas identified, and scene security planned.

The Incident Commander would be Lt. Perry Roth. He and York had the most SWAT experience. Roth would work the mobile command post down the street; York would run the tactical team. Mason and Delgado would direct the search of the home after SWAT secured the premises.

Poppy had called Mason again on his cell, and this time he hadn't returned her call. The call was properly reported, and he took a lot of teasing from Delgado and Fredericks. He tried not to let himself think about her. It wasn't that he was unused to beautiful women. Ginger was a beautiful woman, but he knew her. A search warrant execution was no opportunity to drool over a movie star.

The next day at 6:00 a.m. after a more or less sleepless night thinking about his father, Mason made a left turn off Twenty-Sixth Street following a little parade up to the doors of the Sinclair-Logan enterprise, full of hope and dread. Fredericks and Delgado were close behind.

Mason, Delgado, and Fredericks parked, then convened outside the Logan-Sinclair property beyond the curve of the street. The weather was a variation of June Gloom, which now seemed to last until fall. Or was it his mood right now? The white forensics van and a line of patrol cars filled with uniforms pulled in behind them. Every one of them thrived on the rush of adrenaline. Mason felt alive, charged, up—even happy, if he kept his focus ratcheted down to the task. He couldn't think about his father now. He was there to bring some sort of justice for a pretty girl, who would have grown into real beauty and deserved more than nineteen years of life.

A security officer met them at the gates to the mansion, arms crossed, legs spread wide, mirrored wrap-around sunglasses flashing in the early morning sunlight. He released the gate and walked over to stand at the open window of their vehicle. His eyes roamed over the line of vehicles and personnel. He turned back to lock the door of the office behind him.

Mason gave him a hard look. "You stay here where I can see you. No calls to the house."

They locked eyes. The silent bodyguard nodded. He crossed his arms and leaned back against the door of the security kiosk, watching them assemble, and then progress toward the front door of the house. Was a place this big still called a house? When did a house become a mansion? The uniforms behind Mason had their share of guys who hoped for a real door-kicking, flash-bang-tossing raid. Beat writing traffic tickets. They had rehearsed all the things which could go sideways.

The tactical and search team took their stations at the exits of the house. The six-thousand- square-foot mansion had way too many ways in and out. Plans were available at the city, and they had pored over them, working carefully on ensuring officer safety. They'd hit the house at daybreak for the element of confusion, but now they were at the door, Mason was re-thinking strategy. He could imagine the Monday morning quarterbacking they would face if this went sideways.

Mason knocked and waited. And waited. He stood to one side. The door was opened by Lupe Garcia in a pink housecoat and slippers.

"So early. So early," she complained. She peered around Mason looking for Delgado.

Sinclair steamed down the stairs behind her in workout attire. "Good morning, officers," she said prettily, a hand at her throat. "What is this?"

"We have a search warrant for your premises," Mason said.

She glanced around, then back at Mason. "Search warrant? Whatever for?"

Mason handed it to her, running his eyes over her. Mason noticed Sinclair's start of alarm. He stepped aside as a line of uniformed officers carrying their kit streamed past him. The dogs set up a furious barking.

"Wait, wait a minute. You can't do this. I'm calling my lawyer. You wait here. Detective Mason?"

She came close to him, and placing both hands on his chest she tried to shove him back out the door. Mason looked down at her and saw gray appearing at the part in her hair. He fought against the foolish urge to put his arms around her, draw her close, and comfort her.

"A search warrant means we don't need your permission. Move aside, please."

She looked at Mason with a plea in that beautiful face which had moved millions to believe in a transitory moment essential to the plot.

"Please, can't you give us five minutes?"

"No," he said, hardening his voice. "That's not how this works."

In the hallway at the base of the wide staircase, Poppy Sinclair whirled, took a few steps, reached for the newel post to steady herself, and looked over her shoulder at Mason. It was a look and a move that moviegoers were familiar with. He made himself immune. Mentally he erased the poster of Sinclair half-naked wading through a swamp, the poster which had graced his room as a teenager.

Poppy shrieked and ran up the stairs, calling for her husband. Logan opened the heavy doors which led to their bedrooms, looked out, and yanked her inside.

The house was now full of noise, heavy boots, sharp commands, and dogs barking. Lupe beckoned Delgado into the kitchen with a glass jar of green chili. Delgado ignored her. Mason ordered her to secure the dogs outside. Their canine might need the run of the house without any distraction.

Five minutes later Sinclair steamed into the staff wing where the search was beginning, a challenge in her step. She had pushed past a pair of uniforms who didn't try to stop her. Delgado swung around to confront Sinclair, edging her back in the hallway which led off the kitchen.

"What's happening here?" she shouted. "This is outrageous. Completely unacceptable. My husband and I have important meetings and commitments today. We can't leave you pawing through our house."

"Get dressed, both of you. You can wait outside. Get her out of here," Mason ordered the uniforms.

"I own this house. You can't do this."

Behind her, Mason saw an officer move forward to grab her. Sinclair whirled around to snarl at him.

"Detective Mason, you are an arrogant asshole," she shouted. "I thought you were different."

One of the officers took her by the shoulders, and led her, protesting, back down the hallway. The washing machine and dryer were going. A tech stepped back respectfully as she passed, then hauled everything out of the machines into evidence bags.

Mason turned to Delgado when she was gone and shrugged. "You think I'm an arrogant asshole?"

"Yeah, so what?"

"That really gets me in the feels," Mason said, hand over his heart, following her out to make sure she was gone. Delgado scratched at an itch under his body armor. Mason assigned Fredericks to watch her, along with another couple of uniforms, to make sure she stayed out of the way, but was still available.

♋

Lupe Garcia was in the kitchen close at hand to establish intel about who was home, who was gone, who was expected. They pulled her into Celia Talaveras' bedroom before they began the search. The housekeeper looked around the room, her heavy features shifting.

"Anything changed since Celia was here?" Delgado

said, his eyes on her.

Lupe fingered the bedspread. "La señora said to get a new one. It was old. I buy at Bed, Bath & Beyond. You like it, Mr. Detective?"

"I like it fine. You have good taste," Delgado said. Lupe preened with self-satisfaction.

"And that's the only thing changed?" Mason said, surveying the bedroom, which had all the charm of a Days Inn hotel room. It reflected the blank affect of its current occupant, Nigel Bateson.

"Well, him. Mr. Bateson." The housekeeper nodded, her eyes still on Delgado. Surely she must have seen his well-worn wedding ring. Mason saw a man's toilet kit in the bathroom from where he stood. He pointed. "Who does that belong to?"

"Mr. Bateson. He is here now. I tole you."

"Okay, you can go now," Mason said. "You'll be in the kitchen?"

"Where else I go?" she said, smiling over her shoulder at Delgado, and sauntering out.

"Put her outside in a car to wait. We may need her. Get one of the uniforms to do it," Mason said, seeing Delgado move toward her.

🜂

Chapter Twenty-Five

Mason left the two silent forensics specialists moving slowly around the room Celia Talaveras had occupied, and now Nigel Bateson. They set up their equipment and began the meticulous work documenting and photographing the scene. Just watching the tedious process drove Mason crazy. One of them scraped at the paint on the wall which had a window looking out over the pool area. She pulled the heavy drapes closed.

"What do you make of Bateson staying here?" he said to Delgado.

"Man, he must love his job."

"Or he's keeping a close eye on this pair. That's my guess. Logan must be a real handful." Mason was already searching through Contacts on his phone to put in a call to Bateson. He hadn't come to the door when they arrived. They wanted him on the scene. Now. He had insight into this place.

"You see that thing in *People* with Logan, the interview where becoming a father changed him? How he's become a better person," Delgado asked.

"You read *People*?"

"Hey, I was getting my hair cut. He's also waiting for an invitation to do a Broadway play. Shakespeare maybe."

Mason snorted and took his attention off the celebrity couple's whereabouts to begin the search warrant. They focused on Celia's room. It was the obvious place to start. He ended the call and turned back to Delgado who was standing at the door of the room talking with the two forensic specialists. Women in their mid-30s, they ate lunch together, worked out together, and rumor had it they slept together. Neither of them had anything much to say to anybody else. They were good at what they did, but you didn't go to them for sparkling conversation.

One of the forensic specialists said to the other, chipping a fleck of paint off the walls with a knife. "Oh look. Fresh paint."

"Don't you love it when they think we're stupid?" the other one said. A big smile lit up her face.

"Tell Mason," Delgado said to the one with strawberry blond hair and a big nose.

"I want to show you something, sir. Can you step inside? Stay there by the door."

Mason and Delgado followed them in.

"We don't know if the victim was killed here, but you want us to check it out, so that's what we're doing. We're looking for what's under the paint with this stuff called BlueStar. It's new and better than a chemical reagent like Luminol. If blood was covered over with a good primer of a dark coat of cheap paint, enough biomass would still leech out and give the reagent something to react to. This stuff is amazing. We love it," she said, glancing over at her partner. "You can spray it again and again and not harm the sample."

Her partner hit the lights. She held the spray bottle labeled BlueStar Forensics up to the wall and hit the trigger. Almost immediately a luminescence in a bright shade of blue indicated a positive result. As the luminescence began to fade, she brightened it up with another hit on the atomizer.

"Lotta blood here," she said. "We still have to do a confirmatory test, though. When we finish up in here, we'll look for a blood trail. If she was killed here, she had to get next door somehow. She didn't dig her own grave and crawl in."

"Maybe she leaked along the way," Mason said with a grin. Cop humor.

The carpet looked new, but then everything in this house looked new and unstained and bore a smell of disinfectant and cleaner. Logan was a well-known germ freak, and hated strangers touching him.

Delgado leaned against the opposite wall of Celia's old bedroom, getting out of the way of the two forensic specialists who were wearing white protective clothing. Delgado gave Mason a punch in the arm.

"Dig up the carpet, yeah?"

"Oh yeah. What's underneath?"

Bateson proved hard to get hold of for a guy who lived at this address and had a condo, business address, website, Facebook page, secretary, and numerous cell phone numbers. He must have had a call by now from his guys that they were now inside the house. The story Bruce Draco had told them about the night shots were fired still didn't sit right with anybody.

"Where's Megan and the twins? And that asshole Jake?" Delgado said.

"Find out from Garcia."

Mason finally got Bateson on the phone. "I'm here at the Sinclair house executing a search warrant," Mason heard the security chief draw in a breath. So he hadn't been warned.

"So that's why Logan's calling me," he said finally after a long pause. "I'll be right over."

"You don't answer your client calls?"

"Not when they call me seventy-five times a day."

"Why would they be calling you that often?"

"Celebrities," Bateson said. "They don't operate on ordinary rules. I'll be right there."

"We're told that you have a room here."

"Death threats. She gets stalkers. He gets death threats. I'm keeping a close eye on the place. But I can't be there 24-hours a day."

"Why haven't you told us about this before?" Mason said, angry now.

"It's got nothing to do with your case. It's the usual crazies. You ever heard of crazies?"

"Yeah, I know crazies," Mason said. "Check in with me when you get here."

♌

"Our forensics people learned the whole wing of the house where the staff lives was painted recently. Why was that?" Mason said, getting Lupe Garcia again at the kitchen table.

"Mr. Bateson, he want that before he move in. I come home from visiting my daughter, all the rooms done, all painted Navajo white. Ugly."

"Why were all the rooms repainted?"

Her patience seemed to snap. "I don't know. Because he want. They put new carpet in his room. They do what he likes."

Mason and Fredericks exchanged a glance. Mason tilted his head back on the chair, gazing at Garcia with skeptical eyes. This seemed to unnerve her.

"I do nothing wrong. I do my work. I go to my ESL

class. I visit my daughter. I got no boyfriend. I'm a good worker. Is this over? Nothing else to tell." She stood up.

Mason gave it his last shot, leaning forward. "If we arrest them, there won't be any job, Lupe."

That shook her. Mason wasn't sure it was true. There were the twins, Megan, and the older boy who lived with his mother part-time.

"Have they got relatives who would take the kids?"

"He has mother. Old lady like a *bruja*. Her? Maybe. I read she has a sister. I don't know. I never see family here. Big parties but no family."

"Think about that," Mason said, rising from his chair. "Get dressed. One of the officers will escort you outside."

Her eyes swung to Delgado. "I make you breakfast first."

"No, no, we're fine."

Lupe Garcia was led out past Mason to the incident command trailer parked well away from the house. Her searing gaze following Delgado unnerved Mason. Delgado being the subject of anybody's sexual interest felt wrong, plain wrong.

They'd searched the house for guns immediately on going in, and didn't find any display cases or gun safes downstairs. Either Logan kept them at his shooting gallery or they were all upstairs. SWAT was winding up a felony arrest on the Pier and put on alert.

Logan came out onto the wide landing on the second floor which ran around three sides of the upper floor looking onto the great room and the entry foyer below. He was wearing a pair of black boxer shorts and nothing else. A snort of amusement almost escaped Mason. Logan's physique must be air-brushed or the poundage shot around somehow. Where were the pecs and the six-pack familiar to moviegoers? How much weight did he gain between movies?

"You? What are you doing in my house?" he yelled down at Mason, his face red.

"Search warrant, Mr. Logan, for evidence relating to the death of Celia Talaveras."

"Not this again. Get out. We had nothing to do with that." He gave his head a toss that spoke of a life of ordering people around. "Talk to my lawyer. I'm calling the chief."

"Don't bother calling her. She'll be here soon. Why don't you get dressed and come down and we'll talk about this."

The twins came down the hallway from another wing of the house. They clung to Logan's legs, looking down into the great room filled with strangers. Derek yanked the children into the bedroom with him. With a flounce, Poppy followed them, slamming and locking the bedroom door.

A few minutes later Derek Logan was out of the bedroom roaring at the top of the stairs, "I told you. Get out. All of you get out. Now."

He was wearing a glaring, wild expression, balancing from one foot to another.

Mason and Delgado looked at each other. "Maybe we're in a movie."

Delgado grinned. They'd seen homeowners try to order them out before.

"Calm down, Mr. Logan," Mason said, coming to the bottom of the steps where Logan could see him. "Get dressed and come down."

"Out. Out. Out," Logan screamed. "Get out of my house. You're making my wife crazy. My children are crying. I called my lawyer. My wife and I have important things to do today."

Poppy stood behind him, pulling at his shoulder. Then she caught a glimpse of him, side view, and slapped him in the stomach. "Derek, for heaven's sake. Get dressed. They don't want to look at your saggy old gut."

"My lawyer will have your badge," Logan blasted. He marched back, slamming the door into the double bedroom, his wife and five-year-old twins inside. As yet, there was no reason to set up for a barricaded hostage situation. Logan loved law enforcement reportedly. But Sgt. York and the SWAT team were now nearby.

"There's gates in the fence. Make sure they're locked and get back to me," Mason said into his collar mike to one of the tactical guys. He recalled the spot of OJ's blood that was missed on the gate and wasn't going to make the same mistake.

Mason muttered, a frown on his face. "He's up there with all those guns."

Delgado raised his eyebrows, meeting Mason's gaze.

"Shit," Delgado said.

This wasn't the way it was supposed to go. Homeowners and suspects were supposed to be contained immediately. Celebrity had its own rules and Mason would suffer for this.

He stationed officers just outside the bedroom ready to grab Logan if he appeared again.

※

A few minutes later, Logan eased open the door and roared, "I'm calling the press and telling them about Soviet Monica Nazis locking us up in here while you steal things from my house."

Mason held his breath. The officers edged closer, but not close enough to storm the door.

"You can come out anytime you like Mr. Logan. Nobody's locking you in there. But we will still be executing the search warrant. Why don't you get dressed and we'll all be civilized about this?" Mason said.

"I'm ordering my security people to come in here and supervise your men. We have videos of everything valuable in this house. If anything is gone, you people will have to answer for it."

"That's fine, but nobody is going to be supervising this search warrant except me. Please get dressed, Mr. Logan."

He could hear Poppy issuing sharp mother commands to the five-year-old twins behind the closed bedroom doors. Megan appeared from the end of the upstairs corridor and squeezed past her father, giving him a look of disdain.

"Come back here, Megan," Logan shouted.

"I'm not going in there with you," she said over her shoulder. "You're crazy."

"Nice talk," her father said, slamming the door.

Megan sauntered down the stairs garbed from head to toe in black fleece, her long brown hair twisted up into a messy bun on the top of her head.

"You can't do anything to me now. Just try sending me to fat camp after this," she said, turning to look at him.

"Good morning," she said when she reached Mason.

He too was favored with the look of teenage contempt. Megan Logan looked around the hallway and great room where officers in black SMPD polo shirts were picking up pillows off the blue leather couches and setting them carefully on the floor. In the home of a celebrity suspect, everything would be handled with the greatest care, unlike the squalid quarters of a meth dealer where nothing mattered.

"Don't touch that," Logan screamed, coming out again and pointing at an officer who had a photograph in a silver frame in his hand. The guy looked around at him, startled. Logan had pants on now.

"That's a priceless memento. I'm putting a stop to this until my lawyer gets here."

"We're asking for you to cooperate with us real nice now, Mr. Logan. Let's be reasonable here. Nobody wants you getting hurt, especially your wife and kids," Mason said, as though sweet reason were all that was required to make this turn out right.

He and Logan were now face to face at the bottom and the top of the stairs. Logan did everything he could to intimidate him. Mason watched him puff himself up, an actor at work, calling on everything inside himself from previous roles. It didn't work.

"So what's it to be?" Mason said.

"You don't scare me."

Mason grimaced. This was certainly getting things off to a good start. He paced, stiff-legged, consulting with the SWAT commander, Sarge York. At some point the family had to come out of that bedroom so it could be secured and searched.

Mason should have had them out of the house by now.

🜂

Chapter Twenty-Six

Mason turned away to answer a question from one of his guys. There was so much going on, he had to put Logan out of his mind for the moment. He forced away the situation with his father, his betrayal, the money, the flying lessons. His future.

Right now his job was to direct the search, looking over the shoulder of the scribe who was documenting everything. So was a videographer who had gone through the house at the beginning. The smallest details. If and when this case went to court two years down the line, asshole defense attorneys representing Logan would do their best to make Mason and all the other officers look inept by questioning them on the position of some knickknack on a glass shelf next to the staircase. Logan might have videos on the placement of every precious memento, but Mason would too. It flitted through his mind one of his officers might let his fingers stick to a souvenir from the house, something which looked so trivial it wouldn't be missed. He disregarded it.

The bustle of the search went on around him. Questions flew at him from all sides. Delgado was rumbling from room to room, then left to concentrate on the office. The downstairs of the mansion was filled with loud voices, heavy boots, crackling radios, and shouted orders.

Upstairs it had gone silent. The tension showed on the Lieutenant's face. He had attempted to start a dialogue with Logan and, so far, had failed. Sinclair and their kids were still up there. No word from either of them.

Logan hadn't shown his face again, or anyone else in the family. No weapons had been fired. There had been no overt threats from Logan. There was also the celebrity issue. Was the rest of the family in imminent peril? There were procedures to follow. The time had to make a decision. It was time to bring in SWAT.

♣

The SWAT team arrived in their van, filing out into the house in close order, like black-clad Ninjas. SWAT, under the command of Sgt. York positioned themselves in areas of concealment, weapons trained on the double doors and the hallway to the back of the house around the corner from the bedrooms where Logan and Sinclair and the twins had holed up. Officer safety was the first priority. SWAT trained for this, but it still took time to get the robot equipment set up. Nowadays nobody liked to stick his head around corners to take a look. Robots went in when possible. Or the police dog, but nobody wanted to get the dog shot unnecessarily, especially the handler and the bean counters. They sweated in their gear, creaking every time they moved, snaking the robot up the stairs to listen outside the double doors which led into the bedroom area where Logan and Sinclair had barricaded themselves. Waiting.

York put two SWAT operators out in the security kiosk watching the screens monitoring the house. With sound cameras recording everything, they'd have a record of what went down, who did what, who said what. With the unfortunate exception of what was going on in the master bedrooms, the immediate hot zone.

The Public Information Officer slid in, getting in Mason's face.

"What? What?"

The PIO held out his phone for Mason to see. The actor had posted that SMPD Soviet Monica gangsters were tearing his house apart. Loyal fans were posting they were prepared to storm the house to rescue him.

"There's no way anybody could get close to this house," Mason said, his certainty slipping. "Unless they came up from the back from the golf course …There's fencing all around this property. I've walked it myself."

"He's tweeting we're Soviet Monica thugs who are threatening to shoot him," the PIO said. The comments piled up one after another as he watched his phone.

Mike Rosen showed Delgado his phone. "You see what Logan's posted on Twitter and Facebook?"

Delgado took the phone from him and busted out laughing. Then his face went serious. "Nah. We gotta get Logan down here. He's up there thinking he's running the world off his cell phone."

"This is trending on Twitter. Get him out before he goes crazy. For all we know, the family's in there with him under gunpoint."

Mason wanted to argue it. "He's got a lot to lose if he pushes that."

"How do you know he's not up there stuffing cocaine up his nose?" Vargas screamed, suddenly there in the house with them.

"What are you doing here?" Mason said, startled. Vargas had no role in this. Roth and the Sarge were in command. Vargas was supposed to be outside, observing from the Incident Command trailer.

Vargas was a screamer and now he was high on control. "I'm taking over from York. The situation's going to shit. You know he's got guns. He could come out those doors any second on automatic fire."

"LT," York protested. "We're not even fully set up yet. Let me do my job."

Mason was flabbergasted. He took a step back and rolled his eyes at the Sarge out of view of Vargas. This made no sense. Who let Vargas do this? But then it all came together. Roth, the Incident Commander, had pushed Vargas up the promotional ladder. He was giving his boy a chance to prove himself. Mason couldn't do anything about it anyway. York took himself off to the kitchen, giving the news to his team. He wouldn't leave unless Vargas pushed him out the door. Vargas had trained with them. They knew him and that was bad. Nobody needed to say anything. Mason broke the silence.

Mason pulled Delgado into the kitchen where York was on the phone. They waited until he swiped it closed.

"Roth is pushing this. You know that. He's Vargas' buddy," Mason said.

"Yeah, I know," York said.

Mason overheard tense discussion between Vargas and the Incident Commander about the balcony that led off the bedroom Logan occupied with a view into the pool and backyard area. No sensible person would jump from the balcony to escape, but people under pressure did crazy things. Thick wisteria vines grew up onto the balcony. They stationed snipers behind the pool cabana and in a corner concealed in the bamboo hedge at the back of the property.

If Mason could imagine Logan swinging down like Tarzan, Logan could imagine it too.

♌

"It's her," Mason said. "Poppy." He put it on speaker phone.

"Detective Mason, we need your help," Poppy said. "My husband is …"

Mason heard Logan shout, "What are you doing, you crazy bitch?" Anyone standing close to the stairs could hear him.

The phone call ended. Mason ran out again into the protection of the overhang under the landing outside the bedrooms on the second floor.

A jumble of hisses and squawks could be heard on the headsets the communications team had set up. One of the communications officers managed to get a tiny mic and fisheye camera to the top of the stairs. No way to get the camera under the door, and no way to drill through a wall. They were trying to get another mic across the floor of the balcony and through the open door into one of the bedrooms.

"I know you're out there," Logan said, pounding on the wall nearest the door. "I hear you. Stay away. I'm not letting a bunch of cops push me around. I have to protect my family from you. Cops shoot innocent people like us."

Vargas filled up the rooms with his gum-chewing anxiety. The Lieutenant stood next to Mason, close enough he could smell the cinnamon gum on his breath.

"Mr. Logan," Vargas yelled. "Everything all right up there? It's time for you to show us everybody's there of their own free will. This doesn't have to slide over the edge yet. There's ways to work this out."

"I'm giving him a time limit," Lieutenant Vargas explained to his circle of listeners.

No, no, no, Mason screamed inwardly. "Don't corner

him," he muttered to Delgado.

"Mr. Logan, you have ten minutes for all of you to come out of there," the LT said. "Ten minutes. Then all of you come downstairs. Your lawyer is on his way and you can consult with him. Okay?"

Sweat beaded on Vargas's brow.

"Get a hostage negotiator on his way just in case," Vargas ordered Mason.

Bad had now gone worse. Did Logan have his family at gunpoint? Was Poppy Sinclair a willing or unwilling participant in the standoff? That mattered.

The Lieutenant lit a cigarette against all procedure and then yanked it out of his mouth, but the paper stuck to his lips. Smoke curled into his nose and eyes and his head jerked back. He picked at the paper on his lips and then started coughing. "I need a minute," he said, turning his back, and grinding the cigarette out on the hardwood floor.

Mason wanted to laugh. He also wanted to grab Vargas and say, "What the fuck is wrong with you? Can't you see what's happening?"

They waited for the hostage negotiator to arrive. Logan was surely helping his crazy along with whatever pharmaceuticals he had upstairs with him.

Ten minutes passed and it was quiet upstairs. Mason pulled out his phone to check the time. A call from his mother. He shrank from her.

"I'll bet Logan's enjoying this," he muttered to Delgado. "Depending on how it gets spinned. He loves the publicity this is gonna get. Him--holding off the nazi cops. He's got his own and the studio lawyers who will make him look good--like he's protecting his family from us."

Mike Rosen, the PIO, was restricted to wooden policespeak to tell the story from law enforcement's point of view. He had to write court-worthy press releases:

Logan's people didn't. They could tell the story any way they liked. SMPD would be left to fight off the attacks.

Chapter Twenty-Seven

The crazy train was accelerating. Logan could come out shooting, triggered by a squirrel in the trees, a cloud passing over the sun. A hostage situation involving Poppy Sinclair and Derek Logan made Mason's asshole pucker. And it should have scared the Lieutenant as well, but he was getting off on command, liaising with the Deputy Chiefs who were in Las Vegas at a conference. The Chief was still at her medical appointment. They were trying to reach her. The Captain was there, and consulting with the Incident Commander out in the trailer.

Mason suggested they get Bateson in. Vargas shrugged but didn't say no.

"What do you think is going on here?" Vargas asked Bateson when the security chief was led in.

Bateson shrugged. "Could be a lot of things. Logan's crazy, you know."

"How crazy? We know he likes guns. Likes drugs. Bad combination."

"Yeah, there's that," Bateson said. He slouched against the table. "He's a blender with the top off."

Bateson confirmed the arsenal was upstairs in the side-by-side master bedrooms, accessible from either side, not exactly happy news. Logan and Sinclair didn't share a bedroom or bathroom. The doors visible from the landing led to an interior hallway and two master bedrooms, with a connecting door between them.

"What about her? Sinclair?" Vargas said.

"She tries to manage him. She's her own kind of weird, though."

"Think we can get him to surrender the kids?" Mason said.

"I don't think either one of them gives a shit about the kids. Bad idea adoption. I always said that."

This annoyed Vargas and he snapped, "They probably didn't ask your opinion."

"That's very true." Bateson steepled his hands, tapping his fingers together, waiting Vargas out. Vargas waved him outside. Bateson left. He looked nervous. Mason wondered whether he was worried about a lucrative contract ending.

The last thing Logan had screamed through the doors of the bedroom was that he wanted everybody to go away and leave him alone," Vargas said with a strained laugh to Mason. "Says he's innocent. He'd never hurt Celia."

Mason's eyebrows rose. "We're supposed to believe that and go away?"

"Not fuckin' likely. I want him. I want Logan." Vargas had made this personal. He wanted to bring down a movie star. He wanted to be a movie star.

🖢

The world was watching. News helicopters whapped overhead just beyond the perimeter of the restricted airspace Mason had set up. The communications team still hadn't been able to jam transmission from the house, despite the feverish work going on. TMZ was live, Derek Logan and Poppy Sinclair on selfies from their bedroom.

Everybody wanted to go home tonight with no new

holes in them. But nobody on the first floor believed this would all end in a kumbaya moment. Here were the elements of O.J.'s slow progress up the 405 in the white Bronco to nearby Brentwood. Instead of crowds on the freeway overpasses waiting to see the Bronco pass, news helicopters were broadcasting video of the mansion on Woodland. There was nothing to see except the occasional cop heading out to the packed mass of vehicles, red and blue lights spinning on the top. Social media could keep it alive indefinitely.

Woodland Drive was closed at San Vicente Blvd, and Vargas had threatened castration for any officer who allowed a civilian to get through, especially one with a camera. The story was huge enough on cable TV and social media to shove political coverage off the screen. Everybody loved a celebrity who had overcome personal afflictions: Logan's addictions and a speech impediment. Poppy, well darling Poppy. She suffered over the drowning of her friend in their Jacuzzi. Look how much good she did in the world, sacrificing herself for causes which swung between hotel worker sexual harassment to Syrian war refugees.

The station was besieged with calls. Mike Rosen, the new PIO, was good in reporting day-to-day policing but proving excitable and ineffective in a crisis. "There's a new Twitter feed saying they're white, so you probably won't kill them." He danced up and down, holding out his phone to Mason.

Mason was too busy to look at it. "I don't want anybody getting killed, least of all me."

The drone operator arrived, adding another element to the whap of the helicopters nearby, the rumble of the heavy engines of patrol and personnel vehicles, police radio chatter and loud male conversation.

❧

"They're saying terrible things about us, Derek. Look on TMZ." Poppy Sinclair held her laptop out for him to see. "Look."

"That buh buh bitch interviewed me. I know her. She has fat knees. She was all over me in the Green Room."

"I don't care, Derek. I don't care. Why do you even bother telling me this stuff?"

She watched her husband. He had been locking and unlocking the door to his gun safe where he kept the AR-15 he was so fond of. Once taking it out and fondling it.

"Put that thing away."

"What?" he said, looking right through her, his eyes vacant.

Poppy didn't think Derek would kill her to prevent telling what she knew about Celia Talaveras, but she couldn't be sure. He seemed to be in his own movie now, in which he played an innocent victim hunted down by the police, talking to himself as though he were running lines, nearing the doors to press his ear to the door to listen to the cops. He'd kept his buzz going with a stash he'd managed to keep hidden from her, helped along with Maker's Mark. Poppy ran the scenario over and over again, watching Derek watch clips of himself on cable news, and made a decision. Opinion was divided on whether Logan had gone crazy and was keeping her and the children under gunpoint. Or whether this was part of the publicity for their upcoming movie, the first occasion they'd starred in together for more than five years.

"They won't come in here as long as they think the kids are in danger," Poppy said, flopping down on the unmade bed beside him, just out of reach. She rubbed her nose upward with the heel of her hand. "They're driving me crazy."

"Blow your nose, for fuck's sake."

"They could bash their way in here, though. Kill us all, maybe."

"Nah, we're stars."

"What will we say about that girl? They must think one of us killed her. They must have some sort of proof now, no matter how well we cleaned up the blood."

Logan gave her a sharp look. "We? We duh duh don't have any motive. We'll say Nigel killed her."

"Why would he kill her?"

"She wouldn't fuck him?"

That made Poppy think. "Maybe. No. That won't work. Nigel's got the gun from that night. Remember he took it away? It has your fingerprints on it."

"And yours too. You grabbed it away from me when you came into her room. Remember, genius?" he sneered. "We were stupid to let him take all that stuff. It was evidence."

"You were the one who panicked."

"You didn't? You were a mess."

"Nate could handle it. Reasonable doubt? We're stars."

Poppy bit her lip, thinking. Planning. Nate seemed to have told Logan that moving a body after an accidental death was only a misdemeanor, but Logan had forgotten. He had rewritten it into the movie version in which he was the action-adventure lead in a standoff with the cops.

�

The hostage negotiator was pulled back from a training course, and would arrive any moment. Donny Wakimoto, the hostage negotiator, was one of the little guys on the force. But he had a silver tongue and a golden throat, and last week had defused a nasty situation with a homeless couple barricaded with a knife behind a security fence. Wakimoto gave off waves of cool.

They watched Wakimoto get set up with the SWAT team communications officer in the incident command trailer. Since this had become a barricaded hostage situation, they had continued trying to jam both Logan's and Poppy's cell phones and the landlines in the house. But that wasn't proving to be quick or easy. In the meantime, they fed a throw phone over the balcony that would be the connection to Logan and Sinclair from the moment the lines were cut. For the moment they kept the line open between Logan and the hostage negotiator.

Logan was yammering that he had to show up for meetings on his new movies. They couldn't proceed without him. He had a contract.

"People depend on me to churn money for them," Logan howled. "You bozos don't know how this works."

The hostage negotiator was in the early phase of negotiations where he was making Logan feel he could have everything he wanted, that this could all work out somehow. The team wearing earbuds, exchanged grins and fist bumps.

🕭

Twice there were screams from the children with the sound of slaps and howls. Logan hollered he wanted toys and games brought from the children's rooms. The five-year-olds whined they were hungry.

"Why don't you let the children go, and we'll get them something to eat?"

"I thought you planned to starve me and my children," Poppy said with heavy sarcasm over the one phone line they kept open.

"No, no, no," Wakimoto said in his honeyed, calm voice. "Let me get something set up."

He turned to Vargas for orders. For a concession like this, they needed the targets to give something up. That was the way hostage negotiations worked.

"Let the children go, Ms. Sinclair."

"I want them to have lunch first," she insisted.

But the world was watching. The family had no breakfast. Were the thug police Nazis going to let little children go hungry? Vargas gave in and had sandwiches brought in for the family.

The grocery store sandwiches had crusts on them. The twins would only eat crunchy peanut butter sandwiches: this was creamy. Poppy gave an inelegant snort when she realized there wasn't even a dull kitchen knife to cut the crusts off. White bread. Mayo. She couldn't ask her children to eat this.

�£

Millions of viewers were now watching Logan and Sinclair on a live video feed coming from their bedroom. Poppy had dressed and was in full makeup. Derek wore jeans and a white polo sweater. The twins, hair combed, dressed in matching pajamas. Mr. and Mrs. America's sweethearts had gone live on some morning show and were rebroadcast everywhere. They were innocent of any crime. Held by unfeeling goons working for the Santa Monica Police Department. Terrified they were going to die. How could they have killed their nanny? They loved her. To the public, nanny sounded better than the maid who cleaned the toilets and hung out with the kids.

Two hundred thirty-seven thousand comments on the Facebook page Logan and Sinclair shared and they were still pouring in. Both Poppy and Logan answered questions about the police action taking place at their home. SMPD had rousted them out of their beds before dawn to harass them for no reason at all. They had cooperated with the police to capture the vile murderer who had killed their beloved nanny. And now look what had happened.

Public opinion, as judged from the trending twitter feeds and Facebook posts was solidly on the side of one of America's favorite couples.

Poppy's lovely face twisted in agony as she spoke: "Any mother's worst nightmare has become my reality. I am in fear for my life, and the lives of my husband and children, at the hands of the police."

Mason and Delgado looked at each other, hearing this. They were victims of police brutality, forgetting nobody in blue had laid a finger on either of them.

Logan nodded in the side of the shot. "We will obtain justice and recompense from the Santa Monica Police Department. You may be sure of that."

Tears sprang into Sinclair's eyes. "My children, my husband and I will need treatment to begin dealing with the physical and emotional trauma stemming from what is being done to us."

Mason gave a snort of disgust. He went outside to check on the search of the storage shed. The shed was the depository for the gardeners' equipment, the lawn and pool guy, and luxury toys the kids had discarded.

In an ideal world, he'd find the shovel used to dig the grave next door. This was not an ideal world. No bloody shovel or anything else he could tie to grave digging. In fact, no shovel at all. Proving there had been a shovel there in the first place was hardly something which would shore anything up in court.

He came back in the house to report and checked in with Vargas.

"Get them shut down," the Lieutenant screamed at the communications officers, completely losing it. The last link to the outside world had not been severed. A fuck up with the cell phone provider. Somebody's head was going to roll for this.

The feed from the bedrooms went black. Logan and Sinclair were off the air, and a cheer went up from the communications team. Logan could scream and yell all he wanted now. They were the only ones hearing him. The TV commentators went crazy speculating what this could mean.

Bad publicity for Santa Monica's image and tourist-destination commerce. Somebody would have to pay, and shit rolled downhill.

🦂

When his feed to the outside world was cut, Derek no longer had to pretend to be the loving husband and father. What he didn't realize was there was a tiny camera and transmitter in the box which had gone in with the sandwiches. Poppy and Derek came out loud and clear now on the headsets monitoring the mic. They no longer needed to depend on the robot mic outside on the landing, or strain to hear Logan screaming through the doors.

"Brats," Logan said, shoving the children into Poppy's bedroom. The twins had thrown the sandwiches on the floor.

"Crusts won't kill you," their mother barked, leaving the sandwiches where they lay. "You'll eat if you're hungry."

The phones were out. Derek was the only person to talk to. No TV. Poppy hated books, any kind of reading. She had her PA read lines to her, memorizing lines that way. Right now she'd even talk to one of the media vultures who would beat each other senseless for the chance to get an exclusive with Poppy Sinclair. She was always surrounded by people ready to smile at her and jump to anticipate any want she might have. Now she was alone with Derek.

Her appetite had fled. She thought of asking the good-looking detective who had a thing for her to send up another order of sandwiches without crusts, and then realized how that would play on social media. She had no doubt that somehow, somewhere, there was a live feed going out of the house straight to social media.

Could Nate Silverstein get her out of this? She had no doubt Nigel would turn on them. Would he tell the truth that Derek was the one who killed her? He couldn't possibly think she'd done it? Or did he? How could anyone believe she'd done it? It was an accident.

It would be worth more money to Bateson if he could turn on her too. Lupe would stay loyal. Could Nate represent both of them, or would he choose Derek? She'd met other criminal defense lawyers at parties, balding little Jews who had big reputations for getting stars off. She didn't have complete confidence in the Gloria Allred-like lawyer Nate had recommended for her.

As time wore on, they began to realize the police would wait them out. Maybe they had more power than they thought they had.

♫

Chapter Twenty-Eight

"Mason," Lieutenant Vargas said, swiveling to Mason.

"Yes, sir?"

"Get the arrest warrants."

"It's already started, sir."

Did the Lieutenant think he had been taking pizza orders and checking his Facebook page? Vargas was now in charge with his buddy, Incident Commander Harvey Roth, in the mobile command post overseeing the operation. Roth formerly headed SWAT, so he knew what he was doing, if Vargas didn't. The Deputy Chiefs were on their way back from Las Vegas.

The hostage negotiator needed to get Poppy to say Logan was holding a gun on her and the children and they were in imminent threat. That meant the team could risk busting in. The risk was casualties, and nobody wanted that.

Mason and Delgado's job was still to get the evidence that would jail the pair upstairs for a long, long time. He could see Delgado behind him, documenting everything.

❧

The Chief arrived, looking pale and moving slow. She

looked over the phone log and the running transcription of the dialogue between Logan and Wakimoto, reviewing the negotiator's talking points. She was under pressure too, harangued by the Chamber of Commerce and the mayor. Abruptly she sat down and put her head between her knees, creating a mild flurry. She pushed everyone away, then picked herself up and lurched out the door.

Fredericks sidled over to Mason. "The Lieutenant? Just watch. Vargas is gonna find a way to blame this on somebody else. Shit's gonna get real."

The Lieutenant dogged the hostage negotiator, walking around him in circles, giving him whispered instructions, knowing he shouldn't get in his way but not being able to stop himself. Mark Bratley, the interim SWAT commander, held whispered consultations with his men, keeping them alert and sharp.

Logan's lawyer was led in, huffing and puffing and threatening to blow the house down. Mason stood close enough to Nate Silverstein to smell fresh barbering and appreciate the fine weave of a suit that disguised the bulk of a well-fed body.

Vargas gave Silverstein the courtesy every member of the bar deserved as the attorney read the search warrant. He finally looked up at Vargas. Nate Silverstein was a senior partner with the Los Angeles law firm best known for representing high-end celebrity clients who had found themselves on the wrong side of the law: big names like Schwarzenegger, Bruce Willis, Sylvester Stallone, Demi Moore, Celine Dion, and Jim Carey. Silverstein was the go-to guy for pit-bull lawyering--his clients hired him to silence unwanted press and make accusations of unlawfulness disappear. The Fixer.

"Mr. Logan is free to come out of the upstairs area with his wife and the children," Vargas said. "No one is holding him against his will. But I will tell you we plan to arrest both of them when they appear."

A good litigator is an actor himself. Silverstein could switch from mild to terrifying in a moment according to the intel Fredericks had distributed when they were organizing the search.

"And what would the charges be?" Silverstein said. The lawyer gave an unperturbed smile gazing around the great room of the house. For him, this was another routine tragedy.

Vargas found a way to turn and answer an interruption from an officer but didn't answer. If the blood found in Talaveras' room turned out to be the blood of a dog, or somebody else, they were all screwed.

"The charges?" Silverstein repeated.

"Murder."

"I want to confer with my client privately," Silverstein said, looking toward the stairs. He set his expensive briefcase on the floor.

"That's not going to happen, Mr. Silverstein," Vargas said. "Unless Mr. Logan and his family come out willingly. And soon."

Silverstein didn't look surprised.

Mason looked to Wakimoto who was still, sitting with his eyes closed, staying calm. Logan started screeching again, and Silverstein lifted mild eyes to listen.

"Mr. Logan," Wakimoto said, "You're entirely in control here. There's nobody near the door. How about letting your children come out?"

"Then you use the batt batt battering ram and come in and kill me," Logan shouted. "I know how that works."

"Ah, c'mon, Mr. Logan. You only know it from the movies. In real life it's a lot different from that. We want to work with you. Look, your lawyer's here and he wants to talk to you too. You need to make arrangements if you want to let your movie project go through. He says you're on a deadline to commit. There's a big meeting today. They want you there. Like you say, a lot of people depend on you."

"I've been telling you that!"

"Derek, Derek, Derek," Silverstein said into the headset Vargas handed him. "We need to bring this thing down right now."

Derek screamed. "Nate, Nate? Is that you? They're gunna kill us. You you you gotta make this go away." And he didn't stop howling for two full minutes.

Mason did what he was supposed to be doing, but kept his eyes on the well-fed lawyer who backed away and mouthed, "I'm not going anywhere near Logan."

Vargas smiled.

"You got a direct line to Poppy? She listen to you?" Wakimoto asked Silverstein. He yanked the earbuds out of his ears and stood up, rotating his shoulders.

"Her lawyer's stuck in traffic on the 405. She's been chewing my ears off trying to get here." Silverstein searched his man purse and found a card he handed to Vargas. "How about giving her a police escort over the Sepulveda pass?"

Vargas snorted, then walked around in a circle.

"You think any of these studio people have any influence with Logan?" Wakimoto asked him. "Seems like he's running the show up there."

The lawyer tilted his head back and looked at the ceiling. "He likes control. That's how we keep a leash on him, letting him thinks he's directing everything."

"That's good to know," Wakimoto said. "So how's his relationship with his wife?"

"Look, they're actors. They go at each other.

Everybody knows that."

"Logan knows you're here. Think that'll get him out?" Vargas asked.

"Tell him there's talk of replacing him on his current project. If he cuts this short, there's still some room, but not if he drags this out. Tell him that."

"I will," Wakimoto said. He tucked the ears buds in again. "We might need you here. Can you hang tight? Maybe you could wait in your car?"

"Do you know how far away I had to park?" the lawyer said, eyes popping. "Do you know what it's like out there?"

"I got a pretty good idea, yeah."

Vargas led Silverstein to the room where Poppy had interviewed Mason on a day which now seemed so long ago.

♫

"You started the arrest warrants yet, Mason?" the Lieutenant asked again, jaws moving, the smell of cinnamon gum surrounding him. His jaws clenched and unclenched, tension showing in the veins on his neck which stood out like interstates on a map.

"Yes, sir. Half an hour ago."

Mason knew damn well whenever in doubt, *get a warrant.* There was no way either Logan or Poppy was going to walk out of here without being in cuffs.

"We think it's the victim's blood, but what if it isn't?" Mason said testing out his worst fear on the Lieutenant. "We've started the DNA match …" He stopped himself from adding that it will take time because he figured the Lieutenant would hit him.

"What have you got so far?"

"Way too much blood all over the walls and the floor,

bed covers are new. They're tearing up the carpet. The underlay is new, so are the floorboards. Fredericks is running down the company that did the work."

The Lieutenant turned away, muttering. "What kind of a cover story would you give to people who did work like that? Like how would you explain all the blood?"

"With their money, they could tell them the moon was made of provolone cheese, and they'd nod and yup and believe anything they said. No problem. Yup."

"Still, there's gotta be a trail. You looking at the gate between here and next door?" he said, tilting his head toward the property where the grave had been found.

"We are. If there's any blood trail, we'll find it," Mason said, hoping it was true. "We gotta get this contained," Mason said to himself.

♫

Chapter Twenty-Nine

On the average, domestic hostage situations were over in about an hour. This dragged out, fueled by the show taken online by Poppy's and Derek's iPad. Now the pair were limited to dialogue with the hostage negotiator. Or each other.

Lieutenant Vargas went back to push close to Wakimoto. "Anything new?"

Mason situated himself close enough to hear Wakimoto's response. "They're fighting. The kids' nagging is driving Logan crazy. Boy, if one of these Mama Bears heard what was going on up there, they'd tear the heads off those two."

"What are they arguing about?" Vargas asked.

"The kids want Megan."

Vargas paused to listen and then winced, including Mason in his look. "That's all we need."

Now Poppy was playing the good mother and celebrated social justice activist. The right kind of wrong publicity could exonerate the rich and powerful. The spin was the thing. People could be made to believe anything.

"We gotta get this contained," Mason said to himself because nobody else was listening.

♣

"What are we going to do, Derek?" Poppy said. "We're going to have to come out of here sooner or later."

Derek flung himself down on the bed, tossing the throw phone aside. The children were all over him, wanting to play. They never got this much alone time with Daddy.

He flung them off. Not gently. One of the twins got up and looked at him, his thumb in his mouth.

"You're not nice, Daddy."

"No shit."

"What are we going to do, Derek?" Poppy said again. She'd always been the one making big decisions. Then he had surprised her by going off to start a production company with all the toadies he'd collected to tell him he'd be a great director and producer. Her control over him had slipped. "We might be able to talk our way out of this. Nate's really good. Remember what he did with Stallone. Say we let them take us …"

"No. Soon as we're out of here, you're gonna lie and say I did it …"

She looked at him her mouth agape. "But you did, Derek. You killed her. I didn't."

"It was a mistake. I did not kill her. Besides Nate told me it was a no big deal. An accident. You didn't tell me he told you that, did you? You let me worry, didn't you? I had to find that out myself. Bitch."

"Yeah, well. But if it was an accident…" Poppy said. "That's what Nate said. Besides that, he told me he told you. You just can't remember anything."

"She killed herself. What if there's no proof I did it. Look how we cleaned everything up. Nigel said nobody would know."

Poppy stood up, facing him. Suddenly she ran for the bathroom. She said over her shoulder, "Nigel said he'd dig up the body so no one would find her."

"Fucking Nigel. He's gonna sell us out," Derek said to her through the bathroom door.

"Probably," Poppy said.

The toilet flushed. Poppy came rampaging back into the room and grabbed the throw phone that connected them to the hostage negotiator away from Logan. "I want to see my daughter," she screamed.

♃

Everybody went alert to a new demand.

"Sure, we can arrange that. I can understand that. You want to see your daughter," the hostage negotiator said reassuringly, looking around at Mason. "She's right here." Megan was outside in the incident command trailer.

"Tell her to come up here."

Like that was going to happen.

"Gee, she was right here. Now I don't see her. Why don't you come down with the twins? We can talk this out."

"No, you tell Megan to come up here. I'm not coming out. You'll kill us." She was interrupted by Logan bellowing something incomprehensible. Wakimoto waited out the screaming.

"I'll round Megan up for you," Wakimoto said.

"That little bitch," Derek screamed.

"I'll have to figure out where she went, Ms. Sinclair. Maybe she went to school. Why don't you send out the twins?"

Mason wondered if his suggestion Megan had gone to school sounded as ludicrous to her mother as it did to him. Was Poppy a captive or a participant? If she was a captive, they had exigent circumstances to justify busting in, a scenario nobody wanted to entertain.

Mason went to get a coffee outside and found Megan who sat, seemingly unconcerned, playing on her phone in an interview room in the incident command trailer. Maybe this kind of craziness was the usual in her life. Could that possibly be?

"Mind if I talk to her a minute?" he asked Vargas. "I've got a good rapport with her."

Vargas looked up from one of the many screens he was monitoring with the Incident Commander.

"She won't say a word. You can try."

Megan looked up as he came in, gave him an uninterested look, and went back to her phone opposite him at the long table, scratching at her arm. A spot of blood appeared through the flimsy black material.

"So you worried about your mother?"

"Not really." She looked up at him with a world of experience in young eyes.

"The twins? Your dad?"

"No."

"Why's that?"

"She can handle him. This will all blow over."

"How do you think that's going to happen?" Mason said, genuinely curious.

"It always does. I really don't care what happens to either of them. For once I'd like to get what I want."

"What's that?"

"What I wanted was to be an exchange student in Sweden to get away from all this, but they don't want to do it because it would be a real bother to be nice for a whole year to somebody my age. More work than photo opp benefit. So I'm stuck here."

Mason didn't know what to say to that. "Megan, we found a lot of blood in Celia's room. Somebody killed her. Somebody in this house." He held her eyes, but she looked away.

"I know, but it was an accident."

Mason didn't know what to do or say at this complacent statement. He sat there with his mouth hanging open. "What kind of accident? How do you know that?"

"I heard them talking a week or so ago. I thought Celia left with her boyfriend, but she didn't. She didn't leave me. All that time I spent hating her …" Her face held an expression of triumph.

"Why didn't you say something?"

"I didn't know until a week or so ago. Who's going to believe me? I'm a kid. They're famous. I've seen how they do things. They can ruin people and nobody sticks up for me."

"But somebody you apparently loved died … how do you feel about that?"

"How do you think I feel, cop?"

"Wait. Wait." He left the kitchen and called Vargas over. He wanted a witness.

But Megan Logan had gone back to silence. She grinned at Mason when he came in again with Vargas. Vargas left with a snort of disgust.

"He thinks I made that up," Mason said to her after Vargas left, pissed.

"Poor you. I need my medication." She rolled up the long sleeve on her right arm and showed the angry red eczematous outbreaks.

"I'll see what I can do," he said, wanting to add, "Don't hold your breath, kid."

☘

Chapter Thirty

Delgado found the home office on the ground floor in the back of the house. The sun pored through floor to ceiling windows looking out onto the dazzling sparkle of the swimming pool. The vast room grew hot in the morning sun. He spent some time looking for the air conditioning thermostat and couldn't find one, then realized this was probably a SMART house where the electronics controls were in the cabana by the pool. The sweat poured down his back. He flung off his bulletproof vest on the back of the chair he sank into. His and hers computers and desk set up for both Sinclair and Logan, and two more for their personal assistants. The rest of the house was filled with the buzz of detectives carrying out the search, SWAT team communications, and occasional shouted commands.

Delgado wasn't their best computer guy, but he could figure out basic stuff. He ran the directories on Logan's machine, noting the amount of disc space devoted to his Pictures files. He started on Logan's *Me* folder, ignoring the *Projects* and *Awards* folders, the next biggest files.

His phone vibrated on his belt. Another crisis with his mother-in-law. His wife's hurrying rush to say it all at once. The doctor had hospitalized the old lady, so her Medicare days would start all over again and pick up the bills at least. The old resentment against Maria's brothers and sisters not contributing filled Delgado's mind, and he almost missed it scrolling through the photos. There was a selfie of Logan standing behind Celia Talaveras, one hand over her shoulder casually near a breast. Maybe. Yes? No? Something between them?

"There's nothing I can do right now. You know that. Right? She's safe there in the hospital."

"How can you say that? The last time she got that infection," Maria said in protest.

"I gotta go," Delgado said. "I'll try hard to get out of here, but you know we got a serious situation going."

"I know. I saw it on TV. It's all over social media," Maria said. "You be safe."

"I'll meet you at the hospital when I can. Okay?"

Delgado didn't want to get into another conversation about her mother. Millions of words talking about the old lady already. Crisis after crisis. He found the printer and clicked off a copy of the money shot of Logan and Talaveras. There might be photos that were less ambiguous.

"Ha! Gotcha," he muttered to himself.

The quickest way back to gloat over the photo with Mason was around the back of the house. His mind shot from the photo to the old lady, to his retirement date, to his sixteen-year-old daughter's boyfriend. He spotted Mason across the sloping expanse of the lawn. Mason, Fredericks, and a patrol officer were searching the storage shed. The thought of his daughter's boyfriend shot all caution out of his head. The Harley. The loser boyfriend parked in his driveway.

�♪

Logan's hearing had always been acute. The faint slither

of the moving robot camera fed across the floor of the balcony outside his bedroom sent his outrage stratospheric. They were rushing him. At any moment they would burst in and kill them all.

"I hear that, you bastards." He flew to his AR-15, hefting it and stomping self-righteously to the balcony door.

"Derek, what the fuck are you doing?" Poppy said right behind him. She caught sight of the fat Latino cop crossing the yard as Derek swung the gun up and aimed. "Derek! Derek!"

She pulled at the gun, getting in the way of the snipers taking their shot.

The blast and the bloom of blood on the cop's back came simultaneously. The cop didn't spin around three times, clutch his chest, and fall to his knees as it happened in the movies. He didn't say anything, gasp in surprise, slap a hand over his wound. He just fell down in a heap.

Derek was so high he didn't seem to connect the rapid *bam bam bam* with anything he'd done. He lived in a world without consequences. He whirled heading back into the bedroom, leaving Poppy aghast, still clutching at him, screeching.

"I gotta piss."

"Derek, you shot a cop. You shot a cop."

🜨

Shots fired. Silence. Officer down.

Mason's heart stopped beating, waiting for a further burst of automatic fire.

Every officer present felt the grip of the "rescue the officer at all costs mentality." Nobody gets left behind. They trained for officer extraction situations, but everybody there knew, if it was *his* partner or his buddy, he'd ignore everything and go in risking his own life.

Communications stepped all over each other jamming transmissions. Wakimoto was talking fast to the Incident Commander. Vargas was pacing, deranged.

The snipers should have taken out the target immediately after the shot was fired and a fellow officer fallen. The force level went to lethal immediately with the officer down.

Why hadn't they fired?

"Who? Who's down? What happened?" Mason screamed.

Running like a man on fire, Mason approached a knot of officers outside the office area who tried to shove him back away from the hot zone. His heart fired at a rate that made him pant and sweat.

"What happened?" he said, his voice high. He tried to ram his way through them.

Somebody muttered his worst fear. "Delgado."

Rational thinking went out the window. "I'll go," Mason said. "Let me go."

He struggled against a wall of heavily armored cops.

"Get out of here, Mason. This is our job."

"He's my partner," Mason shouted.

That should have meant everything, but today it didn't. They elbowed him back, riot shields at hand, edging out the door.

Vargas charged in, arguing with SWAT commander Bratley about the best way to pull Delgado out. Precious seconds were ticking away with Vargas running his mouth. Bratley looked as though he wanted to run Vargas' nuts through a shredder.

Finally Bratley gripped Vargas' shoulder and shoved him away.

No time for a debate on a risk benefit of a successful

extraction. Act. Now.

Bratley burst through the door onto the patio under the balcony overhang.

ঔ

Derek hadn't meant to shoot the cop, like he hadn't meant to scare Celia Talaveras into killing herself. It was all a terrible mistake. He convinced himself Poppy had grabbed the gun and made it go off. She was the one who made him shoot the cop. Her grabbing at him.

Nobody would understand that, though. Nate believed him that the maid's death had been an accident. But he was paid to believe him. Would anybody else? Would a jury, if it ever came to that? Nate tried to convince him burying the girl next door wasn't really serious. He faintly recalled Silverstein had emphasized that, but he couldn't remember all the details. Information just seemed to drift out his ears these days. The lawyer had a strategy all worked out if it came to the police actually charging him.

The publicity risk scared Derek. No way he would come out of this looking good. Once they started digging around in the maid's room they'd find something. They always did. He'd chatted up the cop advisor they had on *End Notes*. His fingerprints were in her room, her bathroom. Cops could pull DNA out of the air nowadays.

He needed to think. If he could get away from all this commotion with Poppy and the twins, he could think, find some way of making himself look good. He just needed to think. He held the AR-15 close.

Adrenaline and paranoia flared up like a match tossed onto rocket fuel. A slick of redness pooled beneath a heavy body lying on the lawn in a yellow shirt and brown pants. He couldn't see the cops, but he knew they were there. They'd kill him if they had a chance. Now they had an excuse.

Some guy named Wakimoto who he'd been talking to kept asking if everybody was alright. Of course, they were alright. He didn't intend to hurt anybody. He came out of the bathroom.

Poppy was still screaming in his face, "You shot a cop."

Derek wasn't listening. He was replaying his last movie in his head.

He considered himself impervious, bulletproof, invincible. Look who he was. The fans love me. I was the highest paid action star last year.

Poppy was screaming at him about turning himself in. He put his fingers in his ears dancing up and down saying la, la, la, la like one of the kids. He saw she was afraid of him. It empowered him. Good. The bitch.

"You made me shoot him. The cop," he said, clarifying it for her.

She just stared at him.

"Look, we can still tell them what happened that night … it was an accident like you said," he said, cradling the AR-15 against him. It felt good.

"Are you crazy?" his wife said. She grabbed a handful of tissues and swabbed at her nose.

"Why are you always saying I'm crazy? I'm no crazier than you are."

The twins jumped up and down shrieking *crazy, crazy, crazy*, racing from one end of the room to another, the room which over the last hours had shrunk from being palatial comfort to a lushly carpeted dungeon. The gunshot had excited them. One of the twins jumped on his back and he flung her off with a curse.

He considered his wife, the beautiful Poppy Sinclair. She didn't look so good right now. Her skin had gone gray, her hair bedraggled, and her bitch face wore the nasty frown which pinched her eyebrows together. Her eyes were set too close together, he thought for the five hundredth time. He'd never cast her in the play he knew would make him a Broadway hit. The twins kept trying to climb on her and jump off the bed into an armchair and roll on the floor.

"Get off me, you animals," Poppy screeched, wriggling out of their sticky grasp. They wouldn't eat the sandwiches, so she dug out a gift box of Belgian chocolates and fed the chocolates to them. Probably not a good idea, but it shut them up for a while. She shoved them into her room adjoining and locked the connecting door. They screamed and kicked the door.

"We have to do something," his wife said, casting a glance at the AR-15 he still held. The door of the gun safe was open too, each of its compartments filled with the arsenal Derek collected over the years. The guns made him feel safe. He could protect his family.

"How long do you think we can hold out here before they bust in and kill us all?" Poppy asked. He gazed at her with what he thought was his thousand-yard stare, keeping her at the wrong end of the binoculars, far away, small and insignificant.

Darkness was slowly painting in shadows around the cabana, the lawns. The water in the pool merged from turquoise into indigo. Once darkness fell it would still be a mess, but a different mess. He looked across the canyon to Pacific Palisades.

Legend was that law enforcement was relentless if you shot one of them. Until they'd cut off his phone, Derek had been assured he had nothing to fear if this ended well. But it wasn't going to end well. Not now. Shooting the cop was an accident. It was the drugs. It was

Poppy. Not him.

Chapter Thirty-One

Mason watched, helpless, as the ambulance screamed into the driveway and the paramedics pounded through the house. Delgado made it onto the lawn near the edge of the swimming pool before he fell. The snipers were ready if Logan showed a square inch of flesh. Everything in the house had gone quiet. A knot of officers collected at the back of the office. The plan was now operational. Bratley had shoved Vargas aside and there would be trouble about that.

Wielding a shield, Bratley scissored across the patio stones in a crouch, two other SWAT operators on his flanks. He shouldered Delgado in a fireman's carry and headed back for cover under the balcony overhang.

Mason waited for weapon fire from the balcony, holding his breath. Nothing.

The paramedics had Delgado up on the gurney in a quick practiced movement, bag on his face within seconds, compression on the exit wound on his chest.

When it finally sank in, Mason felt the chill descend from his brain to the soles of his feet. Maria and the kids. Elena, his goddaughter. The years he and Delgado had put in together, the laughs, the stories. The goofs. The Steely Dan concerts. Springsteen. Before Delgado got sober and then afterward. Delgado could not die. He'd come too far.

People needed him.

✦

Poppy shut herself down, going into her room, letting the twins crawl over her. She endured it for a moment, then dug around in her bedside table for her happy pills. Maybe a low dose of Ambien would be okay for them. Who would blame her? The twins would put anything in their mouths she gave them. It didn't take long for them to quiet down. She went into Derek's bedroom and looked at him. He lay on his bed, fondling his gun.

She regarded her husband, a man she'd lived with for sixteen years. Derek's bedroom still looked like a glossy hotel brochure. Rooms staged by a set designer, Derek Logan, her romantic lead, dark, well-built, handsome, his hair cut expensively, his body well-maintained by other people, and except for his histrionic streak, as empty as she was.

She saw both of them reflected in one of the multitude of mirrors everywhere in the house. They were models playing a couple. She stared at her husband, whose eyes seemed to be whirling like pinwheels in his head.

✦

Derek's mind expanded at the rate the universe was expanding. He'd seen that line somewhere. His IQ soared into the limitless, uncontained. The low buzz of police activity in his house, the drone hovering over the windows, the helicopter whapping overhead became quiet and distant. He saw Poppy. The twins beating on the locked door were at the edge of his hearing, somewhere else. Celia Talaveras receded at the speed of light.

Yes, the police might be closing in on him. He knew

that. Poppy would snap like balsa wood. The bitch would babble everything she knew. He enjoyed the rushes of adrenaline on cocaine which made him want to start punching. Until now. Now he needed solitude.

The drugs, the lovely drugs, were running out.

The drugs had drained his sex drive, but he still talked a good game. He still hit up the interns and behind-the-camera crew because it was expected of him, but he'd been surprised to notice he didn't even have the energy to beat off lately. He couldn't face another failed rehab. Another diet. Another painful cosmetic procedure.

He knew Poppy would turn on him like a spitting cobra when – and he knew it was when, not if – the police burst in on them. The cop advisor on *Bitter End* had told him everything the writers got wrong in the script. Trouble was, he couldn't remember anything now. He fumbled through his mind, trying to remember. He could only recall the negotiator would lie and lie and lie to him. Wakimoto seemed like such a nice guy, had kids. He knew how stressful kids could be. Big fan too. Knew all his movies. Wanted to have a beer with him when this was all over. Promised him if he let the kids go, it would count in his favor.

Maybe the guy could make Celia Talaveras go away as well.

An idea came to him. He saw a square on the ceiling of the room and thought of the attic above. He'd noted the attic access square once before when he was lying on his back on Poppy's bed after one of their rare fuck sessions.

With a jolt of soaring optimism, Logan knocked a lamp off the nightstand to the right of Poppy's bed. With effort, he clambered on top of a chest of drawers, hauling the heavy cabinet with him.

Poppy and the twins watched him. "What are you

doing, Derek," Poppy said with a hiss of impatience.

Logan vaulted on top of the chest of drawers. He was still a couple of feet short of being able to reach the access entry to the attic. He upended a wastebasket and set that on top of the nightstand. It teetered.

"I hope you fall and break your neck," Poppy said, her arms crossed, watching him.

With both hands, Logan reached up and pushed the square of light wood upward. Using every bit of strength he possessed he hauled himself up into the attic. It was hot and dusty and quiet. Blessedly quiet.

♩

As soon as Derek got himself into the attic, he heard Poppy pounding on the bedroom door. She snatched up the throw phone Derek had been talking to the police on.

"Hey, you out there. Mason? Mason, I want to talk to you."

Derek went down on his knees and hollered into the square open space below. The twins looked up at him.

"Daddy? Daddy?"

"Poppy, you bastard bitch. You lying cunt. I'm coming down there."

Holding the phone, Poppy returned to stand below him, looking up, her face flat and fixed. Then she grinned. She flung the wastebasket away, then shoved the heavy nightstand off the chest of drawers onto the floor where it landed with a crash. It registered slowly on Derek. He could almost believe he could jump down, spring off the chest of drawers, drag her by the hair into the bathroom and drown her in the marble sink. But not quite.

He hesitated.

♩

Mason followed the gurney which held the gray-faced Delgado through the kitchen to the front of the house.

One EMT muttered to the other, "He's goin' zero on us."

Vargas was still running his mouth, but nobody was listening.

Poppy was banging on the door of the master suite with her fists. The twins were screaming. "Hey, cops. Get me that guy, Mason."

Everyone turned to look at Mason, their attention divided by Delgado's taking a bullet and the new demand from the suspect. The guy's partner went to the hospital when his partner got shot. The partner went with the ambulance to start *The Wai*t. The ER filled, the family poured in, the ER nurses started pushing and shoving. Too many people. In four to seven minutes the wounded cop was in surgery: at least in the big Santa Monica hospitals. And then *The Wait* began. That was the way it was supposed to go.

Lieutenant Vargas grabbed Mason by the shoulder as he raced past the knot of officers gathered around Wakimoto.

"Wait," he said. "Where you goin'?"

Mason looked at him, bewildered. "The hospital. Delgado."

"She's asking for you," Vargas said.

"Who?" Had Maria heard about this already? He had to get there. The ambulance was already screaming away.

"Sinclair." Vargas looked at him as if he'd gone stupid. Too many things all at once. His father. Delgado. The Lieutenant's voice was dim over the beat of his heart.

Vargas handed him a headset. "She wants to talk to you."

"Who?"

"Sinclair."

"Ah, shit. What about Logan?" he said.

Wakimoto touched Vargas on the shoulder. He turned with a grimace.

"What?"

"She says he's gone," Wakimoto said.

"Gone? Where?" Vargas howled. "Where the fuck's he gone?"

Mason turned away to breathe. Breathe. Get himself under control. The only sign the hostage negotiator was under any sign of pressure was an unruly cowlick which stuck up at the back of his head. Wakimoto concentrated on the feed from Poppy Sinclair.

The calm tone of the hostage negotiator. "Ms. Sinclair? Where is your husband? We have an officer down. Give me one good reason why we shouldn't end this thing right now. If we do that, you won't like it."

"We're fine. Derek shot him. Not me. I had nothing to do with that. It wasn't me. I want to talk to that Mason guy. I don't trust any of you. Derek's up in the attic. We're safe now. Let's get this thing over."

The Incident Commander, Vargas, and Wakimoto consulted. The news Logan was in the attic and could be on the move flashed across SWAT communications.

They would have to make a hard entry into the attic space.

Mason's attention span was three seconds long. His head was pierced by a sudden brain- tumor headache so bad his vision blurred. He thought of Delgado, then his mind bounced like a ping pong ball to his father, back to Sinclair.

"Talk to her. Talk to her," Vargas said to Mason, making circles in the air with his hands.

Mason looked to Wakimoto for help. Training

insisted hostages should only talk to the negotiator. Mason ripped the headset away from his ears. He muttered in an aside to Wakimoto.

"What do I say to her? I should be…the hospital … Delgado …" he said.

"You can't do a damn thing for Delgado," Vargas said stepping over him. "Talk to her."

"Ms. Sinclair, it's Detective Mason."

"Where are you? I can't deal with those people. I want you to guarantee if I let my children out of this place, you won't shoot them."

Mason looked to Wakimoto, ignoring Vargas who was pacing in a circle, jamming his earbuds deeper into his ears.

Wakimoto nodded. "Say yes."

"I can guarantee you that. You and your husband are another matter, though."

"I know. I know. I'm not stupid. Derek shot the cop, not me. He killed Celia. I had nothing to do with it. He killed her." She said with the assurance she'd said he was being framed and completely innocent not hours before.

Wakimoto's voice came into Mason's ears on another frequency. His brown eyes held Mason's own with urgency, communicating. "Tell her to let the children go."

"You say he's up in the attic. Is that right?" Mason said, hoping his voice would sound authoritative.

"Yes. Yes. He's gone crazy. You must know that."

"Does he have other weapons?"

"I don't think there's anything up there. He went up through that little thingy in the ceiling. I want out of here."

Wakimoto held up his hands in a stop position facing Mason.

The white bedroom door which had been shut all morning opened. An AR-15 flew onto the carpeted hall floor. The door was slammed shut.

"Thanks, Ms. Sinclair. You're doing the right thing," Mason said.

"Tell her to let the kids out one at a time," Vargas said.

The door opened and both kids were shoved out into the hall, bewildered and scared, and half asleep. SWAT operators grabbed them and hustled away, the kids screaming.

"Follows orders, doesn't she?" Wakimoto said.

"Let her wait a bit …" Vargas said, dancing in one spot, his jaws champing the cinnamon gum.

"Ms. Sinclair?" Wakimoto said.

"What? Don't shoot me. I want to see Detective Mason."

"What the fuck's with you and her?" Vargas demanded.

Mason shrugged, which made his brain tumor headache even worse. "She thinks we got something going. We don't. It's all in my reports. Logan called me too. They're gaming me for insurance. That's what I think."

Vargas' skepticism spoke of contempt for Mason's opinion. "Don't think, Mason. You're no good at thinking." He danced away, talking to his buddy the Incident Commander.

A few minutes passed, cooking the silence from the upper floor. SWAT operators lined up on both sides of the door, ready to snatch her.

A commotion took place as the front door opened. Though the shielded from view, a wave of hysteria went up from the media.

"We don't want anybody else getting hurt, Ms. Sinclair. Open the door and come out slowly with your hands up. Slowly. Let's not rush this and get anybody hurt," Mason said.

He held his breath.

Poppy Sinclair opened the door and found herself confronting hard-faced tactical officers in full body armor; assault rifles pointed in her face.

"Oh, for heaven's sake," Sinclair said coolly, waving her hand in the air as though dispelling a bad smell. "That's not necessary."

"Both hands up," one of them screamed. "Both hands."

"Cuff her. Get her down here," Vargas screamed.

"Here's my hands. Are you happy now? Is this really necessary? You look ridiculous."

When she had been secured, Mason came out into an area of the great room where he could see what was going on. In every other barricaded hostage situation he'd been involved in people came out shattered, in pieces. Traumatized. He and the hostage negotiator looked at each other.

"Where is Detective Mason?" she said, looking around for him. Mason kept himself out of sight.

The tactical operators swept into the room to clear it, as soon as Sinclair was escorted away, Everybody held their breath, waiting for gunfire. Hands cuffed behind her, SWAT officers marched Poppy Sinclair down the stairs.

Vargas bolted a half a can of Red Bull, rubbed his acne-scarred face, and strutted over to scream at Poppy. "Where is your husband?"

She gave him a look of complete disinterest, glancing around her living room.

"He's not here," one of the tactical squad hollered over the stairs. "We've got an opening into the attic."

"Then where the fuck is he?" the Lieutenant

screamed. "You," he said, turning to Mason. "Stay away from her."

"What's Logan doing?" Vargas demanded of Wakimoto.

Wakimoto didn't answer. How the fuck was he to know?

Mason was on the phone checking on Delgado. He knew damn well there would be nothing to say this early. Derek had gone silent. The media was clamoring for comment, some explanation of shots fired,the ambulance arriving and then leaving, the siren screaming.

✦

Chapter Thirty-Two

If Poppy had ever been held at gunpoint by her supposedly crazy husband, the Oscar-winning actress didn't look it. She was perfectly turned out, in filmy white from head to toe. The right shoes. Exquisite earrings. She pretended the handcuffs and search of her person was not happening, holding her head high. They thumped her down into a chair in the crowded area under the stairs. She looked around, peeved.

"You have destroyed my home. It better be put back exactly the way it was when you got here. We have videos. Look what your big boots have done to my floors. These handcuffs are too tight. My shoulders hurt," she complained, twisting to look at Mason for sympathy. He turned his back on her, on hold with the ER. A nurse there might talk to him.

"That's all I'm going to say to you without my lawyer. None of this is my fault." Assured self-righteousness lit Poppy Sinclair's countenance. "My poor husband is the victim of a vicious plot. He is innocent of any crime. You're trying to frame us."

How many times had he heard this one? Mason, long used to being lied to by the best, almost believed her. That's how good she was. But if she thought he had some influence here, she was wrong.

"Where's your husband?" the Lieutenant shouted in her face.

Poppy reared her head back with a disdainful expression. "Don't scream at me. I told you. He was holding us against my will. I knew if I tried to get away he would kill us all. I want to see Megan. Where's Jake? What is he being told about this?"

She held her dignity even with her hands cuffed behind her back. "And where are you taking my children? Lupe goes with them. Or have you arrested her too? Ugly brutes."

"Lady, you don't seem to realize how much trouble you're in," Vargas said in a quieter tone. He could hear the SWAT operators tearing up walls and floorboards above.

Poppy drew herself up. "Do you think I'm stupid?"

"Where's your husband?"

"Where is my lawyer? I'm not saying anything else until I talk to her. If I can't see my children, you can lock me up right now."

It was a great line. A pity there wasn't a more appreciative audience. Mason grinned, knowing sooner or later a Barbara Stanwyck line like that would make it into social media. Even though everybody present had been ordered not to take cell phone photos, the temptation would be too great. Cops were only human.

Mason could have sworn she winked at him as she passed him, head held high. He felt like bursting into applause. Almost.

Mason, held back from the hospital against his will, watched Vargas. He was getting instructions from the Incident Commander.

"You got Logan? Where is he?" Vargas screamed at

Bratley, the SWAT Commander.

"You mean he got away?"

"We don't know that either," Bradley said.

"You stay put, Mason. I might need you."

"Look, we haven't found him yet," Bratley said. "We will. He's gotta be on the property."

"Get him. Or I will get you."

Everything went into high gear after Poppy Sinclair was led through a highly-modified perp walk to the windowless van outside taking her to the station. She tossed her head and lifted her chin. If she'd been visible, it would have created a paparazzi riot as soon as they spotted her on San Vicente Boulevard.

The team had entered the rooms Logan and Sinclair had occupied. It was almost familiar from the videos Mason had seen online earlier in the day. The furnishings were luxury on a scale he had seldom encountered. Sure, he'd got his share of processing crime scenes in big houses in Santa Monica in his days working property crime. But this was another level up. No time to run his eye over things and imagine what it would be like living here. If he released his mind from its steely grip, it went immediately to Delgado, and then home to his father. He made himself a stone statue. Hard and cold. Stone.

Even though Sinclair had said Derek had gone up in the attic, nobody trusted her. No Derek Logan in either of the bedrooms or anywhere on the upper floor. Mason watched them ripping up floorboards. He wasn't in the bedrooms Megan, or Jake, or the twins occupied, or the twins' playrooms. He wasn't downstairs or the canine would have found him long before now.

Vargas pointed a finger at Mason, then jerked it down. If Mason had been a dog, this would be a "sit" command.

"I know he's here. He's here. He's gotta be here." He ran both hands through his hair.

"Sir, we've been over every inch of the house," one of the SWAT operators said to him, trying to calm him down. "We practically demolished the bedrooms upstairs looking for him. You can see that for yourself. He's not there. We're taking the attic now. Give us five."

Delgado's wife called Mason. Maria was stuck in traffic at Topanga Canyon on the 101 Freeway. "Dave, Dave? How bad is it? Are you at the hospital? They won't tell me anything."

Mason felt plugged in, talking to Maria, less distant from Delgado. But she didn't know anything about his condition either.

"I'm still at the scene. The LT wants this all tied up before he'll let me go."

"Dave, I counted on you being there. Ernesto, he works in Anaheim, and he's trying to get there. The traffic," she moaned. "I had to leave my mother with Graciela and she's only a teenager. If anything goes wrong at the hospital …"

At the best of times nowadays, Maria looked like she'd spent the night in a bus station, harried and worn. He remembered when Maria was plump and sweet as a candied yam. Now he could picture her jackrabbiting in stalled traffic to insert herself in the smallest opening to get to the hospital quicker.

"Dave, is he gonna die? I can't stand this. I can't do it without him."

Mason was feeling like that himself. Delgado was his rock. The prospect of losing Ginger, however, would still be worse. Everything was spinning away from him.

Then everything went silent as the tactical operation breached the attic. He could hear them giving commands on entry, the dog barking.

"Maria, I gotta go. I have to. I'll be there as quick as I can. You know that."

Mason ran up the attic stairs, right behind Vargas after the scene was secured.

The attic was unfinished, the house built only five years ago. There were two racks of suits and dresses in plastic sleeves, rows of transparent containers stuffed with Hollywood career memorabilia the officers pawed through. A row of suits and dresses hung on a rack were piled on the floor. They had even pulled up the pink insulation rolls filling the area between the joists to look underneath, and gone over the flooring with heat-detecting radar.

"He's not here in the attic," a wiry young female officer said after a half-hour. "He can't be here."

The attic occupied a space at the front of the house which faced the street. The back half of the third floor hosted an upstairs patio, a deck facing the lawns and the spectacular view of Pacific Palisades. Gas heaters. A swing set for the children. The Jacuzzi where Poppy's girlfriend had drowned. Conversational groupings of white wicker and pastel chintz covers. A seascape mural on the outside wall.

Nowhere to hide.

Mason walked to the edge of the roof looking down. At least thirty feet off the ground. Logan couldn't have rappelled down. Had he flown off into the trees? Did he have an accomplice who spirited him away? It wasn't inconceivable.

"There's been somebody out here watching on the deck the whole time?" he asked one of the operators.

"Of course."

Mason felt like putting his fist through a wall. He

knew it with certainty there would be no news of Delgado's condition yet—unless he'd died on the operating table. He needed to be there. For Maria. For the kids. He'd watched all of them growing up, was godfather to Elena. Would the girl be able to manage her grandmother with Alzheimer's if the old lady got combative?

It was as though Vargas knew what he was thinking.

"I want you here, Mason. Nobody leaves until we get Logan."

It violated every cop norm for Vargas to keep him here at this point. He was being an ugly son of a bitch because he could. Maria's phone was busy every time he tried. His ER nurse buddy was off today, and he was put on hold.

Vargas went storming back down the attic stairs. Mason heard the elevator grumbling. The doors slid open to reveal a uniformed officer.

"You hear anything yet about your partner?"

"Not yet," Mason said.

"That's hard. Logan's gotta be here," he said looking around.

Mason looked around too. "Yeah?"

"He's gotta be here. We've had guys up there since the beginning of this thing. Nobody saw him. Guys up here on this deck too. Hey, heard you had something going with Sinclair? That true, sir?"

Mason gave him an ugly stare. "What do you think, asshole? No. She's using me. That's all."

Mason watched as another team went over every square inch of the attic space again. He couldn't stand still. One more time he lifted the light wood covers which topped the exterior columns flanking the entryway on the front of the house. Four hollow columns jutted up above the floor in the attic. He'd already looked to see if Logan was hanging from the lip of the hollow columns. He wasn't. That was his last idea.

"Where could he have gone then?" Mason thought of the wisteria vines and the balcony. Heavy, mauve blooms clustered thickly, dropping blossoms onto the patio below where Delgado had collapsed.

"Off the balcony?" the uniform said.

"He couldn't have." He could see one guy's attention being distracted for the length of time it would take Logan to get down and across the lawn, but not two. Two snipers at the back of the house secluded behind the cabana with a good view of the back of the house couldn't have missed him. He would be spotted if he'd gone off the front of the house.

"He's gotta be here then," the officer said.

The elevator doors to the third floor slid open to reveal Lieutenant Vargas again.

"Nobody here, sir." Twisting his headset off, the young officer looked at Vargas' wild-eyed face and tried a joke. "Not even a mouse."

Vargas snorted. "Fucking drone guy should have spotted him." His mouth worked as if he were chewing on a tough piece of steak. He had control of his voice, but his eyes were very bright.

Somebody else's fault. That figured. Mason wished somebody would lead the LT away by the hand to supervise the school crossing guards.

If Logan had gotten off the property, he could be anywhere now. But with that well-known face, somebody would have spotted him. But would his rescuer want to be in the movie too? A rescuer could get millions for a story about rescuing and hiding Derek Logan. It would be a manhunt to equal running OJ Simpson down.

Chapter Thirty-Three

Logan hadn't been heard from in three hours and twenty-seven minutes. The search continued but slowed down because there was no place left to look. They had run out of ideas, unless they took up all the floors and pulled the siding off the house. They'd been over everything with the heat-detecting radar and the police dog. Even the cars in the underground four-car parking garage. Nothing.

Vargas had made some bad decisions and showed poor leadership under stress. Everybody had seen him lose his cool, take over an operation that was being handled well, and make a mess of it. More competent officers kept him from the worst consequences of his actions. He could limp along in the struggle to regain whatever reputation he'd once had, but his colleagues would now watch him like wolves, and eventually, he'd be forced aside for the good of the pack.

Mason went outside to get a breath of air which didn't smell like cops. He thumped down hard on the stairs outside the front door, outside the view of the media swarm. He tried calling Ginger. No answer. Had she heard? A call from his father. He couldn't sort through his mixed feelings about him right now. A witness on another case had left a message. The looky-loos and media were out down the street, news helicopters whap whap whapping overhead.

He slumped forward, his head in his hands, still on hold with the ER. Vargas was keeping him there on the chance Sinclair might be willing to talk. So far that hadn't happened. She was waiting for her lawyer. Smart.

Mason was the one who'd put together the case on Logan, then walked away from Logan's mansion without Logan. He imagined a bleak future in which his boss and everybody else on the line would be looking at him too. There was always a chance he could get a job as a security guard at one of the nearby construction sites. His dream of flying lessons and a plane had taken wing. It was the only future he could imagine after he retired from being a cop in which he could be happy.

He leaned against the column fronting the mansion, his aching head in his hands, hearing something, still on hold with the ER. A moan. A scratching.

"Help. Jesus…"

His head swiveled around. He put the phone down.

"What the hell?" Mason stood up from the stairs looking around at the wide steps leading to the entrance of the house. Two four-foot tall stone jars flanked the huge front door. Tall enough for Logan to squeeze into. He leaped to his feet and looked inside the narrow opening of the big amphoras. Nobody could insert themselves through that.

The moaning continued. Mason ran up and down on the six-foot-wide staircase leading into the emerald lawns. Nothing other than the two amphoras in front of the house.

Then he saw it.

Four columns which ran from the lip of concrete in front of the house into the attic. He'd looked down into them from above and seen nothing. He banged on the nearest column, and there was a faint tapping returned.

"It can't be Logan," he said. He hit the column hard with his fist.

But it was.

Logan had dropped down the entire thirty feet from the attic where the narrow columns ended.

The columns were hollow but made of unfinished wood with an exterior stucco facing.

"Mr. Logan?" Mason said, gouging a hole with his Swiss Army knife and peering down into the hollow. He saw a lot of blood, hair, and a naked shoulder.

"That you?" He suppressed a giggle of triumph and nervousness.

A long time before an answer came.

"Fuck you, cop. Get me out of here."

"You okay?" Mason said again, grinning for all he was worth.

"I'm dying."

"How could you be dying, Mr. Logan, when we're having this very interesting conversation?"

He radioed Vargas. SWAT brought in a pry bar. One hard bang made a hole about six feet off the ground.

Vargas was suddenly there, chittering with anxiety. Vargas had his look. Five firefighters replaced him to peer into the column. Much discussion followed on how to get Logan out as soon as possible. With a combination of drilling and demolition equipment, the fire guys excavated an opening. Gradually and very carefully, they enlarged it.

A firefighter peered over Mason's shoulder, shining a light downward. "Man, how'd he even get in there?"

One firefighter started to laugh, and then another.

The situation was not without its humor, and Mason could imagine the stories which would be told when this was all over. Would being the butt of a joke like this on social media bother Logan?

✿

Social media was not the worst of Logan's problems. Clinging to the lip of the hollow column, eventually, he had to let go. Not only had he broken a heel, his left tibia and hip, inflicted major lacerations and contusions on the rest of himself, he had scraped the flesh off his face leaving plastic surgeons little to work with. The square chin could be rebuilt but skin taken from his flanks to rebuild his face didn't match.

He had also shot a cop who was trembling on the brink of death.

✿

An hour after the scene cleared, Vargas released Mason. Mason burst through the doors of the waiting room at the hospital to find it full of uniforms, off duty cops, and Delgado's extended family and many friends. The TV was tuned to the wind-up coverage of the Sinclair-Logan standoff. Maria saw him and pushed her way toward him.

"You finally got here," she said, collapsing in his arms and a fresh flood of tears.

"Is he okay? Is he okay? What do you know?"

She tilted back to look up at him. "They don't know yet."

✿

Mason dragged himself up the stairs of his condo as the shadows fled and dawn was breaking. The Ken and Barbie fitness buffs who lived across the hall from him emerged in cool workout clothes to start their day by running up and down the three hundred stairs which linked up the

Adelaide, the last street overlooking Rustic Canyon's floor. He'd spent all night at the hospital in the waiting room with a bunch of glum cops and Delgado's large family. Time would tell if Delgado would be okay.

The last twenty-four hours had passed in a blaze, the tense minutes longer than the hours. The adrenaline crash came midway through the night. He fell into a sleep state like a light being turned off. From there he descended into dream sparkles of his father in flash frames, Delgado at the Friday night barbeques in his backyard. Poppy snarling at him as she was led away.

Court for his father? A trial? Nobody knew at this point. Mason would withdraw money to pay the lawyer from his pension fund. Of course, his parents wanted to pay him back. His mother said she would see if the school district would hire her full time. His father would apply at Ace Hardware. It was too soon to tell whether he'd ever get hired anywhere again. There was talk of them moving out to Santa Monica to be closer to their son and only granddaughter. Right now, Mason didn't even want to look at his father.

Neither did his mother apparently. She had moved into her sister's basement back in Grand Rapids.

The strain he remembered in his parent's faces made him want to fold up and bury his face in Ginger's neck, sleep for a week, and make time stop.

He wanted to go back to the way it was. His dad had never been his hero. He was gone too much for that. George Mason was the big joker around the neighborhood, fixed everybody's lawnmowers, and had a compliment for all the pretty girls. He had been blind.

Nothing was ever going to be the way it was again. It had never been the way he persuaded himself it was.

For him or for Derek Logan. Logan's dream of a

Broadway hit, in which he was recognized as a serious actor, was over too.

Too bad. So sad.

꩜

That was only the beginning of the beginning of the end. Ahead lay the reams of paperwork and reports to assemble to take the case to court. The DA's office was still deciding on whether to prosecute a death that could be labeled homicide or accidental. Prosecution on shooting a cop was a certainty, though. Logan was in the hospital and would be there for a considerable period of time, shackled to a cot. Resources spent protecting the actor from fans cost the department heavily, and there was no enthusiasm for keeping a guy safe who had shot one of their own.

Justice was a squishy concept. Cops got sick of seeing people they'd booked in the morning waving at them from the streets that night. Especially in California. Taking cases to the District Attorney's office that were declined because they weren't a sure conviction.

But Logan's case was different. Was it an accident? Or not? Bateson kept the bicycle hook which had embedded itself in Celia Talaveras' eye socket but, out of context, it meant little. The cause of death was a metal object through the eye socket into the brain. That was obvious, but was it this metal object? The pathologist quibbled. The lawyers haggled it one way, then another. It might be a long time before the case went to trial. Shooting Delgado would move it along, though. Logan wasn't going anywhere soon.

Mason got Nigel Bateson in an interview room days later, along with his lawyer, a thick-necked bodybuilder. He couldn't charge him as an accomplice in a felony because concealing an accidental death wasn't a felony.

Conspiracy to commit a misdemeanor? Aiding and Abetting? Bateson didn't seem worried, wearing smugness like a new Armani. He denied any involvement but claimed that Logan had told him about it. Logan had told him where to find the bicycle hook.

"Because he was so eaten up with guilt and remorse, I suppose," Mason said.

"Something like that," Bateson said stone-faced.

"And Logan told you where he put the shovel? Right?"

"Right."

"You're a lying piece of shit, Bateson. Poppy and Derek say you were in this up to your ears."

"And your proof?" Bateson looked at his expensive watch and then at his lawyer. He rose with a grin. Mason put his hands flat on the desk.

"Hey, what was it like working for them?" Mason said, plain curiosity getting the better of him.

Bateson remained standing, a different expression on his face. "The money for one. And there was no hassle getting paid. They were fun to watch."

"Fun?"

"Yeah. You're a normal person and they're so far beyond normal, you get to see crazy up real close, but you're not going to get hurt. Right? Both of them, their heads are so far up their asses, they can't see daylight. It was a laugh."

"A laugh?" A sense of humor was the last thing he expected from Bateson.

"The press won't hurt me either. I can use the business."

"Your billings tripled four months ago," Mason said, not willing to let him go without something after an hour's sparring. "What was that for?"

"I needed to be on-site. I live in the same house as those two goofballs, I'm going to get paid for it. Like I said, it was a laugh."

Mason snorted, a dry, bitter laugh. Too soon yet to break the guy down, he thought as he watched Bateson and his lawyer walk across the lobby of the Public Safety Facility that housed SMPD and the Fire Department. Among all the *he saids/she saids* of Logan and Sinclair's story, there might be an opening yet to put a stick in the wheels of Bateson's operation.

"You I'm not done with," Mason swore under his breath as the beefy lawyer held the door open for Bateson. Bateson turned and gave Mason a long look.

Fredericks continued buying the *Enquirer* every Thursday and slapping it on Mason's desk when she'd finished reading the latest Logan-Sinclair think piece. She loved it. Bateson looked good with his raptor nose and lean and rangy body. Accusations against their security chief had leaked out, which wouldn't hurt his business. It showed how far he was willing to go to protect his clients.

Months later, an alert photographer got a pic of Derek escorted out of a dermatologist's office looking like a gargoyle. Prison doctors, ah, not the same as Beverly Hills plastic surgeons. Nor was the HIV specialist care.

♎

The LT managed to obscure the fact he'd lost Logan, and Mason had turned him up. Logan had been close to dying. A little longer and it was likely they wouldn't have found him alive. But everybody at the station knew Mason had made the collar. His dream of taking the accelerated flying school program had evaporated, but he was only thirty-eight. It hurt remembering the feeling of the drone of the engine under him, and the liftoff above the single runway of the Santa Monica airport, the sky and the sapphire-blue ocean spreading out below him. So many good times at the Spitfire Café with Ginger bullshitting around with all the others who were as fly crazy as he was. Still, he'd filed the paperwork to turn the money over to his parent's lawyer back in Grand Rapids. He was the good child.

Ginger said he should talk to somebody about it. His head was a mess. That probably wouldn't happen.

♋

The fate of the children was still tied up in the courts, and except that their parents were in jail, their life had pretty much stayed the same there in the house with Lupe and one of her friends taking care of them. Derek's mother, a legendary piece of work, was brought in. It looked as though Poppy might be released soon, if charges were dropped. If ...

She would be wearing an ankle bracelet along with her Jimmy Choos. Megan was enrolled in a boarding school in Sweden, seeing a therapist.

Would Celia Talaveras be remembered? Mason hoped so. He had formed a picture of her in his mind when he'd interviewed Megan, who was grieving all over again. A loneliness of spirit had drawn those two together. Celia never mentioned the fifteen extra pounds that made Megan's thighs rub together, her asymmetrical face, and the bump on the bridge of her nose her mother insisted she have a little work done on. Celia didn't gush over her famous parents. She knew Megan didn't have any friends. Celia was her friend.

Megan kept alive a dream Celia had of working in the studios when her English was better. She saw the way her father looked at Celia. It was only a matter of time before he ruined her. She was working with a friend of her mother's, little by little, to get Celia out of that house. All Celia wanted was some kind of job behind the camera—other than craft service. It wasn't that much.

All they needed was time to work it out. Just a little more time. They could have been so happy.

𝕷

One afternoon when Mason sneaked by to visit Delgado in the rehab hospital, he heard Delgado take a call from Lupe Garcia. The entire eight years he'd worked side by side with Delgado, he'd seen his partner look, but never step out of the narrow Catholic Church-going, Latino family thing, or cheat on his wife. Maria. They made marriage look easy. He grabbed a handful of get well cards off the nightstand next to his bed, and pretended he was reading, rather than listening to their conversation.

It wasn't a conversation he could ever initiate with Delgado. Out of all the smart, pretty Latinas in the station, his partner chose Lupe Garcia? There was some deep cultural thing going on here he couldn't figure out. Other people's relationships were deeply private, and mysterious. He knew Delgado liked the attention from Lupe Garcia, but was he really going to take it farther now that the case was over?

Delgado swiped the phone closed, grinned at Mason and scratched his stitches.

"That was Lupe Garcia, huh?" Mason said as casually as he could, swinging around in his chair.

"Yup." Delgado took his comb out of his back pocket and ran it through his thick, silver-streaked hair. He was grinning. "Lupe, yup."

"You gonna jump the wall here to go see her?"

"That's what you think, huh, Mason?"

Mason shrugged.

"I fix her up with *mi primo.*"

Delgado had a number of *primos* all over southern California, and Mason envied the way they were all close to each other. Not like his wreck of a family.

Relieved, he smiled. "Nah, I never thought that. So which one?"

"The one with the kitchen fixtures business in Sylmar. He likes the flashy ones. She'll like him."

The End

Mar Preston
By Accident / Preston – 1st edition

ISBN: 978-0-9988583-4-0

Also by Mar Preston

No Dice

Rip off

On Behalf of the Family

A Very Private High School

Payback

The Most Dangerous Species

Available on Amazon in paperback and Kindle
format as well as in Kindle Unlimited

As well as the EBook series on

Writing Your First Mystery

Acknowledgments

No book is ever written without the involvement of other people. My editor, Elaine Ash, provided inestimable help in restructuring the story, suggesting ways to amp up the action, and shaping the characters until they were as alive on the page as they were in my head.

In *Rip-Off* and *On Behalf of the Family*, I read Chechen and Turkish newspapers (in English) for years as a preparation for writing the books. To write *By Accident,* I read *People* magazine and *Us*, watched *E!online*, and *TMZ*. My favorite sources came and went, along with becoming expert on celebrities whose careers soared and then frizzled in the maelstrom of celebrity gossip. I still pick up *The Enquirer.* I still want to know who's doing who, and how. Celebrity gossip can become addictive.

My law enforcement guru this time was Sgt. Bill Lewis, Ret. Of the Oxnard Police Department. He corrected my mistakes in police procedure without laughing too hard. Sandy Browne from the National Transportation Safety Board has directed me away from some arguable assumptions. I am deeply grateful to them.

Judith Cassis has been my most important influence over many years, a cheerleader, book coach, and nudge when the flame of creation flickers low. I cannot thank her enough for always being there.

Special mention of thanks to Bruce Spargo. Anyone who knows Bruce will recognize a dim facsimile of him in these pages.

This book was written over a long period of time, so I have forgotten many of those moments when you said something that gave me an idea and made my ears go ping, ping, ping. There were many of those moments when I probably went blank, and you wondered where I'd gone. Thank you.

And my thanks again to Howard Colf who made everything possible.

This Book is Dedicated

To

My Pine Mountain & Santa Monica Friends

Manufactured by Amazon.ca
Bolton, ON